DINOSAUR WARRIORS

The closest dinosaur's armor looked more ornate than the others'. Aaron straightened to his full height and tried to look as formidable as he could. He kept his hand on the hilt of Otomo's sword, though Aaron figured he was as likely to cut himself with it as anyone else.

"You're in charge, right?" he said, feeling more than slightly ridiculous. "My name's Aaron. I'm a friend of Jennifer and Struth's."

The Mutata bellowed and trilled; the others answered with sharp cries from their nasal horns . . .

. . . and they charged.

R A Y   B R A D B U R Y
P R E S E N T S

DINOSAUR
WARRIORS

Ray Bradbury's Dinosaur Series #1
DINOSAUR WORLD
by Stephen Leigh, illustrated by Wayne D. Barlowe

Ray Bradbury's Dinosaur Series #2
DINOSAUR PLANET
by Stephen Leigh, illustrated by John Paul Genzo

Ray Bradbury's Dinosaur Series #3
DINOSAUR SAMURAI
by Stephen Leigh and John J. Miller,
illustrated by Brian Franczak

Ray Bradbury's Dinosaur Series #4
DINOSAUR WARRIORS
by Stephen Leigh, illustrated by Nicholas Jainschigg

Ray Bradbury's Dinosaur Series #5
DINOSAUR EMPIRE
by Stephen Leigh and John J. Miller,
illustrated by Nicholas Jainschigg and Cortney Skinner

Ray Bradbury's Dinosaur Series #6
DINOSAUR CONQUEST
by Stephen Leigh, illustrated by Cortney Skinner

TIME SAFARI, INC.
SAFARIS TO ANY YEAR IN THE PAST.
You name the animal. We take you there.

R A Y   B R A D B U R Y
PRESENTS

DINOSAUR
WARRIORS

A NOVEL BY
STEPHEN LEIGH

Illustrated by
Nicholas Jainschigg

A Byron Preiss Book

J. T. Colby & Company, Inc.
Purveyors of Time Travel Instruments and Accessories™

J. T. Colby & Company, Inc.
Purveyors of Time Travel Instruments and Accessories™

Dinosaur Warriors

"Time Safari, Inc." is a trademark of
Byron Preiss Visual Publications.

Library of Congress Cataloging-in-Publication Data
Leigh, Stephen.
Ray Bradbury Presents Dinosaur Warriors.
        (Ray Bradbury Presents) "A Byron Preiss Visual
Publications book."
p. cm.
        [1. Science Fiction—Time Travel. 2. Fiction—Science
Fiction—Adventure. 3.] I. Jainschigg, Nicholas ill. II. Title.
III.
        Series: Ray Bradbury Presents.

J. T. Colby & Company, Inc.
Purveyors of Time Travel Instruments and Accessories™

Manhanset House
Dering Harbor, New York 11965-0342
bricktower@aol.com
bricktowerpress.com

ISBN: 978-1-59687-747-4
January 2019

**This one's for Christopher & Kyle
from their Ogre Steve**

The author would also like to acknowledge Johanna Broda, David Carrasco, and Eduardo Matos Moctezuma, authors of *The Great Temple of Tenochtitlan* (University of California Press, 1987), from which a portion of the information regarding Aztec rites and language has been drawn. Because this story is fictional and takes place in a vastly different world than ours, great liberties have been taken with the information they presented: any errors of historical fact—intended or otherwise—are mine, not theirs.

Table of Contents

Prologue

A Synopis of the Previous Books

Aaron Cofield and Jennifer Mason are sitting on the hill behind Aaron's house in Green Town, Illinois, enjoying the summer afternoon. Their affectionate talk is interrupted by a commotion in the woods below. Goading each other, Jennifer and Aaron investigate. Rather than the expected bear, they find a clutch of very large and very odd eggs. The two call their friend Peter Finnigan to help document the strange find, but they are suddenly hit from behind by a running, badly injured man.

The reason for the man's flight becomes obvious as a charging allosaurus crashes wildly through the trees. The stranger kills the beast with his rifle; as the dinosaur crumples, so does he.

The trio takes the man back to Aaron's house, and confers with Aaron's grandfather Carl. The stranger—Travis—regains consciousness long enough to tell the three teenagers his story. Travis tells them that he is a

1

time safari guide from two hundred years in the future. While escorting a group of hunters through the Mesozoic era in order to kill a *Tyrannosaurus rex*, there was an accident: a man named Eckels went blundering off the special path laid down by Travis. On their return home, the time travelers found history changed—for the worse. When Travis attacked Eckels in a rage, Eckels fled for his life in the time machine. Unfortunately, the machine met itself in the Mesozoic, and the resulting paradox caused the explosion of Eckels's machine *and* the destruction of the floating path.

Travis, in pursuit of Eckels in another machine, came upon the wreckage. Infuriated and despairing, Travis was about to return to his own time when the allosaurus attacked. Running from the beast through the jungle, Travis came across a piece of the path still floating a few inches above the ground. Instinctively, he leapt upon it—

—and landed in the Green Town woods with the allosaurus close behind.

Travis lapses again into unconsciousness after this lengthy and strange tale, and the trio retires to the kitchen to eat lunch and talk. A few minutes later, Jennifer goes back to check on Travis but finds the man gone—slipped out of the open window.

As they sit in the kitchen wondering what to do next, Aaron spies a triceratops nibbling on the grass at the edge of the incline. In a second, the three are up and out of their chairs; the triceratops snorts in surprise and fear and makes for the cover of the trees with the teenagers in close pursuit. Grandpa Carl hollers at them to be careful, but he can't stop them.

Once in the woods, the three are separated: Aaron, out ahead, literally falls on a section of the broken path—and finds himself with Travis and the body of the dead T-rex in the Mesozoic.

At the same time, Jennifer and Peter, growing more concerned at Aaron's silence, have found a section of the path themselves—another piece entirely. Jennifer insists that they step onto the path. She's certain that Aaron must have done the same. Despite Peter's reluctance, they do so . . .

. . . and enter a world they have never seen before, lush with primitive plants and strange reptilian life. Jennifer is excited—certain that this is the Mesozoic that Travis was talking about. They explore and find footprints leading into a cave. Entering, they are ambushed by Eckels. The man is raving about talking to dinosaurs, rambling on and on about things that make no sense to the two. He ties them up and leaves the cave, saying that he's going to offer the two teenagers to the dinosaurs. While Eckels is away, Jennifer and Peter manage to escape.

They are trying to return to the section of path when they are captured once more—this time by a group of sentient man-sized dinosaurs armed with spears.

After their capture by the dinosaurs, Peter and Jennifer are herded down from the hills toward the valley. The two are placed within a barricaded compound. The dinosaur placed in charge of them, Jennifer learns, is a female named SStragh (called Struth by the humans).

Over the next several days, Jennifer attempts to learn the dinosaur language, though it is extremely difficult for her human throat to reproduce the various honks, trills, and bleats with which the words are sprinkled. Jennifer and Peter learn that the Mutata (as the dinosaur tribe is called) are one of two sentient species of dinosaur, that they have been troubled recently by invasions from what they called Floating Stones and by someone they name the Far-Killer. The Gairk, a tribe of warlike, sentient dinosaurs similar to the allosaurus, are also upset by the changes within their valley, and the Gairk are also searching for this Far-Killer.

It also becomes obvious that SStragh is not exactly in the best graces of the dinosaur called the OColi—the Eldest—who is the head of this Mutata tribe.

SStragh captures the Far-Killer and brings him back to the encampment. The Far-Killer is Eckels. Eckels claims not to remember abducting Jennifer and Peter. In fact, he gives a very different telling of Travis's tale. According to Eckels, *Travis* is ultimately responsible for the destruction of the path and the time-stream. The explosion of the time machine knocked Eckels here, where he wandered confused and a little mad for a time—that is why he can't remember their first meeting. He asks for their forgiveness. Peter shrugs; Jennifer is not quite so inclined to believe him.

The three plot to escape, though Jennifer holds back, not wanting to do anything which might hurt SStragh, with whom she is beginning to share a friendship.

There are other forces at work, however. In particular, Frraghi (or 'Fergie,' as the humans call him), the OColi's second-in-command, is pressuring SStragh to dispose of the humans. The Mutata are set in their ways, following a half-instinctive set of rules called the OColihi, or Ancient Path. The recent disruptions have threatened these old ways. Complicating this is the fact that SStragh's mentor, whose name is Raajek, once attempted to upset the outmoded Ancient Path. Raajek wanted to lead the Mutata on the OChiihi, or New

Path. Her attempt failed, and Raajek left the Mutata, exiling herself.

The OColi gives SStragh one boon—if Jennifer can show that she is "intelligent" (and thus knows the Ancient Path), he will allow them to live. Eckels had killed one of the Mutata during his capture. The OColi insists that Jennifer be brought in to perform a part of the ceremony they call Giving, though SStragh is instructed not to teach her any of the rites. Jennifer will succeed or fail entirely on her own.

Confronted with a ceremony she doesn't understand, Jennifer manages at last to stumble through well enough to impress the OColi. Peter, on the other hand, has not been so fortunate. Eckels and Jennifer can live, the OColi rules, but Peter is to be killed and his body shown to the Gairk as proof that the Mutata have done something about the Floating Stones. SStragh is unable to conceive of disobeying the OColi. She has only one option—to allow Jennifer and the others to escape, even though that will mean her own death. SStragh makes that decision, but before she can put the plan into action, they are interrupted. The Gairk have sent an emissary who insists on seeing the humans. They are presented to him, but before the Gairk can act, a strange lightning storm begins. Devoid of rain, coming upon them with no warning, the lightning flashes display shifting patches of other realities, both known and unknown. One of these small worlds happens to appear where the Gairk is standing, and half of him simply disappears, killing the creature. Fearful, Frraghi orders the humans killed.

SStragh, in desperation, seeks out Raajek, who, though blind, has sensed the omens. Raajek agrees to return to the Mutata to help SStragh. In a confrontation with the

OColi, Raajek uses a clever deception to save the humans.

If only for the time being . . .

In the Mesozoic, Aaron deals with a badly hurt and rather unstable Travis. In a rage, Travis orders Aaron into his time machine and they return to Travis's "present," finding only a desolate, cold waste utterly devoid of anything human at all. Travis goes mad, shouting that Eckels has destroyed known history entirely; Aaron is also shocked, wanting to disbelieve all of this since it also means the end of Green Town and his own time. When Travis is nearly killed by the plant life of this odd future, Aaron convinces the man to take the time machine to *Aaron's* HomeTime. Aaron is certain that he will find Jennifer, Peter, his family, and Green Town intact. He must.

But he doesn't.

This world is far too much like the world they just left. Aaron is shattered. His entire past is gone, all of it. Eckels has destroyed the timestream entirely, changed the past so much that nothing is the same. His family has never lived, nor Jennifer, nor any human at all . . .

As the two, despondent, are about to return to the Mesozoic, where at least things are familiar, a whirlwind attacks them, changing shape as it comes. Worse, there is no sign of the time machine—it has disappeared.

In defiance, Aaron strikes at the whirlwind, which dissolves into a fantasy-cover wizard. The creature—whom they address as Mundo, though it actually has no name— is an extension of the World-Mind, a consciousness that spans all living creatures in the world. Mundo doesn't understand much of what Aaron and Travis are worrying about, doesn't understand their "alone-ness" at all, and certainly doesn't share their concerns. However, Aaron convinces the being to return with them to the Mesozoic—since if they *don't* do that and Eckels is still alive back there, then Eckels will change history yet again and destroy Mundo in the process. Aaron convinces Mundo there's no danger, since not only can they return him via the time machine, but the section of path that leads from the Mesozoic to Green Town now must connect to *Mundo's* present, not Aaron's.

The strange trio returns to the past, but the trip is very disturbing to Mundo, who goes into a shrieking fit as this part of him is suddenly disconnected from his greater whole. Aaron calms him, and they go off to find the pathway. Before they can do that, however, a time storm much like the one witnessed by Jennifer and the others assails them. When it passes at last, Aaron—more desperate than ever now—sets off with Mundo.

They find the section of broken path and step on it.

It's with incredible surprise that Aaron finds himself in the Green Town forest once more. Mundo, angered, bolts and runs, cursing Aaron for having tricked him. Aaron starts to go back to get Travis, then stops. He's home now. If he goes back through, he might find himself trapped once more.

Instead, Aaron moves through the familiar, comfortable forest toward his house. He spies Grandpa Carl on the porch. Waving, shouting, Aaron goes to greet him.

BOOK TWO

Aaron finds that Green Town isn't exactly the familiar place he remembers. The house is run-down, Grandpa Carl is strange and irritable, and the newspaper he reads has odd headlines about time storms throughout the country. Worst of all, Aaron finds that twelve *years* have passed in this world, and that his parents are dead.

Carl is visited by an officious-looking man from a place called the Compound—evidently a quasimilitary establishment near Green Town. It's obvious to Aaron that his grandfather is in trouble with the authorities and is being blamed for the time storms and odd visitations. Aaron decides to go into Green Town himself.

Green Town is as strange as Carl and his house. A statue of a dinosaur dominates the square, and Aaron meets a schoolmate of his, now thirty years old. When the man becomes suspicious of Aaron and the way he looks and threatens to call Sheriff Tate, Aaron flees. On the way back to his house, Sheriff Tate's car, with two sinister passengers, one male and one female, passes him as he hides in the weeds at the side of the road. Back at the house, he finds that the three are waiting for him to return. Aaron watches from the woods for hours—and then, in the middle of the night, he sees Mundo approaching the house. Tate and the woman see Mundo as well, and the woman shoots at the creature, pursuing it into the woods. Aaron flees too, since they're heading right for him, and eventually finds himself near where the piece of roadway to the Mesozoic is waiting.

Aaron decides he needs help and returns to the Mesozoic to find Travis—while back at the house, Carl is arrested. If Aaron needed any more encouragement, a time storm hits as Aaron and Travis are talking—odd fragments of alternate realities go flickering past them.

Even though they spend only a few minutes in the Mesozoic, months have passed when they return to Green Town with the time machine. Carl is gone, and the house looks deserted. Aaron is furious, and he decides that they must *do* something.

Travis performs a small experiment with the time machine—he finds that he can't go any farther UpTime than the present. This tells him that Green Town is *not* Travis's past at all, but another alternate reality entirely. Things start to fall into place: evidently the pieces of roadway cross not just time, but various shadow worlds where history has taken other turns.

Aaron convinces Travis to send the time machine back to just after Tate and his two cronies took off after Mundo. They do so, and materialize just in time to see Carl being put into a car. The two are fired upon, and Aaron is shot. He falls unconscious.

Carl sees Aaron fall back into the time machine, but the car drives away then. The woman in charge of the mission, Captain Michaels, takes him to the Compound. There, he is shown the piece of the roadway the authorities have found—the roadway that Jennifer and Peter stepped on, though Carl isn't aware of that. Carl, taking advantage of a momentary lapse, jumps up onto the path and is transported . . . somewhere.

In the place Jennifer and Peter call Dinosaur World, the attacks continue from the Floating Stones. More persistent than even the samurai are the huge pterosaurs (called saorods by the Mutata), who attack recklessly and fearlessly from the sky after crossing over from one of the pieces of roadway. The OColi and Frraghi are getting more impatient each day, and SStragh and Raajek do what they can to keep the OColi from ordering the death of the humans. Peter and Eckels seem to have their own plan, and Jennifer finds herself alone in wanting to trust SStragh and Raajek.

The conflict is affecting the entire Mutata community—Jennifer witnesses a ritualistic duel to the death between one of Raajek's followers and another Mutata. It is clear to her that the fragile peace is falling apart.

It is worse than she thinks. The OColi himself is under pressure by his counterpart among the Gairk. The Gairk OColi has issued his own declaration: the humans must die by the day called OGhielas (the summer solstice), or the Gairk will declare war on the Mutata.

SStragh and Raajek redouble their efforts and find the piece of path that Jennifer and Peter came through. They take Jennifer to see it for identification. On the way, they meet a Gairk, who tells them that he has just killed a "soft, pale thing" just like Jennifer a bit up the path. Jennifer is horrified, afraid that Aaron is dead. The Gairk guides them back to the body. Jennifer does indeed recognize the person lying there:

Aaron's grandfather Carl.

Aaron returns to consciousness still at his farmhouse in Green Town, but several months in the future. Travis tells Aaron that he pulled him into the time machine, returned fire, and then brought them here after the car, with Carl inside, took off. Aaron and Travis spend a few weeks recuperating, then return to that fateful night a bit later. There they find a dying man, Tate's crony, who tells them that Carl was taken to the Compound. Troops arrive from the Compound then, and they capture the time machine and Travis. Aaron escapes into the woods, and there he meets Mundo. The two decide to join forces: an uneasy alliance. Aaron and Mundo attempt to get into the Compound via the storm sewer system.

Jennifer buries Carl as SStragh and Raajek look on in puzzlement—that is not the way the Mutata deal with their dead, after all. Then the three go on to the Floating Stone. Jennifer reluctantly decides that with all that has happened, she should take this opportunity and go for help. She breaks away from SStragh and Raajek and jumps on top of the Floating Stone.

Nothing happens. The pathway between the worlds is closed.

OGhielas arrives, and with it the Gairk Envoy. SStragh and Raajek attempt to demonstrate that Jenny has done what was asked of her—she has found a way to seal up the pathways between the worlds, Raajek says. Look, she's closed up the one to her own world. The Gairk seems unconvinced, and at that moment, Eckels and Peter play their own hidden card. When the Mutata captured Eckels, they broke his rifle, but they didn't take the cartridges, not understanding the technology. Eckels and Peter have made a small bomb with the gunpowder, and they light the fuse and run, calling to Jennifer. Jennifer is forced to make her own decision. None of the dinosaurs understands the danger, and Jennifer sacrifices her own chance at escape to save the Mutata and Gairk. Thrown away, the bomb explodes harmlessly while Peter and Eckels disappear into the jungle.

A death sentence remains on Peters and Eckels, but Jennifer is spared.

Travis is interrogated by Captain Michaels as Aaron and Mundo steal closer to the Compound. A time storm hits as well, and a gigantic creature of lightning and cloud escapes from one of the passing realities. It rages through the Compound, tearing down walls and creating chaos— a confusion that allows Aaron and Mundo to reach Travis. The piece of floating path has been hurled somewhere by the storm of the creature's passage, though.

They have one choice: they take the time machine and use it to move back a few hours. Captain Michaels turns out to be more sympathetic than they'd realized. She tells them how they've learned that the gateways are powered by fragments of Eckels's temporal mechanism, embedded in the pathways by the force of the explosion when his time machine met itself. Take away the fragments, and the gateway is sealed; put them back, and it reopens. Grateful, Aaron, Travis, and Mundo get into the time machine.

In the laboratory a few hours before, they move the time machine through the pathway and into a new world:

Dinosaur World.

BOOK THREE

Peter and Eckels have holed up in Eckels's old cave, trying to elude the search by the various Gairk and Mutata hunting parties that are out after them. Peter, out hunting for food, is surprised by a Gairk, and is followed back to the cave. To escape the Gairk, Peter and Eckels escape out a natural chimney in the rear of the cave. Peter, his claustrophobia kicking in as he maneuvers through the tight, dark crawlway, quickly loses Eckels, who is already up and out of the chimney. Peter is nearly at the top, but almost falls. A hand grabs him—the hand is Mundo's.

Mundo pulls Peter out of the crevice, and he is greeted by Aaron and Travis. They heard Peter calling for Eckels and came to help. The reunion is shortlived—they hear the distinctive sound of the time machine in its local travel mode: Eckels has stolen the vehicle.

Jennifer, with SStragh, is out searching for Peter and Eckels herself when they see the Gairk Klaido rushing past. Realizing that the creature is in hot pursuit of some-one and desperately afraid that she knows who, Jennifer and SStragh follow as quickly as they can, but lose him. They find themselves very near where the Mutata are guarding the Floating Stone to the samurai world. Real-izing that a time storm is about to break, they stay there, waiting for the storm to pass. The storm hits, and in the chaos of fleeting realities and strange visions, Jennifer sees the time machine heading for the Floating Stone with Eckels at the controls. The machine glides over the Floating Stone and disappears.

At the same time, she sees something that lightens her mood: Aaron. The two reunite quickly, and then every-one—Aaron, Jennifer, Peter, Travis, Mundo—follows Eckels through the portal to the world of the samurai.

They emerge on the other side of the stone in the inte-rior of a Shinto-like temple. Eckels has been here—the bodies of dead priests are a vivid reminder of his presence, as are the bodies of several samurai warriors outside.

Following, the group meets a Japanese peasant boy named Katsu. Jennifer, who can speak Japanese a bit, talks with him. Katsu is impressed with the sight of all these strange beings. Mundo especially impresses him—not only can Mundo speak the language, but he very much resembles a figure in Japanese mythology: the Mon-key King.

A group of samurai warriors is riding quickly toward the temple. Katsu tells them that they are led by Captain Otomo, who serves the Lord Akira. Aaron wonders if they have somehow found themselves in Japan, but a sight at the edge of the woods seems to indicate other-wise. Looking out at them are figures that can only be American Indians, evidently scouts for the samurai.

The group has little choice. They surrender to Otomo, who takes them back to the castle. The land is untamed and wild, but the topography hasn't changed. Jennifer, Aaron, and Peter all realize that this is Illinois. Green Town.

SStragh has also come through the portal, but later than the others. They have already gone when she emerges. The path of Eckels is very evident to her keen senses—she follows the track of the time machine off into the forest.

Eckels and SStragh are both captured by the Indians. Eckels, in an effort to win favor with them, gives their leader—named Gray Raven—a rifle he's taken from the time machine.

The land may be Green Town, but the history isn't. Katsu tells them how the Japanese—whom he calls Nipponjin—came to the continent they called the Endless Lands, and were slowly spreading out across it. They had encountered several tribes of Indians, with whom they had uneasy truces. Aaron realizes that in this timeline, the Europeans never made it to the New World; instead, the Japanese did.

The group is presented to Lord Akira. Mundo, with the twin advantages of his appearance and language skill, quickly impresses Akira, and wheedles his way into the Lord's good graces. Mundo finds out that a "two-legged dragon" has been spotted near the Indian encampment, and that Lord Akira greatly desires the dragon. Mundo begins to plan.

Jennifer tells Aaron about his grandfather's death. The news steels Aaron's resolve to find a way to fix the mess Eckels has made.

In the meantime, Mundo has made contact on his own with the Indians, making arrangements through Lord Akira to trade the "dragon" they've captured; they would trade it for more rifles to make war upon a rival tribe. Aaron and Travis, working through Captain Otomo (who is not particularly fond of his Lord Akira) learn that SStragh has been brought to the castle.

Mundo isn't done yet, though. Learning that Eckels has been captured by the Hill Makers, as the Indians are called, he goes there, telling Eckels that he'll get him out in exchange for the time machine. Eckels, always one to look out for his own skin, agrees.

Through SStragh and Jennifer, however, Lord Akira has learned about the time machine also, and finds that he desires it. The Hill Makers and samurai end up in a battle over possession of the vehicle, with Travis turning the tide toward victory when he uses one of the rifles. In the midst of that fight, realizing that the Hill Makers are going to lose, Eckels changes sides.

Through a series of adventures, Aaron, Jennifer, and the others learn that Lord Akira is planning his rise to fame from his "banishment" to this miserable outpost, manipulating the Hill Makers and everyone for his own designs. Akira is ambitious, and is planning to take the "Steel Turtle" back to the cities of the west coast (along with SStragh and Mundo, as curiosities), there to make his fortune.

With Captain Otomo's grudging help, they steal the time machine back and make their escape from Lord Akira. In the ensuing battle, the boy Katsu is killed protecting them. Finally, at the shrine, in the midst of a terrible time storm, the group deals with Akira and flees back on the Floating Stone. As Jennifer, Mundo,

SStragh, Peter, and Eckels go through inside the time machine, Aaron and Travis stay outside to close off the gateway by removing the pieces of temporal machinery embedded in the path. It works: a sparkling, glittering barrier rises up, and Aaron and Travis leap through the collapsing portal into Dinosaur World once again.

However, they enter Dinosaur World to find a rather unfriendly reception awaiting them.

1

A Deadly Reception

"Talk about jumping out of the frying pan . . ."

Everything was happening far too quickly as far as Aaron was concerned. Aaron wasn't certain what he'd expected to find in the place Jennifer and Peter called Dinosaur World, but the scene in his mind had never been like this.

He and Travis had just closed off the opening to the Japanese timeline, tumbling through the portal as the gateway between the worlds snapped shut almost at their backs and threw the two of them several feet from the pathway. He was on his hand and knees, nose to nose with greenery as delicate as lace, and Otomo's *katana* in its *sai* lay just beyond his fingers. Aaron could still feel the tingling remnants of the sparking, flaring barrier they'd erected. The back of his shirt was hot despite the frigid passage through time, as if he'd been standing in front of a bonfire.

At least I don't smell smoke . . . Aaron grabbed the sword and picked himself up from where he'd fallen into a thick cushion of low-growing ferns and tried to orient himself. *Where's Jenny?* Aaron shook his head, trying to clear away the cold, whirling confusion of the passage between worlds. A few feet away, Travis was groaning as he tried to stand. "You seen the time machine?" Aaron called to Travis.

Travis, still clutching the glowing pieces of temporal machinery, nodded his head to Aaron's right. "Yeah. Over there."

Aaron looked. His breath went out in a long sigh. "Oh, no . . ."

The time machine, with—Aaron knew—Jennifer, Peter, Eckels, Struth, and Mundo inside, was snared like a steel moth in a spider's web. Struth's dinosaur friends had obviously been watching for them. They'd erected a net of vines and draped it on long poles around the piece of floating roadway. Eckels had driven their vehicle directly into the waiting trap; the poles had fallen, then snagged in a stand of cycads fifty yards away.

It had been simple enough, and all too effective.

The time machine's engines, never designed for heavy work, had been unable to break free of the thick tangle of leafy ropes. Someone inside had shut off the power to everything but the repulsors, leaving the machine sitting silently in its trap at an odd angle. A crowd of what looked like small hadrosaurs wielding spears bristled around the machine, and Aaron caught a glimpse of Jennifer's concerned face pressed against the windshield. She was mouthing something and pointing, but Aaron couldn't understand what she was trying to tell him.

He wasn't given much time to puzzle it out.

In the same instant, Aaron realized that he and Travis were themselves surrounded by several of the Mutata. Aaron's first close-up glimpse of a Mutata other than Struth was definitely not destined to make him feel at home. The dinosaurs wore heavy chest armor of beaten copper plate, and each of them grasped a spear in its right hand, the black obsidian points aimed at the two humans. The Mutata were a formidable sight, their massive, brightly scaled bodies tilted forward, the thick tails held out stiffly behind them, counterweights to the great, wide chests. Their expressive, stem heads gazed down at Aaron. He wondered what they were thinking behind those luminescent, gold-green eyes.

The closest dinosaur's armor looked more ornate than the others'. Aaron brushed uselessly at the dirt on his knees, then stopped. Jennifer had told him that stance was an important component of Mutata speech. He straightened to his full height and tried to look as impressive as he could. He kept his hand on the hilt of Otomo's sword, though Aaron figured he was as likely to cut himself with it as anyone else. "You're in charge, right?" he said, feeling more than slightly ridiculous. "My name's Aaron. I'm a friend of Jennifer and Struth's."

The Mutata hooted something over his shoulder to the others and then glared at Aaron again. His nostrils widened and he snuffled, sending a waft of spice-scented breath toward Aaron.

"Uh . . . that's good, I guess," Aaron began. He glanced back at Travis. "At least they're not attacking. That's a start. So what do we do now—shake hands? Kiss? I've never had any lessons in dinosaur etiquette."

The Mutata gave Travis no chance to answer. The leader bellowed and trilled; the others answered with sharp cries from their nasal horns . . .

. . . and they charged.

The leader rushed directly at Aaron.

Two years of aikido training had gifted Aaron with an instinctive response to a direct attack: as the Mutata thrust its spear at Aaron's chest, Aaron shuffled to his right and then pivoted on his front foot. At the same time, he blocked the spear with Otomo's sheathed *katana*, dropped the sword, and grasped the shaft of the Mutata's spear with both hands. Facing now in the same direction as the onrushing dinosaur, he stepped forward, adding his own momentum to the Mutata's charge. With the movement, he twisted the shaft so that the obsidian blade of the spear came back and down, at the same time bringing the lower end up, as if Aaron were turning the wheel of a car.

The Mutata went tumbling past Aaron with an odd, high-pitched shriek of distress, leaving Aaron with the dinosaur's spear in his hands. The creature landed directly on the piece of floating roadway, which went slowly floating off a few yards with the impact of the collision. The Mutata lay stunned on top of the piece of white plastic like a green-scaled, roasted turkey on a platter, the translucent underlids of its eyes blinking.

"Whoa!" Aaron said, almost as startled as the Mutata. "Hey, that stuff actually *works*!"

The other dinosaurs had skidded to a stop, unsure. They hooted and shrilled as they conferred among themselves while Aaron recovered the *katana* again.

"That was interesting," Travis said in the respite, as both humans watched the Mutata carefully. "Now you only have to do it, oh, a dozen more times or so. And you'd better teach that move to me, too, while you're at it." Travis gave Aaron a quick, uncertain grin.

"I hear you." Aaron shook his head—the technique had been one he'd practiced often enough in class, but he hadn't expected it to be quite so effective. He wished now he'd paid more attention to his classes. "Maybe we'll get lucky and they'll decide it's not worth trying . . ."

Aaron had no chance to savor his success.

The others were gathering to charge again, and there were far too many of them. Travis dropped the pieces of temporal machinery, fisting his hands in defiance, but Aaron knew that his and Travis's stand would be a quick and final one. Travis was unarmed, exhausted, and weak from his wounds; Aaron was nearly as tired as Travis, slightly wounded himself, and, even though at the moment he was holding both a spear and a sword, he had no skill with either weapon. The Mutata were armed and ready, and there were far too many of them.

And then there was simply no time to think at all.

"SStragh!"

SStragh heard her name being called by Jhenini, the voice sounding as if it came from some deep well. "SStragh!" The sound cleared the Mutata's head, which was throbbing from the blow she'd sustained after the strange device SStragh thought of as the Flying Room ran into the trap waiting for it. The impact of the Flying Room with the Mutata net had tossed the craft wildly as Jhenini and Eikels tried to break loose.

Jhenini had also been hurt. A nasty bruise was turning purple under the bangs of her odd yellow headfur. The human female was striking the windshield in frustration, shouting at SStragh in atrociously accented Mutata: "Frraghi's out there. He's going to kill Aaron and Travis! You've got to stop them!"

SStragh managed to find a handhold and levered herself upright, her tail lashing about for balance. The Flying

Room was canted over heavily to the left, and the rear end of the compartment was much higher than the front. SStragh looked around groggily. The young male Peetah and Eikels had been knocked heavily against the sidewalls of the topsy-turvy cabin: both seemed unconscious. The strange, white-furred creature they called Mhundo was sitting stunned but open-eyed in one of the pilot seats.

"SStragh, come on! We have to help them!" Jhenini's seat restraint was stuck; she was pulling and tugging at it futilely. "*SStragh!*"

"Open the door, Jhenini," SStragh told her calmly. "I will see what I can do."

I will never understand humans, SStragh told herself. *Never.*

SStragh allowed herself a sigh. Humans refused to submit to the fates given them by the All-Ancestor. They fought and tried to change their destinies. The worst thing was that SStragh had found herself doing the same more and more often. The humans' presence, for good or ill, was changing SStragh in the same way it was changing their world. "The door, Jhenini," SStragh said again.

Jhenini was jabbing at odd-looking pieces of what seemed to be bright stones on the shelf at the front of the Flying Room. SStragh heard the door—which was now the "roof" of the Flying Room—hiss like one of the limbless lizards the Mutata called Slitherers, but it opened only a hand's width and then jammed. The door shuddered and groaned, but wouldn't open farther. They could hear the Mutata outside hooting and whistling in fury, and Frraghi's strong voice ordered the attack to begin.

"*SStragh!*" Jennifer shrilled in panic.

SStragh grasped the edge of the door and braced herself against the seat supports, levering at the opening with her arms and powerful leg muscles. The door shrieked in metal protest and then slid open fully. SStragh poked her head out of the machine.

She was just in time to see something utterly astonishing.

Frraghi gathered himself and charged toward Aaron. The young human male turned aside at the last moment and did something with his hands and body that sent Frraghi flying tail over head on top of the Floating Stone. Even more astonishing, Aaron had plucked Frraghi's spear from the Mutata's hands.

The surprise at this new tactic halted the others momentarily, but they gathered themselves again and made ready to finish what Frraghi had started. SStragh noted immediately that all of them had their spears in their right hands, as they would if they were killing any unintelligent animal.

SStragh could see Frraghi looking around for his lost spear, finally noticing that Aaron was holding it and using Frraghi's own weapon to threaten the other Mutata.

Worse, the human—just like the Mutata—was holding Frraghi's spear in his right hand, the Hand of Animals, as if he considered the Mutata to be beneath him. A snort of mingled anger and frustration came unbidden from Frraghi. The Speaker shook himself. At that moment, Frraghi also realized for the first time that he was lying on top of the Floating Stone. Frraghi howled in distress and scrambled off the white roadway as if it were a baking stone in the ovens.

Frraghi glared at Aaron and shouted to the Mutata.

"Kill the animals!" he screamed to the others.

"Yeie!" SStragh bellowed. *No!* "Wait!"

Grunting, she levered herself up through the opening, in the Flying Room, tumbling ungracefully out of the vehicle, vines catching at her as she tried to straighten up. She managed to throw off enough of the pliable strands to stand up. She hardly looked dignified, standing there wrapped in greenery, but Frraghi was already getting to his feet again.

Frraghi was fuming: that was easy to see. Aaron's unexpected and—to SStragh—nearly magical tossing of the Mutata, as if Frraghi were a puffwort being blown by a storm wind, might not have injured the dinosaur greatly, but it had seriously wounded Frraghi's pride.

"Yeie?" Frraghi bellowed back to SStragh, but SStragh could hear the undertone of uncertainty in his voice. "So SStragh returns and immediately thinks that she's the OColi."

"I have seen more than you can imagine on the other side of the Floating Stone, Frraghi Speaker-for-the-OColi," SStragh answered stiffly. That was certainly true. SStragh's mind still reeled from the strange sights she'd witnessed in the world of the hard-shelled humans, the ones Jhenini called Japanese. SStragh understood now how lost and bewildered Jhenini and the other humans must have felt when they first came to SStragh's own world. There had been no Mutata beyond the Floating Stone at all, only the tiny, stupid lizard cousins that scurried under rocks and hid in dark places. SStragh had seen the loud, deadly weapons of Eckels and Travis, which could kill from hundred of tails away and which could puncture armor like a spear point ripping through a leaf. SStragh still wasn't quite sure exactly what the humans were or how the All-Ancestor intended the Mutata to respond to them, but she *was* certain now that they were not animals. They were something that the OColihi, the Old Path of rituals and etiquette the Mutata and the Gairk had followed for long centuries, had missed.

"Jhenini has done what she promised the OColi she would do," SStragh continued, looking at all of them. "She and the other humans have closed off the path through the Floating Stone."

Jhenini had managed to release herself from the seat. SStragh heard her scrambling down the side of the Flying Room behind her. Like one of the agile tree-swingers the humans resembled so much, Jhenini slipped easily through the gaps between the strands of netting. The Mutata gathered around the net moved forward to stop her.

"I'm not running away," Jhenini told them. "I'm just untangling SStragh . . ."

Lhath was leading the group around the Flying Room. He looked at Frraghi, then at SStragh. "Jhenini will not flee," SStragh said. "Lhath, if you kill us now when we have the secret of the Floating Stones, you will have also killed the OColihi forever."

"I—" Lhath began, then his odor changed from cinnamon spice with a sour musk. "Go ahead," he said to Jhenini.

With the Mutata watching her carefully, the young female human shrugged toward Aaron, then helped SStragh break loose, grunting as she tore at the emerald ropes of the vines. The rest of the Mutata waited, shuffling nervously and smelling of distress. For the moment, SStragh's appearance and Aaron's odd defeat of Frraghi had stopped them—whatever was going on, this was certainly *not* behavior covered in the OColihi they knew so well. They were confused.

SStragh knew that all it would take would be for one of the pack to make an aggressive move—the others would follow. They balanced on the spear edge of a fight that could only end in death for the humans.

Frraghi hissed in wordless fury. Even at this distance, SStragh could smell the insanity of anger in him. "Where

is my OTsio Raajek, Frraghi?" SStragh said as soothingly
as she could. "Where is the OColi? Bring them here.
You've captured the humans and the Flying Room. Let
that be enough credit to you for now. The decision of what
to do with them should be the OColi's, not yours or mine."

"Our old OColi *had* made that decision, twice before,"
Frraghi spat back. "So has Gairk emissary Klaido. They
have *both* said that the humans are *iado*. Animals." With
the word, Frraghi shook himself and roared wordlessly.
His armor clashed with the sound of a distant storm. "As
for Raajek, you will find that she is no longer the ally you
expect."

A strange scent wafted on the breeze as Frraghi said
the last words, and his stance was one of triumph. SStragh
wondered at that, but there was no time to worry about
it. "The Floating Stone has been *sealed*," SStragh said
again, as soothingly as she could. "*Think*, Frraghi: the
human Aaron threw you onto the stone, yet you didn't
disappear into the world of the hard-shelled humans. You
lay there, and *nothing happened*. Nothing, Frraghi."

Frraghi didn't seem to like the reminder of his hu-
miliation, but SStragh persisted. "Jhenini and the others
have deciphered the secret, as Raajek and I have said all
along. Animals—*iado*—could not do that, Frraghi. *Iado*
could not create the Floating Stones, could not make the
Flying Room, could not have learned to speak our language as Jhenini has. The humans are not simple animals;
in fact, what I have seen of their world frightens me
because I wonder who is more advanced: them or us. At
the very least, the OColi should learn of what has happened here."

"The OColi . . ." Frraghi snorted, and that strange
scent came again. "Our OColi has ordered them to be

Given to the All-Ancestor. That is what I *think*, and it is also all I need to know."

The voice that answered was a new one in the argument.

"Then, Frraghi Speaker-for-the-OColi," said the voice, "you should also know that I'm holding the weapon you call a Far-Killer, and I will quite happily take your head off if you move."

The voice—speaking the Mutata language better than Jhenini ever had—came from the Flying Room. Mhundo was standing up in the open door, holding one of the humans' rifles in his hands. The ugly, multibar-reled end was pointed at Frraghi.

At the sight of the white ape, Lhath charged the Flying Room brandishing his spear. Mhundo turned at the sound and fired. The percussive report was loud in the clearing, sending flying lizards screeching from the tops of the fern-trees as dark earth fountained up at Lhath's feet. Lhath, startled, went sprawling as the Mutata tried to scramble backward as quickly as he had advanced.

Mhundo clicked his tongue reprovingly.

"Uh-uh-uh, you big dumb lizard," he said in English, then switched back to Mutata. "I think we have a stand-off," the ape told Frraghi and SStragh.

"No, we do not," answered a soft voice.

Jennifer knew the form that had emerged from between the fern-trees nearest the time machine. The Mutata's blind, ancient face seemed more sad and care-worn than before, and a young Mutata stood at her elbow guiding her. For the first time, Jennifer noticed that the gray-white mounds of the Mutata village could be seen through the ferns. Evidently the Mutata had moved the Floating Stone close to the village since she and the others had gone through into the Japanese timeline; she wondered how long they'd been gone from here—far longer than the week or so it had been for them, Jennifer suspected.

"Raajek!" she said. "It's good to see you!"

"Jhenini," she said. "I smell your presence, and the presence of several others of your kind. SStragh, is what you say true?"

"Yes, OTsio Raajek," Struth answered. "It is. The humans can seal off the pathways through the Floating Stones. You must convince the OColi to rescind his order and to have the Gairk do the same."

"The OColi . . ." Raajek's normal sour odor became more prominent with that, and her stance became more erect. "That could be interesting. It is amazing how your thinking changes like the clouds when the burden suddenly falls to you. The way I used to rail at poor Tiafer . . . and I find that now I understand what he was feeling all too well . . ."

Struth realized it first. "OColi Tiafer has died," the Mutata blurted out. *"You're* the OColi now."

"Yes, she is," Fergie said. "And she has been a good one, despite my fears."

"OTsio—" Struth began, and Raajek corrected the younger Mutata with a shiver of her body.

"Not 'OTsio,' SStragh. Not any longer. The OColi cannot be an OTsio to any Mutata; you know that law as well as I do. I am no longer your mentor, you are no longer my student. I release you from that burden. The OColi's duty is only to the OColihi."

"OColi Raajek," Jennifer asked. "What about the OChiihi, your New Path? Don't you see? All the same problems are still present . . ."

"Forget that. What about *me?*" shrilled Mundo. The ape brandished the rifle, the ugly barrel glinting in the bright sun. "Talk, talk, talk. Don't forget who's holding the weapon here."

Raajek's wrinkled snout twitched as she lifted her head in Mundo's direction. "Your scent is odd," Raajek told Mundo. "You're nothing I have met before. You smell of bravado and confidence, but not of wisdom."

"I don't need wisdom," Mundo said. "That's the beauty of a gun. All you have to do is point it the right way. Boom—I win and you do what I say. No wisdom needed."

Aaron moved quickly across the clearing toward Jennifer. The Mutata watched him carefully and Fergie growled, but none of them made any move to stop him. The two hugged each other fiercely.

"Jen, what's going on? Who's on whose side here?" Aaron whispered.

"I'm not quite sure," Jennifer answered. Reluctantly, she released Aaron, calling out to Mundo. "Mundo, listen to me. Raajek is Struth's teacher, her mentor. She's saved me and Peter several times over."

"I am *so* impressed," Mundo answered sarcastically. "Then I'm sure she won't mind calling off her spear-carrying friends."

Mundo turned to Raajek, his dark snout wrinkled, and spoke in Mutata. "You understand me, OColi Raajek? I want you to tell Fergie and the others to leave right now or I start taking out people, starting with you. *I'm* getting out of here—I'm going through portals until I find *my* world again."

"No, you are not," Raajek said softly and quietly. "The moment you make the Far-Killer speak with its deadly mouth, each Mutata here will attack. You will certainly kill me, as you say. You may even kill several of us. But you will not kill us all, and those you do not kill will be ready to give your spirit to the All-Ancestor, if She will take you."

"You're all crazy," Mundo spat out. "Half of you would be committing suicide."

"We would be protecting the eggs to come. We would be following the OColihi." Raajek seemed to smile at Mundo. "We would do it, each of us. That is our wisdom—we do not have *ghunss.*" Raajek used the English word, slurring the syllables and half whistling the end.

"Believe the OColi, White-Fur," Fergie snorted. "There are four hands of Mutata here around you. One of us will reach you."

Jennifer had been quietly translating for Aaron and Travis. Travis added his own counsel. "Mundo, even if that's a fully loaded weapon—and given what we've been through, that's doubtful—you're not going to take them all out. If they all rush at once, you won't be able to pull the trigger fast enough; put the rifle on full auto that long and it's going to overheat and lock up."

"You're lying," Mundo spat.

Travis shrugged. "You're the one who can read minds. Read mine. Read the dinosaurs'. Or just call the bluff. It's your life." He coughed and went silent.

"Mundo," Jennifer said. "You can trust Raajek. You can."

Mundo shivered, snared in indecision. His finger curled around the trigger—tensing, relaxing, then tensing again. Jennifer thought that the ape would fire, that she would see chattering, explosive death rip through the Mutata.

But Mundo finally gave a cry almost of pain and tossed the rifle aside.

"You'd better be right," he said to Jennifer as the Muta-ta swarmed over the time machine and pulled him out, as Frraghi came to stand behind Jennifer, Aaron, and Travis.

Raajek's blind, unreadable face was turned toward Jen-nifer. And what she said then scoured away the relief she felt.

"I am not the Raajek you remember, Jhenini," she said. "The OColi is not the OTsio. I give you your lives, but nothing else. You will seal off the Floating Stones. All of them. And the first one you will seal is the one which brought Jhenini here."

2

The Death of the OColi

Under Fergie's direction, Peter and Eckels were brought out of the time machine. Peter was conscious, though bruised, groggy, and in considerable pain from his healing gunshot wound and the rough ride; Eckels simply looked angry.

"Oh, this is just great," the man said as he stepped down from the machine, flanked by two Mutata guards. "We should have stayed where we were. These damn lizards tried to *kill* me the last time."

"You tried to blow them up. What'd you expect them to do?" Jennifer asked him. Eckels glared at her, sullen.

Raajek called out to Fergie. "We'll go to the Floating Stone you brought from the hills," Jennifer heard the new OColi say.

Fergie lifted his head briefly to Raajek in acknowledgment, then arranged the other Mutata around the rag-tag group of humans and began herding them through the screening ferns. Aaron touched Jennifer's arm. "Jenny, what's going on? Is Raajek on our side or not?"

Jennifer shook her head. "Right now, I'm not sure."

"Well, Struth sure doesn't look happy." Aaron nodded to the front of the group, where Struth and Raajek were conversing earnestly. Struth's scent was sour, and her stance was slumped—that was enough to tell Jennifer that whatever Struth was hearing from Raajek wasn't pleasant.

"Stay here. I'm going to try to talk to Raajek myself," Jennifer told Aaron. "Keep an eye on the others; you may need to give Travis a hand."

"Jenny . . ." Aaron began. He exhaled loudly. "One thing . . . I'm not about to trade one kind of captivity for another. I don't think any of us is willing to do that. I want to find a way to set all this right, and I suspect that's what they want, too, but we can't do that if we're prisoners. You tell them so, okay?"

Jennifer put herself in front of Aaron so that he had to stop. The Mutata nearest them squawked in irritation, but Jennifer ignored the protest, hugging Aaron. For a second, he just accepted the embrace, standing there unmoving, then finally he put his arms around her.

"We'll be okay," she whispered, then reluctantly let him go. She gave Aaron a quick kiss and then moved forward with a worried glance at Travis, who looked as if he were about to collapse.

". . . you do not preach the OChiihi anymore?" Struth was asking as Jennifer approached. "Why, OColi Raajek?"

Raajek smelled of damp earth and musk as they moved through the fronds, and her ancient body shivered with a palsy worse than anything Jennifer remembered. Jennifer might not know the Mutata physiology, but it didn't take a medical expert to see that Raajek was ill. She would not be OColi long, Jennifer feared.

"Do you know how OColi Tiafer died?" Raajek said in her trembling voice.

"No, OColi."

"Then let me tell you . . ."

The Dreaming Storm which took you was worse than any we had yet experienced (Raajek said). Not only did the human's steel bird attack those guarding the Floating Stone, not only did Jhenini and you, SStragh, follow it, but the storm left its mark on our *jhaka* itself. I was half-sleeping, the grumbling of the storm as it approached having stirred me from my rest, when the Breath of the All-Ancestor, the wind, suddenly whistled through the halls of the dwellings. I woke fully and felt my way to the window. In that moment, lightning flashed—close enough that even though my blind eyes could not see it, I could feel the heat of its passage. The thunderclap came in the same instant, a storm-shout so loud that it deafened me and I could hear nothing for several breaths after that. I could smell the knife-scent of the strike in the air.

The thunder spoke a few more times and, through the wind and the noise of the storm, I could hear voices shouting in distress. There were strange cries and cries of pain. I called out, but no one came to tell me what was happening; after a time, I could hear nothing. The wind calmed, the storm passed.

Not long after, Frraghi—smelling of fury and sorrow—entered my chamber in the Elder's Dwelling. "OTsio Raajek," he said without any politeness, his voice clipped and rushed. "The OColi desires to speak with you. Unless I return for you before then, you are to come to the OColi's Hall as soon as the skyfire shows its face above the hills. That is the OColi's will."

"What has happened?" I asked Frraghi, but he acted as if I were a youngling asking impertinent questions, sending me no scent of respect. I didn't hear him move, so I knew he was standing there with his head low, as if he were the elder of the two of us. "I have done what was asked and spoken for the OColi," Frraghi said. "I must return to him. I don't have time to waste with you."

I should have insisted that Frraghi give me the respect due my age, but I did not. I was weary, tired of it all. I had never felt so far from the All-Ancestor, and I knew, I *knew* that you had gone from me, SStragh, you who were my last *otsioiue*, even though no one had yet told me what had happened. I knew because there was an emptiness to the night, a void in my heart. So I simply nodded toward Frraghi and listened to him walk away. For a long time, I stood in front of the window. As soon as I felt the warmth of the skyfire, I felt my way down the halls of the dwellings to OColi Tiafer.

Or at least I started to do so.

I came to the doorway to the OColi's Hall. I thought I could smell Frraghi somewhere nearby, though he said nothing to me. There was another scent, so strong that it masked all the others, something sharp and astringent that I couldn't identify.

In that moment, my hand, which had been guiding me along one wall, touched something slick, wet, and unfamiliar. The comfortable old walls had vanished, and I could hear the breeze moving in open air and feel the sun warming my body even though there should have been a stone roof over my head. I pulled my hand back, and the slime clung to my fingers like the meat from a *guijia* melon. Some of the same clinging material fell on my shoulder and neck at the same time, as if it had dripped from above. I shook my neck, flinging some of it off, but it clung stubbornly. For several seconds the mess felt simply wet and cold on my skin, but suddenly I could feel my skin prickling and heating where it touched. I shook my body violently, trying to get rid of the burning.

"Frraghi!" The OColi's ruined voice croaked from nearby, the very fact that he chose to speak audibly telling me how agitated he was. "This is not the Way!"

Frraghi's scent became stronger as he came near me, and his hands roughly grabbed me and pulled me back. I heard the sound of wood against stone, and suddenly cold water was flung over my hand and neck. The burning lessened. I heard the bucket being refilled, then I was doused again, and one more time before the burning finally ceased. Shivering and wet, I stood there gasping.

"OColi," I said. "What has happened here?"

"Tell her," the OColi grunted to Frraghi, and I could hear pain in Tiafer's poor voice, deeper and more intense than anything I had ever heard in him before. The breeze brought me his scent then, and I could smell nothing but sickly-sweet corruption, as if I were smelling meat rotting in the sun. I felt sadness, for though Tiafer and I had always been on opposite philosophical sides, I respected him and I never wished him ill. He was suffering now, and I could not see him to know why.

"It was during the Dreaming Storm," Frraghi said. "I was in the OColi's Hall with him, listening to the howling of chaos and watching nightmare landscapes appear and disappear around us—all caused because we listened to SStragh and you, Raajek. Because we did not follow the OColihi and allowed the human abominations to live when the All-Ancestor cried for their souls. This is *your* fault, Raajek."

"Frraghi—" Tiafer interrupted warningly.

"I am sorry, my OColi," he answered, and took up his tale again. "The storm hurled its lightning directly above us, the thunder screaming at the same time. Something hit the roof, a heavy sound and yet not quite solid, as if whatever had landed there was soft, as well. I went to the opening to look out; the OColi remained among the warming rocks. Maybe if I had stayed near him . . ." Frraghi stopped, and I smelled regret.

"There was a sound from above, not unlike water boiling in a clay pot, and a smell unlike anything else," Frraghi continued. "There was no warning past that. The sizzling became loud and then the roof was *gone*, melting away like the hard, white rain that fell one winter when I was young. A curtain of translucent, gelatinous material cascaded heavily from above, coating the rocks and ground and covering the OColi as well. He . . ." Frraghi stopped, and I knew that he must be looking at the OColi, for his scent had gone all soft and respectful, tinged with a mourning that I did not yet understand.

"Continue," Tiafer grunted softly, and I heard Frraghi lift his head in mute obedience.

"I heard a sound that will haunt my nights," Frraghi said, "for the OColi screamed in terror and pain. 'It eats me!' he shouted. You know how the effort of speaking rips at the OColi's throat, OTsio Raajek. You know how his voice has been ruined by the nodules in his throat, and how they send searing agony through the OColi if he raises his voice above a whisper. Yet not only did I hear him plainly, but several others came running from nearby rooms. I rushed to the OColi, and I tried to brush away the mess, but it burned my hands—here, feel them."

Frraghi thrust his hands into mine. I brushed my fingertips over them. They were blistered, raw and tender and oozing fluid. "Frraghi," I said, "I am sorry. They must hurt—"

"Imagine your whole body that way, OTsio," Frraghi raged back at me. "Imagine that kind of pain, and then think of the OColi, for that is what he feels. Whatever the Dreaming Storm brought, it could melt stone and flesh both. Lhath heard both the OColi and me screaming, and he brought water and threw it over us. That eased the burning, and I plunged my hands into the next bucket, rinsing away the awful stuff. We scrubbed the OColi with water and leaves, but. . ."

Frraghi stopped, and I shuddered. He didn't need to say more. I could smell the rot. I could hear the distress in the OColi's asthmatic, labored breath.

I could sense the presence of Amath, the All-Ancestor's left hand, who comes to take away the souls of the dying. I could feel Amath lurking. Waiting.

"Thank you for pulling me back," I told Frraghi. I felt cold and weak, and Frraghi's disdainful scent wrapped around me like a choking vine on a tree.

"I would have let you blunder into the mess, OTsio," Frraghi said bitterly, "even though the dream-stuff no longer burns as harshly as it did. I wanted you to feel some of the pain of the OColi. I wanted you to hurt. I wanted you to feel the results of what your New Path and your tolerance of the humans have brought us. But the OColi would not permit it."

"Frraghi . . ." I stopped.

There were no words for the way I felt. None at all. I think my beliefs began to shatter in that moment, SStragh. I felt the OChiihi dissolve under the impact of this dreamstuff the Dreaming Storm had sent. You had disappeared, sneaking Jhenini out of her encampment when you knew that doing so might cause her death if you met with Gairk. The guards we'd set around the Floating Stone of the hard-shelled humans had been attacked by the steel bird of these other humans, and they had seen you and Jhenini following them through the gateway in the midst of the Dreaming Storm's confusion. You were gone, the humans were gone, and the Dreaming Storms of the OChiihi had attacked the OColi. I felt betrayed, SStragh. I felt sick.

"Raajek," the OColi whispered in his quavering, lost voice, and I felt my way over to him. He hissed as I approached, like a female youngling approaching her first heat, warning me not to touch him. The sound of his voice came from low, and I knew that the OColi was lying down on the stones, too weak to rise.

"OColi," I said as I crouched alongside him. "I am sorry."

"Bend down, Raajek," he whispered. His sour breath filled my nostrils. "Listen to old Tiafer while you can. You and I have fought our war of words for hands upon hands of years, Raajek, since we were both named OTsio back when Iyaati was OColi, and then Weria and Shiasi after her. When Shiasi died and I was suddenly Eldest, I would have stood aside for you, Raajek, because the need to be OColi was strongest inside you. It was only your arrogant belief in your New Path that made me accept the burden. Did you understand that then?—I became OColi because I did not want *you* to take that position. So we continued our fight over the years. Now it ends."

"Tiafer," I said. "Rest. We don't need to speak of this now."

Tiafer gave a short bark of amusement. "And when would you rather we speak, Raajek? When is the last time you had a conversation with a pile of bones in the Giving Hall? I *have* no other time," Tiafer continued urgently. "You never lied to me, Raajek; if anything, you spoke your true thoughts harshly and you make a poor liar now. Amath is waiting for me; you know that as well as I do. Your OChiihi has killed me." Tiafer stopped, gasping for breath, and even though I could barely hear his next words, each of them was like the blow of a Gairk's war club. "You *will* be OColi now."

Tiafer remembered all too well, SStragh. I *had* wanted to be the OColi. I'd wanted to be the Eldest, the Mutata whose least word was law, and I'd wanted it because I was so full of myself, so certain that I was right and all the old ways and all the old teachings were wrong. Tiafer had named me rightly: arrogant I had been, arrogant I still was.

"Tiafer—"

"No, Raajek," the OColi said with a trace of his former heat, "you have no choice in this. This is my final curse on you, my revenge, and I *will* have it. You will be OColi."

"Why, Tiafer? Aren't you afraid that I will abandon the OColihi that you've followed for so long?"

"I am very afraid. I am afraid to meet the All-Ancestor at last. I am afraid that no matter what anyone does, this will be the last generation of Mutata and Gairk in our valley. I am afraid that I will die poorly. But I'm *not* afraid to call you the OColi, Raajek."

The OColi's voice had become weaker and weaker, until I could barely hear him through the liquid exhalation of his breath. For a long time he did nothing but lie and recover enough strength to speak again, but always,

always his scent was that of a victor in *ciosie*, as if he'd won some unseen battle between us. At last I heard the rustle as he lifted his old head once more. I could feel the stare of his one good eye on me.

"I have learned a little wisdom in my time as OColi," Tiafer said. "Just a little. But it's enough to know that being the OColi will change you, Raajek. It will change you as it changed me. And if you don't . . ." Again, the laughter, and the scent of strange victory. "Well, what does it matter? If the Dreaming Storms continue, if the Floating Stones keep sending strange creatures to trouble us, then there will be no need for an OColi, since there will be no Mutata to follow the Eldest."

"Tiafer," I began again, but once more the OColi interrupted me, and I went silent so I could hear his words.

"There is one other curse I lay on you, Raajek," he said.

"What is that?" I asked him.

"You will stay with me until Amath comes to carry me back to the All-Ancestor. You will stay."

I lifted my head in submission. "You are my OColi," I told him. "I will always do as you ask."

I lay down alongside Tiafer. His body was as warm as the stones of the hills in summer's heat, as if a fire were consuming him from inside. He said nothing more, and by the time the skyfire had risen high enough to touch us with its warmth, Tiafer had begun to shake with a fever, occasionally murmuring words that I could barely understand. He seemed to be talking with the ghost of his OTsio Khiar, who had been killed long ago. "Khiar," he gasped, trembling with the burning of the fever, "I know she disturbs you with what she says. But she is my friend, and she will make a better OColi than me, if either of us is given that long a life."

I knew that Tiafer spoke of me.

I stayed with him all that day, and through the cold dark after the skyfire hid itself behind the mountains beyond our valley. When I heard the *saitie* announcing the coming of dawn with their chirping, I thought the time had come. Tiafer groaned and his body convulsed, as if Amath were inside the OColi, tearing the soul from the living body. "Frraghi," I called softly. Frraghi had stayed with us as well, and now he came and lay down on the other side of Tiafer. We both laid our hands on him, asking Amath to give us some of the pain of Tiafer's death. Under my fingertips, his body felt skeletal, and where his scales had fallen away, huge liquid-filled blisters marred the skin.

I kept hearing Frraghi's accusing voice in my head. *This is your fault, Raajek.*

Maybe Amath had listened to our plea, for Tiafer stirred, and he spoke coherently for the first time since the fever had come. "Frraghi," he said, "listen to me. On you I put this burden: serve OColi Raajek as you served me. Be her Eyes as you have been my Voice."

I heard Frraghi's hiss of displeasure, and I knew that he gave me a glance of hatred. "OColi Tiafer," he began, "I cannot—"

"You *must*. I give you no choice. Do you hear me now, Frraghi, you who were once Speaker-for-the-OColi?"

A sigh. "I hear you, OColi."

"Good. And you, Raajek . . ." Tiafer paused, and I wished I could see him. I wanted to see his old face one last time. I wanted to see the expression in his eyes.

But I could not. I could only listen, and hold his dying body.

"You must find the way, Raajek. Find the way . . ."

Those were the last words he spoke. His body relaxed as he gave up the inner struggle and surrendered to Amath. For a long time, he continued to breathe, but the sound became fainter and fainter until I could no longer hear it. His body, so warm before, began to grow cold. At last I heard Frraghi stir from his seated position. "He is gone," Frraghi said. "What is your wish, OColi?"

OColi. I had never expected to be addressed by that title.

"Who is Amath's Hand now?" I asked Frraghi. "It's been so long since I attended a Giving."

"Jokata is Amath's Hand for us."

"Then go to Jokata and have her bring OColi Tiafer to the Giving Hall." I heard Frraghi lift his head and begin to go, but I called to him. "Frraghi . . ."

"OColi?" He said the word so easily, so mockingly.

"Will you Give Tiafer when it is time, Frraghi?"

"I will be honored, OColi," Frraghi answered, and though I searched his voice, I found nothing there: not respect, not resignation, not even hatred. His words had the barrenness of someone who was beyond emotion.

Frraghi left me.

I stayed behind, clutching Tiafer's dead body to me as if I were trying to hold back time itself, until Frraghi returned.

"OColi Raajek," Struth said after a long silence, during which the column of Mutata and humans moved through the lush jungle near the Mutata village. Jennifer looked back at Aaron, who cocked his head quizzically at her. Jennifer shrugged and moved closer to Struth, listening. "I'm sorry to hear of OColi Tiafer's death, but I would have thought . . ."

Raajek chuckled sadly—a melodious trill of notes through her nasal horn—as Struth's voice trailed off.

"You thought that I would have used my position to replace the OColihi with the OChiihi I preached for so long. I would have thought it too. Maybe I would have: if you and Jhenini had not disappeared, if Eckels and Pee-tah had not used their horrible magic on the Gairk, if the Dreaming Storms had not continued or if the attacks from the Floating Stones had ceased. But none of those things happened, SStragh. The Raajek you knew died with Tiafer, SStragh. I am not her."

Fergie, at the head of the group, pushed through a last barrier of ferns just ahead of them. Through the verdant lace of the fronds, Jennifer could see a small opening and another piece of the roadway. The place was nowhere that Jennifer remembered, but the shape of the fragment of roadway was all too familiar. It seemed years ago that she and Peter had first stepped into Dinosaur World through that opening between worlds.

Fergie led Raajek into the clearing, until the old Muta-ta stood alongside the broken path hovering a few inches above the ground. There she turned to face the group straggling in. Her blind eyes seemed to search each one of them sternly. "SStragh, you will take the one called Aaron and seal this stone. Jhenini and the others will stay here with us. The burden is on you—return by the time the skyfire leaves, or the others will be sent to the All-Ancestor as Tiafer wished."

Thunder answered her declaration.

3

A Race in Time

In other circumstances, Aaron would have found the hike fascinating, as they passed through a lush world that was only a dim, fragmented memory locked in stone in his own time, as creatures that—to him—had existed only in brittle, silent frames of bones skittered away, screeching and chittering as they fled from the small army of Mutata and humans. A miracle of paleontology was taking place before his eyes, and he had no interest in it.

His attention was almost entirely on Jennifer, who was talking with Struth and Raajek. The old blind Mutata seemed to be doing most of the talking.

"Jenny—" He called aloud and began to push forward, but the nearest Mutata thumped him between the shoulder blades with the end of his spear. Aaron stumbled and started to get up, ready to strike back, but Jennifer shook her head at him, giving him a worried smile.

Peter had come to a halt as they thrashed through the last curtain of ferns. "Aaron, that's *our* stone, man!" he exclaimed. "We can't let them close—"

The Mutata alongside the redheaded youth lifted his spear warningly, and Peter subsided into sullen silence.

Raajek moved out into the clearing, the old Mutata walking painfully. She stood in front of the fragment of Travis's path and said something. From the look on Jennifer's face, it was nothing pleasant. With the words, like a portent, thunder grumbled in the clear blue sky.

"Oh no," Aaron said. "Here we go again."

Aaron remembered watching storms roll in from the hill in back of his house. Thunderclouds, glaring achingly white in the sun, would lift above the horizon like drifting, snow-clad mountains. As they approached, the dark outriders of the front appeared below: rolling streaks of gray-black; violet so dark it was almost black; or that strange, ugly, green-black that the worst storms could produce. The true heralds of the storm—the wind, the jittery flash of distant lightning, and the trailing kettle-drum rumbling of thunder—would make their appearance on the stage of the sky. As Aaron made his retreat to the back porch, they would stalk closer and closer until the wind forced the trees to bow down before the storm's majesty, and the thunder crashed while lightning reached out with broken fingers of glaring blue electricity as hot as a welder's torch. And then the rain came, rushing across the tops of the trees like a pale gray curtain. . . .

The time storm was like that, only in fast motion. Seeing the apparition approach was like watching time-lapse photography of an Illinois thunderstorm projected on the giant holographic screen of the sky.

"This is like the last time," Jennifer shouted into the rising wind. "Remember when we left Dinosaur World the last time, and again a few minutes ago when we came back? The time storms show up when a portal's about to be activated."

Aaron didn't like the implications of that at all. The logic—or rather, the lack of it—made his head spin. The wind was picking up; the lightning flickered faster, and the clouds were nearly overhead. Aaron had to shout to make himself heard. "Jenny, that's crazy. The portals would have to be able to know the future, if that's true. Besides, who says anyone's going through now?"

"Raajek does," Jennifer answered. She translated what Raajek had just said: *SStragh, you will take the one called Aaron and seal this stone*. The protest came from all of them at once. "No!—" "That's insane . . ." "No way, man, I ain't getting stuck here again—" "I won't—"

"Tell Raajek that we can't," Aaron said insistently in the hubbub, glancing up worriedly at the darkening sky. "Jenny, the time differential alone might make that impossible. I mean, *years* went by in Green Town in the few days I was in the Mesozoic, and while we were in the Nipponjin timeline, months passed here. The time on either side of the portal is chaotic. If Struth and I go through, even for a few minutes, that might be hours or days here. That's assuming we don't hit any trouble on the other side—and I don't know *what* kind of reception we're going to find there this time. Captain Michaels had the path in a guarded lab; and even if Michaels turned out to be okay in the end, her friends weren't the least bit shy about shooting before asking questions. Heck, Captain Michaels might not even *exist* there anymore. Tell Raajek that."

"Lie to her," Peter interjected. "Tell her that you need *all* of us to do it. Then we'll just pop through and never come back. At the very least tell the lizard that Aaron needs you and me, Jenny. That'll get us back *home*, no matter how strange Aaron claims it is."

"Hey!" Eckels and Mundo shouted simultaneously; Travis, sinking down wearily on the ground, just shook his head.

Jennifer gave Peter a look as angry as the sky. "Then Raajek will ask Struth if that's true, and Struth can't lie to her, not to Raajek."

Jennifer looked back to Aaron, and her gaze was help-less. She turned to Raajek and spat out a series of grunts and whistles; the Mutata replied in kind, and Aaron knew what had been said by the way her shoulders sagged as the old dinosaur spoke. "She doesn't understand the time differential problem," Jennifer said to them. "The whole concept escapes her. She won't change what she's ordered. Aaron, I don't see that we have a choice. You just have to do the best you can, as fast as you can."

"Jenny, there's one thing I *do* need," Aaron said. The swirling wind snatched at his words and hurled them away. "If it has to be Struth and me, fine, but I can't com-municate with her, and that's a necessity. I need you to translate. Explain that to them, and hurry; the storm's gonna be on us any second."

"Hey!" Peter protested, his face coloring as the wind tousled his hair. "Then you and Jenny go through and leave *me?* No way!"

"That's not what I'm after—" Aaron began to explain, but Raajek interrupted with an insistent hoot.

Jennifer spoke desperately with Raajek, who snorted. She lowered her head, saying something to Jennifer, who—strangely, to Aaron—lifted her own chin before turning back to Aaron. "She said Mundo can translate. Mundo's to go with you, not me."

"Hah!" Peter exclaimed. He almost sounded pleased.

"No problem," Mundo answered before Aaron could speak. The wind was whipping his long white fur around, like a hundred invisible hands stroking his body. The sky was entirely overcast now, the clouds an ugly, impossible purple, and the lightning was strobing nearer. "And if this storm is an indicator, we're going through the portal any second. Let's get *out* of here."

Aaron blinked dust from his eyes. The Mutata were shuffling around them nervously, making strange noises and glancing at the sky warily. "Jenny—"

"Aaron, right now we don't have a choice."

"Yeah, and it doesn't look like the blind dragon's about to give you an extension on her deadline, so we'd better move," Mundo added.

"All right," Aaron said. He hugged Jennifer to him fiercely, knotting his fingers in her hair as he brought her to him. He tried to memorize the feel of her, the smell of her hair, the sound of her voice. He wanted to curse, to rail against fate. It all seemed so unfair, to have finally found Jennifer again only to be forced apart once more.

"I'll be back as quickly as I can," he told her as he let her go. Jennifer looked up at him and smiled.

"If you see my mom, tell her I'm okay."

"Sure." Aaron looked at Peter, at Travis and Eckels. "I won't waste a second. I promise."

Eckels sniffed; Travis nodded wearily. Peter wouldn't look at him. Lightning crackled as Aaron turned to Struth and Mundo, throwing harsh shadows across the glade and leaving the sharp scent of ozone. With the flash, the visions of broken timelines began their erratic dance, living images of strange worlds flung down to live for a few seconds and then disappear again in the strobo-scopic flashes of the time storm.

As Aaron, Mundo, and Struth stepped onto the float-ing roadway, Aaron saw a pale slug the size of a subway car, with what looked to be an adolescent boy's torso grafted onto the top of it, appear where fern-trees had once been. Black sewer pipes stabbed the body like monstrous pins, pinning it to a section of tiled floor. A penguin wearing what looked like a funnel for a hat and ice skates on its flippers stood in front of the gigantic apparition. The scene looked like something from a Hieronymus Bosch painting. The boy/slug seemed to wave to them . . .

. . . and then the apparition was gone as Aaron fell into the cold emptiness between the worlds.

Despite everything he knew, despite the fact that he'd already seen history twisted and warped, Aaron had hoped to see Green Town—restored, familiar, and plain. He'd hoped that somehow, magically, everything would have been restored, even though he understood that if that were the case, it would be very difficult for him to perform the task he'd been sent to do and close off Green Town from Jennifer, Peter, and himself.

He needn't have worried about it.

The Green Town he remembered wasn't there. Neither was the lab.

They stepped down from the roadway onto untouched prairie. The wind swayed tall grass bluestems and indian grass. Waist-high to Aaron. Sunflowers dotted the rolling plain, with a grand assortment of other flowers providing splashes of blues, oranges, and reds. Rabbits bounded away as Struth came down to stand alongside Aaron; upwind of them an elk stared in their direction as it pulled up grass; meadowlarks and plovers performed acrobatics in the sky as they gave their distinctive calls. The meadow ran down to a wide, meandering creek; in the distance, the Ohio River could be seen through a line of trees.

Humid summer had returned: the sun glared down from an open sky and sweat immediately broke out on Aaron's forehead. Struth was snorting and whistling in her own tongue as she gazed around.

And Mundo was loping away like a white lion, charging through the high grass.

"Mundo!" Aaron shouted. "Damn it, Mundo . . ." *You half expected it*, he told himself. *You knew you couldn't trust him. Mundo's out entirely for himself.* At Aaron's cry, Mundo stopped already a hundred yards away. He stood there for long seconds without moving, then turned and came slowly back to Aaron. He glanced at Aaron without apology, his black muzzle wrinkled and burrs snagged in his fur. "It's all gone," Mundo said. "All changed. Not your world, but not mine, either. All I hear is silence in my head."

"You were going to run. You would have left me here."

Mundo snorted derisively. "Tell me you wouldn't have done the same. Tell me that if it were Peter and your precious girlfriend who were here instead of me and Big Horn-Nose that you wouldn't have left the rest of us behind with the Mutata."

Aaron hesitated. *You might have*, he admitted to himself, even though he knew that Mundo could pick up such surface thoughts. *You would have been tempted.*

"I thought so," Mundo said scoffingly. "Well, this isn't your home *or* mine. Neither one of us has anywhere to run."

"Maybe that's just as well," Aaron answered, though the ache that was swelling up inside him denied his statement. He knew what must have happened, what *had* to have happened: the Compound's experiments into the past had continued after Aaron and Travis had left this timeline. The scientists in charge hadn't understood that

each time they performed such an experiment they
changed the very history around them. One of those
experiments must have changed history drastically,
almost as radically as Travis's world had been changed.

From the untouched appearance of this prairie, the
Compound's mistake might have erased humanity from
history entirely.

*Everything we knew is gone. There has to be a way to get
it back. There has to be . . .* "Let's get this done and get
back to Jenny and the rest," Aaron said.

Struth whistled, evidently saying something as he
pointed to a small nearby hillock. "What's bothering
him?" Aaron asked Mundo.

"Something's there," Mundo said. "A tree branch with
a light, he says . . ."

Where Mundo was pointing, Aaron saw a stick like a
slender, twisted tree stem, knobby and curved like a
branch broken from a tree and stuck upright in the soft
ground. Among the sea of grass, it would have been easy
to have missed it entirely; looking at it caused Aaron to
shiver. The branch didn't seem entirely natural; the
brown surface was shiny, and there was indeed an
amber light at the tip, pointing directly toward the
piece of roadway—a light bright enough that it was
noticeable even in the sunlight. Aaron had seen
strange things in the last few weeks, but the light spoke
more of technology than biology gone awry. This had
seemed an empty, pastoral land; suddenly Aaron had
the hunch that they weren't quite as alone as they
thought. He had the sense that something, someone,
was watching.

"We can't be bothered with it," he said, more to himself than Mundo and Struth. "If we've set off some kind

of alarm, fine. Come on, let's finish this before whoever set it shows up."

Aaron went to his knees, pulling away the grass and weeds that cloaked the piece of roadway on this side. He lay down to peer under the path; mice scattered from under the shelter of the roadway. "I can see the stuff glowing. It looks the same as it did before," he called to Mundo. "Last time we came through here we had to put the fragments back in; now we'll just reverse the process. Shouldn't take more than a minute or so. Mundo, give me a hand here."

On his back, Aaron reached under the roadway. "I sure hope this junk isn't radioactive," he muttered as he tugged at the closest of the pieces of Eckels's wrecked temporal machinery. The charred, misshapen metal had embedded itself deeply into the softer material of the roadway—instead of coming out fairly easily, as had happened with the Japanese path, Aaron's efforts to dislodge the material only resulted in the roadway's bouncing up and down like a car with a bad pair of shocks. The glowing metal stayed firmly attached.

"So much for my estimate on time. If I were an auto mechanic, I'd lose my shirt. Mundo," he called out from under the path, "tell Struth to brace the edge of the roadway with her body, so it doesn't move while I pry the piece out." There was no answer. "Mundo? Hey . . ."

Turning his head to the side, he could see Mundo's and Struth's legs, so he knew they were still there. "Aaron, you'd better take a look at this," Mundo's voice said.

"Now what?" Aaron asked, annoyed, but he rolled out from under the roadway and stood up, blinking in the sunlight.

Struth honked something, pointing to the hillock with the light-stick.

The light was no longer glowing on the end of the branch. The brilliant glow was now resting on top of the stick, and there was a body attached to it, a body that looked as if it had been fashioned from burnished chrome and polished brass. Gossamer wings flickered above a shiny, wasplike body, the light still turning from the abdomen like some fantastic, deadly firefly. As Aaron watched, the insect seemed to grow, stretching until it was the size of a small bird. "It's been getting bigger since it came out of the stick," Mundo said. "I don't like it. It looks made, not natural."

"I'd agree, but it's not bothering us at the moment, and we're wasting time. How about giving me a hand—"

The wasp took flight. Like a sleek fighter jet, the creature arrowed toward them, its wings invisible in motion. Of nature or machine, there was a decided purpose in the thing. A high-pitched whine shrilled from its wings, dropping rapidly in pitch as it approached them. It rose, then banked and dropped like a bomber starting a strafing run.

Aaron and Mundo ducked instinctively. Aaron didn't know if Struth lacked the instinct—maybe insects didn't bother the Mutata, or maybe there weren't that many insects in their world to worry about—but Struth didn't react. She stood her ground, swatting at the attacker with a hand. The creature demonstrated an uncanny agility, dodging Struth's swipe and landing on the dinosaur's chest. The glowing abdomen raised threateningly and then stabbed down, a needle the size of a hypodermic sliding out of the body with the motion. Struth howled in pain.

She smashed the thing against her chest, crushing it.

It fell to the ground like a broken toy. Something greenish, that might have been bodily fluids or might have been an oily lubricant, dripped slowly from the broken joints.

A moment later, Struth fell alongside it.

4

Hypothetical Solutions

"He might not be back for hours yet, no matter how quickly he manages things."

Jennifer started at the sound of Travis's voice, realizing that she'd been staring sightlessly at the fragment of the path, trapped in moonlight as thick as milk. She wondered how long she'd been standing there, and a slight heat colored her cheeks at the realization that Travis had noticed. She was glad it was dark so that he couldn't see her embarrassment. "I know," she said. "But there isn't much else to do. How are you feeling?"

"Okay," the man grunted. "Thanks for your help."

"You need to be careful. I don't like the look of those wounds. I think you may have an infection starting, and I *know* some of those ribs are broken."

Travis gave her a wan grin. "You're the doctor—or the closest we have to one around here. I'll be careful."

The conversation faltered. Around them, the Mutata slumbered in the dark while several nocturnal guard-lizards prowled the perimeter of the camp. Eckels and Peter had fallen asleep while Jennifer had been brooding.

The world was just as active in the night as in the day, swirling with strange cries and calls from the animal life around them, with rustlings in the leaves around the edges of the meadows, with eyes that stared at them from the branches above. At the edge of the clearing, like a wart on otherwise unbroken skin, a small patch of rocky sand glimmered—a legacy of the time storm caused by Aaron's passage through the gateway between worlds. Two startled kangaroos had been transported along with this patch of what looked to be Australian outback. The 'roos had scattered off into the fern-tree jungle. Jennifer wondered if they were still alive, and what they thought of this primeval world in which they'd been marooned.

The sky was crowded with stars; the few clouds were luminous with the glow of the full moon behind them. A wind fragrant with the emerald scent of the prehistoric forest lifted the long strands of her hair appraisingly. "I've been thinking about what Aaron was saying about the time differential," Jennifer said softly. "If years went by in Green Town while a few months passed here, then—"

She stopped, biting her lower lip. "—then even a few days over there should only have been a minute or two here," she continued. She looked at Travis; under the dark ridges of his brows, she could see the gleam of his eyes, watching her. "He's been gone for hours," she said.

"I understand what you're saying," Travis answered. "But I'm not worried yet. With the time storms and the boundaries breaking down between timelines, nothing's constant. It may be there's *no* time difference between here and Green Town anymore, or maybe the timestreams have reversed so that their minutes are days here, or maybe it's totally chaotic and everything's a dice roll as to the way time works in any location."

Travis's words didn't help. Jennifer felt herself blinking away tears. Travis pulled Jennifer to him; she fell into the comforting embrace gratefully. "You're here and he's there, Jennifer. You can't change any of that. All you can do is make sure that you stay safe and alive until he gets back."

Jennifer tightened her arms around Travis, just wanting the feel of another human being close to her. "Hey!" he grunted. "Remember those ribs, Doc." He chuckled.

Jennifer found herself laughing with Travis. "Thanks," she said. "Thanks, Travis. You've helped. You really have."

"Least I can do. I'm partially responsible for this mess in the first place. You kids didn't ask to get trapped in this."

With the words, Travis glanced angrily at the slumbering Eckels. *He'd still kill the man if he was given half an excuse*, Jennifer realized. *Eckels murdered Travis's whole world, and Travis won't ever forgive him for that. . . .* "Besides," Travis continued, "I gave Aaron a pretty rough time at first. I was a little crazy there myself for awhile. I'm sorry. I was hurt and mad and . . . well, *frightened*."

Travis coughed, and Jennifer watched the way the man hunched over with inner pain. The rattling wheeze of his lungs worried her. "I guess I still am," he said. "But right now, the truth is that I'm too tired to feel much of anything."

Travis hugged her again, then moved away to lie down on the mossy black earth under one of the cycads. Jennifer continued to watch the path, trying to bring Aaron back with just the intensity of her desire.

But sleep overcame her will at some point. Jennifer was awakened by a sudden peal of thunder and the movement of cool air on her face. By the time she woke fully, the quick time storm had already passed, though the fronds of the fern-trees were still swaying with the memory of wind.

One thing else had changed.

Where there had been only moonlight on the roadway a moment ago, there was now something far more substantial.

"Struth!" Jennifer called, starting toward the roadway. Two of the guard-lizards immediately interposed themselves between Jennifer and the path, snarling and hissing angrily. That stirred Fergie from his sleep. The Mutata looked around groggily, several seconds passing before he seemed to come fully awake.

"There was a time storm and Struth's on the Floating Stone," Jennifer shouted to the semicomatose Mutata. "She looks . . . hurt." *She looks dead*, she told herself. Struth wasn't moving at all, lying on her side on the white surface. "Please, let me go to her!"

Fergie snorted something unintelligible, then snapped a command to the lizards, who backed away, still hissing. "Go ahead," Fergie snapped. Behind the Speaker, Raajek's blind eyes were opening, her head tilted as she listened to the commotion, and a few other Mutata were struggling to get to their feet in the cool night air. Peter was rubbing his eyes; Eckels was watching cautiously.

"Come on," Travis said to Jennifer. From his tone, Jennifer could tell that the man was as concerned as she was. "Let's get her off the roadway."

"Not with those ribs, you're not," she told him. "Peter, Eckels," Jennifer called. "Give me a hand."

This time it was Fergie who stepped in front of Jennifer as she, Peter, and Eckels approached the roadway and Struth. The Mutata glanced at Struth's motionless body, then at the humans, his spear facing toward them grasped in his left hand. "You cannot touch the Floating Stone," Fergie said. "I will not let you escape that way."

"Struth hasn't disappeared, so the Floating Stone is either sealed or won't work again until we move Struth," Jennifer insisted. "Look at her, Frraghi—she's just lying there. She needs help. Please."

"If SStraagh is dead, then such is the All-Ancestor's will. There is nothing you can do to help her."

"You don't know that."

"Let them go, Frraghi," Raajek called from the side. Fergie hesitated, then brought the spear back to his side and stepped away. "Yes, OColi," he said respectfully, then his great, muscular head turned back to Jennifer. A strong scent came from him, and Jennifer knew that there was some message being given her beyond the words. "I will be watching," he warned Jennifer. "Tell the other humans that."

Jennifer nodded, and translated for Peter and Eckels. Peter snorted defiantly, but Jennifer could see the caution in her friend's eyes as he sidled past Fergie. "I'll make you into a belt and a pair of boots if I get half a chance," he said, looking up at Fergie's stem gaze. Then Peter shrugged at Jennifer. "You don't really need to translate that for him, Jen."

Struth was huddled at one edge of the roadway. Jennifer was glad to see the slow rise and fall of her rib cage as they approached. "She's not dead, at least." Jennifer reached out and touched her helpless friend, half-expecting something to happen as she did so. Her hands tingled as she touched Struth, as if she'd touched a badly grounded appliance. She drew her hand back reflexively.

"What happened?" Peter asked.

"I just got shocked. Real mild, though. Hang on . . ."
Jennifer reached out again, and this time kept her hand
on Struth's side. The tingling continued, but there wasn't
any pain, nor did the sensation get any worse. "Her skin's
awfully cool, but that's probably because she just trans-
ferred between times. The path must still be open since I
can feel something tingling, but I don't think anything
will happen unless we're standing fully on it. Let's get
Struth off so I can see what's wrong with her. Peter, you
get by her head. You shouldn't do too much or you'll tear
that wound open again—just help us guide Struth. Eckels, can you handle her legs? It's like sticking your hand
on a bad wire, but it really doesn't hurt—just grab Struth
and pull her onto the ground. Okay, slowly now . . ."

Groaning with the strain, the three of them pulled
Struth to the edge of the broken path. Once the Mutata's
tail swung over the edge, the weight of it helped bring
the rest of her down. The roadway rocked gently as
Struth's inert body slid the few inches to the ground. Jennifer knelt beside Struth immediately. "I wish I had more
light. Her chest is all puffy on the right side, and there's
something wet there—"

Jennifer stopped. Eckels had whispered something to
Peter, and the redhead nodded. Jennifer knew what Peter
was going to do. She knew from the way his leg muscles
tensed, the way he crouched slightly, the way he was
looking at the broken roadway.

"Don't, Peter," she said. "You won't make it." Jennifer
could also see Fergie, his scaled body flashing in the
moonlight, as he drew his hand back. Starlight glimmered in the obsidian head of the weapon, both beautiful and menacing. Both Fergie and Peter were balanced,
held in the embrace of danger, each of them poised to

move. Eckels backed away, not caring to put himself in the same peril.

"*Peter*—" Jennifer whispered.

Her voice broke the spell.

"Fine!" he shouted at the night, his hands slashing through the air in fury. "Aaron and Mundo are probably—" He stopped.

"Probably what, Peter?" Jennifer demanded.

In the darkness, she could only only see a darkness under Peter's mop of unruly red hair, but she felt his stare. It seared her, as angry as a bonfire's flames. "Dead, Jennifer. There, I said it, okay? *Dead*. That's a damn good possibility, and you know it. And you know what else—the only way to find out is to go through: you, and me, and Eckels." His voice was suddenly eager. "If we all jump right now, I think we can make it before Macho Lizard here figures out which one of us he wants to shishkebab—and even if he *does* get one of us, the other two make it easy. So what do you say, Jen?"

"What about Travis?"

Peter's head jerked to Travis, who listened silently to one side, and back again. "He can try if he wants, too."

Travis said nothing; he only looked calmly at Jennifer, giving her no visual clues as to what he was thinking, though she knew that he could hear what Peter was saying. "He's hurt, Peter. He can't move fast enough."

"Then that's too bad. I'm sorry. I really am. But this is our chance. We may never get this close to the path again. Come *on*, Jen!"

She was tempted. Almost, she nodded. But she knew that the decision meant Travis's death, at the very least. Struth stirred then, groaning as if in some deep pain even though she remained unconscious, reminding Jennifer that her Mutata friend, too, was hurting. *Aaron, I'm sorry.*

"No," she told Peter. "I can't. Go on if you have to, but I'm staying."

"The lizards will kill you."

"Maybe. They haven't yet."

"Jen—" Peter loosed an exasperated sigh.

"No."

Fergie stood poised, the tip of his spear targeted for Peter's chest. Peter turned away from the path abruptly, stalking past Fergie and knocking the Mutata's spear aside with a hand. The dinosaur snorted.

"Your mother was a pair of cowboy boots," Peter answered as he walked back to the periphery of the encampment, Eckels following. The two were soon engaged in a whispered conversation, their backs to the others. Jennifer ignored them, going to Struth.

Fergie stood over the Mutata's prone body, watching wordlessly as Jennifer examined the unconscious dinosaur, though Jennifer was certain that the strong odor coming from Frraghi was an indication of an unvoiced irritation. At least she hoped it was just irritation and not something worse.

"Your youngling male is very stupid," Fergie grumbled at last.

"*Geedo*," Jennifer agreed. "He works very hard at it, too." Jennifer sighed, cursing the darkness and trying to see if there were any wounds on Struth's body. She dipped her finger in the strange stickiness on Struth's chest, sniffing the substance—it almost smelled like oil. There was a small puncture wound there; even by moonlight, Jennifer could see that the skin around it was swollen and puffy. Struth's breathing concerned her as well—she sounded as if she were laboring for breath, and there was a distinct wheeze as she exhaled.

Anaphylactic shock? Allergic reaction? What I need right now is a vial of epinephrine . . .

"Is she going to die?" Frraghi rumbled above her.

Do you really care, or is that what you're hoping? Jennifer wanted to ask. "No," she said quickly. Then: "I don't know. She looks like, well, like she was stung by a wasp— an awfully big wasp." Jennifer had to use the English word, not knowing if there was a term for the insect in Mutata, or if wasps even existed here. "They're like your *saitie*, only with a little stinging spear for a tail . . ."

And we don't have wasps huge enough to have done this in Green Town, either. Jennifer stopped, realizing the truth of the thought. *Whatever happened to Struth, it isn't from anything I remember in Green Town.*

Which meant that whatever trouble Aaron, Mundo, and Struth had run into wasn't something they were expecting. She wished Struth would wake up, so she could ask her—so she would *know* . . .

"Travis," she called. "Do you have epi or adrenaline in your medical supplies?"

"I'd guess so," he answered. "I never used the medkit, but they were supposed to be well stocked."

"Jhenini . . ." Raajek's quavering voice came, and at the same time she smelled the scent of rot from the sores on the blind Mutata's body. Fergie moved to support the new OColi, whose blind gaze stared out above her. "This is a sign. A portent from the All-Ancestor."

"What are you talking about? This isn't a *sign*," Jennifer answered heatedly. "Struth is hurt, that's all. She's having a reaction to a sting, or maybe there was some venom in it. That's all. I need to get to the medical kit in the time machine, Raajek. There might be something in there . . ."

"We will not allow you into the *maa-cheen*," Raajek said.

"You have to. The medkit—"

"Humans *lie*." It was Fergie who answered this time. "The OColi is wise. Jhenini would go into the *maa-cheen* and leave."

"If I don't get that kit, Raajek, I can't do anything for Struth. Don't you understand?"

"I understand that SStragh is in the hands of Amath and the All-Ancestor," Raajek insisted softly. The ancient Mutata's voice was gentle but stern, and Jennifer could see by the way her tail was held that she was speaking as an OTsio might: a teacher giving her student a lesson. "Jhenini, the All-Ancestor always speaks in signs. All of us know that, both Mutata and Gairk."

"When I last knew you, Raajek, you didn't *believe* in the OColihi. You kept telling the old OColi how wrong he was, how he needed to break out of the chains of the OColihi."

"Even when I preached the OChiihi against the OColihi, New Path against Old Path, I still believed that the All-Ancestor spoke to us, Jhenini. I never questioned that."

Jennifer sighed. "I guess I'll have to accept that. So . . . what does this sign of yours mean?"

Raajek stared into darkness. "It means that the All-Ancestor has grown tired of waiting for us to do what is needed. She sends SStragh back to me to tell me that we should do what OColi Tiafer always knew we must. Even in my blindness, I can hear this vision. Look with your eyes—Struth has nearly given herself to the All-Ancestor's hand."

It was true, Jennifer saw. Struth's breathing had become shallow and quick, her ribs barely moving.

Jennifer knew that, in a few moments, the Mutata's breathing would stop entirely.

"Struth . . ." she whispered. "Oh, God, Struth . . ."

"Jhenini, I am sorry, but your companions have failed. Now it is time for you also to make your peace with the All-Ancestor. Be glad. Go to Her with a joyful heart, and She will embrace you."

With Raajek's words, Fergie loosed a trill that sent the jungle momentarily silent while its echoes faded. He raised his spear in triumph.

Aaron lay on his back under the path, tugging desperately at the pieces of temporal machinery. Panic made his head buzz. A thousand thoughts threatened to sweep away his concentration. Sending Struth back had seemed the only solution, but now Aaron worried about how the Mutata would react when Struth showed up without them. What would Jennifer and the others think? Just how long had they been gone to those on the other side—seconds, hours, days?

It doesn't matter. All that matters is getting your job done here as fast as you can. "Mundo!" Aaron called. "What's going on now? Are there any more wasps forming?"

There wasn't an answer. Aaron turned his head to look out from under the shadow of the path, half-expecting to find that Mundo had left again. No, the ape was still there—he could see the white fur of Mundo's legs. Muttering in frustration, Aaron rolled out from under the path. "Look," he began. "I want to get this done and get out—"

Aaron stopped. Mundo was staring up the hill; following his gaze, Aaron let out a soft curse. Where the wasp's branch had sat, a wedge of ground had suddenly tilted, like a trapdoor being lifted. Rising from underneath was a silver apparition. Honeycomb eyes sparked on either side of a metallic wedge of a head. The mouth opened, and white mucous dripped from razored jaws. Triple pairs of appendages hung from a broad, glittering chest; the legs were great grasshopper springs, coiled and ready to leap. The thing looked to be every bit of ten feet tall.

Aaron decided that whatever it was, it wasn't likely to be friendly.

"I can't hear it," Mundo said. "There's no words in its head, just static."

"Mundo," he said softly. "Listen, my friend. We have to close the gateway *now*."

With a last glance back at the still-silent monstrosity, Aaron rolled back under the path, pulling at the glowing wreckage with the strength of desperation. There was a strange rhythmic pounding sound from outside. A moment later, Mundo was with him, and with the ape's greater strength, the misshapen metal groaned and came loose. "*Yes!*" Aaron exulted. Sparks suddenly hissed and spat along the under surface of the roadway. "Let's go!" Aaron cried. "The gateway's closing!"

The two of them rolled from under the pathway. Even as a glittering fireworks barrier formed around the fragment of path, the source of the pounding became apparent.

The silver creature was bounding toward them. A time storm was howling behind it, the wind flattening the prairie grass and tossing the branches of the trees.

The thing had already covered most of the distance to them, now bare yards away. It covered another thirty feet in a leap, its appendages stretched out toward them, its powerful legs crushing grass underneath it.

"Jump!" Aaron called to Mundo and dived for the path himself.

The beast of silver leapt at the same time.

"You can't mean that, Raajek," Jennifer said.

"I do," the OColi answered calmly. "The All-Ancestor asks for you with Struth's death. And I will give Her what she asks for."

"All you have to do is let me get the medical kit—"

"No."

Jennifer could see that Peter and Eckels had turned around to see what all the snorting and hooting was about; Travis was also watching carefully, sitting with his hands around his injured ribs. Jennifer judged the distance between herself and the open door to the time machine, which the Mutata had untangled from its net of vines. The interior glowed invitingly in the dark. *Peter was right. I blew our only chance to get out of here, unless I can get to the time machine now.*

Jennifer wasn't quite sure what she'd do once she got there—somehow try to pick up the other three and escape before the Mutata managed to stop her. It wasn't much of a chance, but it was all they had. "Peter! Travis!" she called. "Get ready!"

And she ran.

Fergie shrieked behind her, rushing to cut her off. Travis was already limping toward the time machine, anticipating her. Peter and Eckels stared, then Peter leapt to his feet with Eckels behind. From the corner of her vision, Jennifer saw the other Mutata responding, moving to intercept the humans.

The other three weren't going to make it, she realized. There were Mutata between them and the time machine. Only Jennifer had a clear line to the vehicle.

Then Fergie's spear—thrown—struck the ground in front of her. Even though the deadly point had missed by a few scant inches, the falling shaft slammed into and between her driving legs, tripping her. Jennifer fell hard, the breath going out of her in a loud *oomph!* Her head banged the side of one of the cycads around the clearing; her hands caught in the tangle of roots around the base of the fern-tree.

She tried to push herself back up before Fergie recovered his weapon. Her fingers, scrabbling in the loose dirt under the roots, touched something: something artificial, something round and smooth, something wrapped in an envelope of stiff paper that crinkled noisily as she touched it.

Dazed, trying to make her head stop spinning, Jennifer clutched at the strange object as she pushed herself to her knees. She looked at it reflexively as she stood, as she readied herself to run again, to flee the death that was rushing down on her in the form of Fergie.

And she stopped.

Through the thin paper, she could feel the unmistakable outline of a hypodermic vial, and on the paper were words she could read even in the dim moonlight:

DISPOSABLE COMPRESSED-AIR SYRINGE
—Adrenalin—

"My God . . ." Jennifer breathed, staring at the impossible thing she held, not daring to believe that it was real. Fergie was nearly on her. Jennifer shouted. "Raajek! Please! *I have your sign!*"

"Frraghi—" Raajek grunted. The Mutata stopped at the OColi's command, the claws of his hind legs tearing the soft loam of the glade. He snorted, the tip of his spear trembling as it remained pointed directly at Jennifer's heart. Everyone had stopped: Mutata and human. They all looked at Jennifer and at Raajek, waiting for the OColi's command.

"Tell me what you see, Frraghi," Raajek said. "What is Jhenini talking about?"

"OColi, the human has something in her hand—"

"What are you holding, Jhenini?" Raajek asked.

"Struth's life, I hope," she answered. "But you'll have to trust me, Raajek. You'll have to let me go to her."

Raajek made a gesture to Fergie, who stood aside, though Jennifer noted that the Mutata kept his weapon ready and kept himself carefully between Jennifer and the time machine.

Her head was still spinning. Part of her denied the reality of what had just happened.

This is too strange. This is the kind of thing you don't believe when you see it in a movie, when the cavalry comes rushing out of nowhere to save everyone, or the monster just happens to have a fatal flaw that no one knew about and the script fails to mention. Everything's too convenient. How did a hypo—and one that's already loaded with just the right medication, no less—get there, right where I'd fall and find it?

But she was holding it, and it felt real and solid. Jennifer tore open the waxed paper that held the device and looked at it. It was shaped strangely: a button instead of a plunger, and the needle must be hidden inside a small metal tube at the business end of the thing, but its purpose was obvious enough. *You still have a problem*, she reminded herself. *You don't know the right dosage. This could be too little. It could just as easily be too much and you might kill Struth with it. The Mutata might not react to adrenaline at all . . .*

But what choice do you have? If someone hands you a miracle, you might as well go with it, right?

While everyone watched, Jennifer placed the hypodermic on Struth's chest and pressed the button. Compressed air hissed, the needle darted forward from the tip as the amber liquid in the vial rapidly disappeared.

For several long, agonizing seconds there was no response at all. The sudden burst of hope she'd felt began to fail. The adrenaline had no effect on the Mutata, or maybe she'd simply sent Struth into irreversible shock. Then Struth took a shuddering, gasping breath. The folds of skin around her eyes fluttered; her mouth opened in an explosive exhalation.

"Struth!" Jennifer shouted.

Struth blinked and grimaced. Her snout wrinkled and she blew a long, low note from her nasal horn that sounded like a trombone. "Jhenini," she said. She saw Raajek then and tried to stand to give the OColi the proper respect, but her legs would not yet support her. She glanced from Raajek, to Frraghi, taking in the Mutata's aggressive stance and the way he threatened Jennifer with his weapon. "OColi Raajek, what is happening here?"

"SStragh . . ." Raajek began. She gave a contemplative, bass drone, her head raising as if she were gazing at something in the stars that only her blind eyes could see. "I thought—"

Thunder grumbled, cutting off Raajek's words, and the stars were masked by sudden clouds. Lightning tumbled harsh shadows across the clearing.

"Jennifer!"

Jennifer turned to see Aaron and Mundo stepping down from the Floating Stone, each of them holding a small piece of phosphorescent stone. Aaron kept looking back at the path as if he expected something to follow him at any second. At last he heaved a sigh of relief and grinned. "We sealed it," Aaron said. "How long were we gone?"

"Very nearly too long," Jennifer said. She laughed from relief.

Aaron barely managed to put down his load on the grass before Jennifer was on him, hugging him as if she fully intended to break every rib in his chest.

5

Attack from the Stone

"It's definitely one of the hypos from a time machine medkit," Travis said. "Or at least it's from my world— they look like every other hypo I've seen. Whether it's actually one from the medkit on *my* machine, well, that'll have to wait until they let us back into the machine."

Jennifer twirled the empty syringe in her fingers. Travis stared at the device hungrily, as if he were afraid to take his eyes away from it. Maybe he was, Jennifer decided. The rest of Travis's world was gone; this might be a link to something he thought dead.

"So how did it get there?" Jennifer asked.

No one answered. The five humans and Mundo were sitting around a small fire near the now inert Floating Stone that had once led to Green Town. Struth was talking with Raajek across the clearing, and Fergie, who looked half-asleep but still dangerous, was crouched near them. Guard lizards surrounded the little group, hissing and snarling whenever one of them moved too quickly. It was nearly dawn; all but the brightest stars had fled the cobalt sky, and the treetops were noisy with stirring life.

"Did one of us kick it out of the time machine?" Peter ventured. "Maybe when we hit the net, the medkit broke open and stuff fell out. Then in all the confusion . . ."

"Maybe," Travis shrugged. "That's plausible enough, anyway. The medkit was secured, though. Even if it fell, anything inside should have stayed put."

"It's still the most likely explanation," Aaron said. He and Peter exchanged glances; Jennifer couldn't quite tell what they were thinking. "Otherwise . . ."

"There could be another time machine around," Mundo ventured.

"Yeah, but *whose* time machine?" Eckels asked. "And where is it now?"

"Why, Eckels? You planning to blow up that one, too?" Travis retorted angrily. "You've destroyed everything you've touched since all this started. I swear I'll use you for Allosaurus bait if I get the chance."

"Oh, the Great Hunter speaks," Eckels answered sarcastically. "You don't scare me, Travis. You never did. I had enough money to buy someone like you a thousand times over."

"There's no money here, Eckels. Your only assets are your wits and your courage. I've seen you demonstrate exactly how much courage you possess several times now, and I suspect that you have about the same vast store of intelligence."

Eckels, his cheeks burning as ruddy as the fire between them, got to his feet, his hands fisted. He looked ready to charge Travis, and from the eager anticipation on Peter's face, Jennifer suspected that Peter would back Eckels as well. Travis, grimacing, started to rise in response. Jennifer knew that a fight now would destroy whatever fragile shreds of cooperation still existed between the marooned parties.

Aaron must have sensed it as well, for even as Jennifer put a restraining hand on Travis's shoulder, Aaron stepped between Travis and Eckels.

"Stop it, both of you!" Aaron barked. "This bickering doesn't help us. Maybe the syringe is a remnant from another time storm, maybe there's another time machine, or maybe Peter's right and it's just one of ours that got kicked into the right place. *It doesn't matter.* Don't you understand that?—it just doesn't matter. The syringe was there for Jenny to find—well, I'm grateful for that coincidence. What matters is what happens now. Where do we go from here?"

Aaron's question was answered the next morning. Under Raajek's direction, the recovered fragments of Eckels's temporal mechanism were gathered up into woven bags. Their shimmering emerald radiance gleamed fitfully from between the strands of netting as the Mutata bore them away. The humans and Mundo were placed in the middle of a phalanx of Mutata guards. Behind them, more Mutata pushed the now-inert Floating Stones that had led to world of the Nipponjin and to Green Town. This odd parade was led through the jungle in the wake of Raajek and Frraghi. SStragh was not allowed to come near any of the humans—she remained near the front of the procession at Raajek's side, helping the blind OColi through the pathless, lush fronds.

They walked for hours, stopping a few times to forage for berries and roots, as the sun made its daily rise to the zenith and began to fall once more. As they walked, the humans saw more evidence that the world-barriers were falling apart. Several times, they passed through landscapes that were obviously foreign to this world, circular patches of otherworlds that were small enough to be crossed in a few strides and others that seemed to take many minutes to traverse: a hill of cobbled, polished stones; a stretch of desert; a perfectly circular lake of brine; and, once, a portion of what looked to be a medieval castle, with the remnants of a silken banner drooping from the battlements.

"Raajek tells me that the Dreaming Storms come almost daily, and each time they are stronger and more violent," Struth said during one of the brief rest periods. "Now, too, they always leave behind a part of another world, another time. There are reports all over the valley of strange creatures: the Gairk kill them when they find them. The saorods plague the Gairk constantly from their Floating Stone."

As Struth went back to Raajek and they prepared to move again, Aaron nodded. "That's consistent with what I saw in Green Town. Little pieces of other realities are there, too. If we're right about there being many parallel histories, then the walls between them are starting to fall apart."

"And what happens when they go entirely?" Jennifer asked.

"Then everything dies," Mundo answered for Aaron. "Chaos rules. Nothing lives."

No one seemed inclined to argue with that dire prophecy.

They continued on. Jennifer noted that they were moving south, away from the Mutata *jhaka,* and toward the low pass where the twin flanks of steep hills that bordered the valley came together. Toward the place, Jennifer realized belatedly, where the Gairk dwelled.

"Look at *that*!" Aaron cried suddenly.

"Klaido!" Jennifer recognized the Gairk who suddenly pushed through the undergrowth alongside them. Aaron and Mundo, who had never seen a Gairk, had nearly run over the Mutata guarding them in an effort to get away from the thing, followed quickly by Eckels and Peter. Klaido looked every bit as frightening and imposing as Jennifer remembered. The *broaii*, the Gairk war clubs, dangled from his waist; the copper armor glinted in the sun. He leaned down like a striking snake, the massive, knife-toothed jaws opening in a steam engine hiss. The gold-flecked lizard eyes regarded first Jennifer, then spotted Peter and Eckels. Klaido's taloned back feet gouged furrows in the dirt, tearing away leaf and twig and earth as he stamped in satisfaction.

"OColi Raajek, you have brought the *iado* to me. They are a fine gift. The Giving will be a joyous time. It has been too long since Gairk and Mutata have celebrated a Giving together, and these . . ." Klaido loosed a contemplative, satisfied blare like someone blowing through a tuba mouthpiece as he glanced again at Peter and Eckels, his dangerous gaze brushing past the rest of them as well. "I have searched for them for hand upon hands of days, and each day my anger at what they have done has grown. At last . . ."

"What's the lizard saying, Jennifer?" Peter asked.

"Nothing you want to know about." Mundo said before Jennifer could decide whether she wanted to answer that honestly or not. "Basically, he thinks of you and Eckels the way you'd think of a bucket of fried chicken. He just can't decide whether he wants you regular or extra crispy."

"Shut up, Mundo," Peter said uneasily. "Jen—"

Klaido had unslung one *broaii*, swinging the blade-studded club easily in his right hand. "These two are mine," he said to Raajek. "The rest you may Give in the Mutata fashion if you like, but these two I alone claim. It will give me great satisfaction to kill them like the animals they are. I would ask that you also give me the female; I would Give her as I would Give one of my own nest, for having been the All-Ancestor's hand in saving my life. I would like to honor her for having been so blessed."

Klaido stopped. The smell of satisfaction didn't leave him, but he suddenly lifted his head for Raajek. "Forgive me, OColi Mutata, I forget politeness with my pleasure. You have come to us, and you should properly speak not with me but with my OColi." Klaido's scent was fragrant with his satisfaction as he looked at the humans. "I will escort you to our *jhaka*. OColi Nakia will be as pleased as I am, I know."

The Gairk village was as unlike the Mutata *jhaka* as anything could get. There was no maze of interconnected white domes here, no careful fencing around the area, no orderly streets. The Gairk *jhaka* reminded Jennifer of a turn-of-the-century London slum. They came out of the jungle into a clearing that sat between tall, green-clad, and steep hills—the pass out of the valley. The streams that trickled out of the hills farther north here had merged into a swiftly flowing river. On its muddy banks, some untidy giant had tossed a random handful of lean-to shelters, rudely covered with thatch roofs or entirely open to the sky. The Gairk, Jennifer realized, must not care about the weather. It was obvious that these dwellings were designed merely to keep the worst of the rain off, or perhaps they existed only to define the individual Gairk's territories within the tribe. That seemed most likely—as Jennifer watched, a nearby Gairk urinated carefully at each corner of its dwelling, like a dog marking its yard.

Excrement and garbage rotted where they dropped in the muddy, rutted lanes; impossibly large flies and other insects swirled around the grisly feast. A large ore-smelting furnace and forge were set up under an over-hanging ledge of the hill to the right. Tailings from the copper-producing operation fouled a nearby pond with green scum, and fumes smeared a blackness over the ferns above the forge. In the midst of the dwellings was a tall mast of wood like a flagpole; suspended from it were the skeletal remains of several of the saorod pterosaurs like the ones who had attacked the Mutata *jhaka*.

Jennifer wasn't sure how many Gairk lived here—no more than fifty or sixty, she thought, gathered in a space about the size of a city block. A small tribe, but a fearsome one. Each of the Gairk, brightly colored males or dun females, seemed to her eyes to be a ferocious killing machine. The stares that followed their strange proces-sion into the Gairk *jhaka* were cold, unsympathetic, and harsh. At Raajek's command, the Mutata piled the glow-ing temporal machinery in a clear space, and the Floating Stones were placed near them. Jennifer, Aaron, and the others crowded together. At the moment, their own quar-rels seemed small. They all wanted the comfort of their own kind—even Mundo stayed close.

Klaido stood alongside Raajek and, swinging his *broaii* with his left hand, crashed the weapon against an oval of copper suspended between two poles in the center of the *jhaka*. The crude gong sounded like a barrel of silverware hitting the bottom of a cliff.

"Hope that's not the dinner bell," Mundo commented.

"Shut up, Mundo!" The command came simultaneously from nearly all of them. "Why don't you concentrate on figuring out what they're thinking," Aaron added.

"I thought I was," Mundo answered.

A Gairk had emerged from another of the caves, moving at a deliberate pace toward the group. She was elderly, her tan-colored scales dull and marked with the scars of old wounds. The copper plating over her chest was decorated with ornate swirls and curlicues, the beaten designs gleaming in the westering sun, and the two *broaii* slung at her waist were more ornamental than functional, the wooden bludgeons intricately carved and only one immense inset blade of obsidian at the tip of each. She walked with a limp—*she has arthritis in the hip joints*, Jennifer realized—but the intensity of her arrogant stare was no less cruel and stern than that of Klaido. Another Gairk walked alongside her: a multicolored male with strangely shriveled arms and no copper plating at all. The female dwarfed the male, in size as well as presence.

The Gairk OColi. . . Jennifer knew her instantly. Klaido had lifted his snout in the same gesture of submission she'd seen in the Mutata, and the other Gairk had done the same. Even some of the Mutata, taken by her presence, had done the same. Only Fergie and Struth, along with OColi Raajek, met the Gairk OColi's eyes as she stalked toward them like a vision of regal, inevitable death.

"My God," Aaron whispered beside Jennifer. "She has to be about the cruelest, the most *awesome* thing I've ever seen . . ."

"OColi Mutata Raajek," OColi Nakia said. Her voice was the beating of kettledrums, the rumbling of an earthquake. The tiny, misshapen male huddled beside and behind her, his dwarf head peering from behind her flanks.

"OColi Gairk Nakia," Raajek answered, and the brassy sound of the Mutata sounded weak and thin in comparison. "I regret that I no longer have the sight to take in your magnificence. I heard that you had become OColi after Kjiti, as I did after Tiafer."

OColi Nakia gave a ground-trembling bray that might have been laughter or might have been derision. Nothing changed in her stance, and Jennifer could not decipher the scent that came from her. "*Not* as you did, OColi Raajek," she answered. "I defeated Kjiti on Challenge-Day last. I tore the sweet life from him with my own claws and teeth, as Gairk have always done. OColi Gairk do not die of old age, as OColi Mutata often do."

Raajek nodded, and she gave the openmouthed grimace that was a Mutata smile. "Mutata ways are different," she admitted. "But the Gairk OColi should not forget that we have *ciosie*, too. Mutata, like Gairk, sometimes die in honorable battle with each other."

"Sometimes." Nakia rolled the word around in her mouth as if tasting it. She looked from Raajek to the humans, and there was nothing in her eyes remotely like compassion. She stared at Jennifer and the others as if they were insects on display in a museum. "So these are the creatures Klaido told me about, the things that had the fire magic that nearly killed him." Her great head swiveled around, cocking sideways like a lizard's. "They don't look so dangerous to me, Klaido."

Klaido stepped forward. "OColi, they cannot be trusted," he answered. "You must not be deceived by their weak appearance. I have already told Mutata OColi Raajek that those two are mine to Give." The Gairk gestured at Peter and Eckels.

"You *told* her, Klaido?" Nakia echoed dangerously.

"Yes," Klaido said. His snout was still lifted, but his eyes watched his OColi carefully, and his hand stayed near his *broaii*.

Nakia glared at him dangerously, her eyes narrowing. For a moment, Jennifer thought that the OColi would attack Klaido, but then the moment passed as Nakia hissed slowly. "You are too independent for your own good, Klaido. You will make an excellent OColi, if you manage to live that long. But I am OColi here, and you are not yet old enough to challenge me. You will let *me* make the decisions, or I will request that you Give yourself back to the All-Ancestor so that some other eggling with more intelligence may have your soul. Do you understand?"

Klaido's gaze never left the OColi's. Nor did his stance change. "I understand, OColi," he said. Paused. "As long as those two are still mine to kill," he finished.

This time, Nakia barked bass laughter. "You *do* have wonderful spirit, Klaido," she said. "I might allow you to fertilize my next clutch, if you still live then. You are lucky that I feel in a good mood today. Yes, the humans are still yours."

"OColi Gairk Nakia, the humans—all the humans— are not Gairks' at all. They are *mine.*"

Raajek's voice snapped Nakia's muscular head around as if it had been pulled. The Gairk OColi's neck widened, her chest expanded; in instinctive response, Raajek's spinal frill flared erect. "I must have misheard the OColi Mutata Raajek," Nakia said. "In fact, I'm sure of it, for I heard nonsense."

"You did not misunderstand," Raajek answered calmly. "I said that the humans are mine, and they are. Mutata captured them, so Mutata will deal with them."

"*I* claimed the humans long ago," Klaido thundered alongside Nakia, "when they tried to kill me."

"You declared them *iado.* I remember, Klaido, and you said that you would hunt them and kill them if you found them. I had no problem with that. But you did *not* find them. We did."

"Then prepare to defend them, OColi Mutata Raajek," Nakia said. "For if you wish to keep them, that's what you will need to do."

The OColi Gairk's left hand was on her *broaii*, ready to draw the weapon, when the small male at her side stepped forward. His coloring had deepened and brightened with emotion, and he looked up at the OColi Gairk fervently. "OColi Nakia," he said, speaking for the first time. "You are making a mistake."

Jennifer expected that Nakia would simply smash the impertinent dwarf with her *broaii* and be done with it—none of the Gairk seemed particularly adept at taking criticism. But she didn't. She just glared down at the little male.

Even Aaron, unable to follow the conversation, noticed the sudden change in Nakia's attitude. "Who's that," he said, leaning close to Jennifer.

"He must be their *zhiotae*," Jennifer answered. "Klaido talked about him once. The Gairk have them; Mutata don't. He's their priest, the one who interprets the Ancient Path for them."

Nakia had lowered her body, her massive, armored tail extending out stiffly to balance her weight. She cocked her head toward the male. "Explain yourself, *zhiotae*," she said.

"The OColihi is in tatters," the *zhiotae* said. His voice was higher-pitched, sounding like a child in the middle of an adult conversation. "The Ancient Path is a ripe *gatha* fruit that has fallen to the ground and broken. These humans have destroyed it, and the Dreaming Storms and the Floating Stones are all signs of their destructive magic."

The *zhiotae* paused and looked at the pieces of path and the glowing shards of temporal machinery brought by the Mutata. "The All-Ancestor spoke to me last night, OColi. In my dream I walked upon a Floating Stone and it was a stone and nothing more. I saw a Dreaming Storm rise above the horizon in black waves of clouds and then dissolve into nothing, shredded by a sudden clean wind. I looked behind me to see where the wind had come from, and I saw the All-Ancestor. She had lifted up the soft ones, the humans. She held up her hand. There were five fingers on the All-Ancestor's hand, and each finger was a human, writhing and twisting. One of them was bleed-ing, and the All-Ancestor tilted her hand so that the blood pooled and then dropped like a red rain to the ground. The blood flowed, a river over our land, and where this river passed, I saw the wounds in the earth healing themselves."

The *zhiotae* stopped. He looked up at Nakia, slackjawed. Jennifer decided that the male was simple or brain-damaged.

"Does this mean that we should give the blood of one of the humans to stop the Dreaming Storms?" Nakia asked the *zhiotae*.

"No!" Jennifer could no longer hold back her protest. "*Yeie!* If you think that, you don't understand your *zhio-tae*'s dream at all."

Nakia's head drew back as if in surprise, then she leaned in closely again, peering at Jennifer curiously. "Klaido had told me that the female youngling could almost speak, but I didn't believe. What is this mockery, OColi Mutata Raajek? She gives me the shape of the words, but not the smell, and the way she stands contra-dicts her voice entirely."

"Humans cannot speak well," Raajek answered. "They can give only the shadow of language."

"Then they are poor imitations made in mockery of Gairk and Mutata. The All-Ancestor's joke."

As the two OColi spoke, Jennifer corrected her stance, lifting her head slightly as a subordinate should, tilting forward at the same time to show the importance of her words, and widening her stance to lend an air of solidity to what she said. "I am sorry that I cannot speak better, OColi Gairk Nakia," she said. "As OColi Mutata Raajek told you, I can't give scent to my words, and the All-Ancestor . . . well, She has given me a shape that makes it difficult to add to the sound of the words with my body. But I ask you to listen."

Jennifer paused. Nakia snorted once, but remained silent, waiting. "Humans are not Gairk. We are not Mutata. We do not think as you do. We have an OColihi, too, a path that we follow, but just as a Gairk's path is not exactly the same as a Mutata's, ours is also distinct. That's not to say that one of us is right and the other wrong—we're just *different*. But in one thing, we are identical. We—all of us—want to stop the Dreaming Storms. We want to find a way to end this chaos."

"That is why I brought them here," Raajek added. "They have found a way to seal the Floating Stones." Raajek smiled in Jennifer's general direction, and she lowered her body, indicating humility. "The All-Ancestor spoke to me, too, OColi Gairk Nakia. She gifted the humans with magic when I was ready to Give them myself. My *otsioiue* SStragh is alive because of that."

Nakia swiveled on her great clawed feet, and her head came even lower, the long fingers of her hands clenching. From a few feet away, she looked at Jennifer, who knew that those jaws could snap her in half in a moment. "Is that true, soft one?"

"It's true that we can seal up the stones, OColi Gairk Nakia. *Geedo*. And it may be that when all the stones are sealed, the Dreaming Storms will end."

Nakia grunted. "I must think on this," she said. "OColi Mutata Raajek, it is too late for Mutata to return to their *jhaka*. You will stay here under our protection tonight. I will ask the All-Ancestor to give our *zhiotae* another, clearer dream-sign tonight, and in the morning we will decide what to do."

For most of the night, Aaron played an elusive game of hide-and-seek with sleep. He tossed fitfully, waking every few hours. The humans and Mundo had been placed in one of the hillside caves, and nocturnal guard-lizards had been set on watch in front of it. Peter and Eckels had quickly discovered that the cave dead-ended a few dozen paces in—the only way out was the entrance. If any of them had harbored thoughts of slipping past the lizards somehow, a quartet of Gairk slumbered just beyond the cave's mouth, and Aaron had quickly noticed that their eyes opened with the slightest sound. The Gairk might not *like* being awake at night, but they definitely came alert quicker than Mutata.

Aaron sat at the entrance to the cave, two of the lizards watching him as if they were hoping he'd do something that would permit them to have an early breakfast of Aaron-leg. Beyond the hills, the sky was tinged with orange and yellow to the east with the advent of dawn. Downslope toward the river a hundred yards away, the two Floating Stones hovered in the center of the Gairk hovels with the small pile of glowing temporal machinery fragments stacked alongside them.

The rest of his companions were asleep—Jennifer closest to him, curled near the small fire the Gairk had kindled for them against the night chill. Mundo snored at the rear of the cave, a white bulk in the darkness; Peter and Eckels were lying on the opposite side of the fire. Travis lay on his back on the other side of Jennifer. The man moved uncomfortably, and he groaned in his sleep. Aaron frowned—Travis's condition worried him. The guide's face was drawn and thin, and he seemed to be getting worse rather than better. The man certainly bore his pain without complaint, and he didn't let it slow him down much, but Aaron wondered how much more he could take.

Or how much more any of us can take. . . We have to find a way out of here, and quick. Jenny's managed to keep these creatures off us for the moment, but these Gairk look like they'd kill us if we happen to breathe the wrong way. I hope this zhiotae *guy had nice dreams . . . What IS that?*

Aaron heard them a moment before he saw them. An image of wet sheets snapping on a clothesline popped into his head, or of his mother—no, more like ten, twenty, thirty of his mother—all shaking out throw rugs on the front porch.

Then Aaron saw them against the orange-red sky: a V-shaped squadron of prehistoric kites, their leathery wings beating a slow rhythm as they half glided, half flew around the flank of the nearest hill. They circled the Gairk settlement once in formation; then in a graceful, unison turn, they banked and swooped. "Pterosaurs," Aaron whispered. "*Big* pterosaurs."

The guard-lizards had seen them as well. They yelped and spat, literally scurrying over the bodies of the sleeping Gairk to wake them and then yapping at them in their strange language. Aaron heard the word saorod repeated several times. The Gairk shouted alarm as a half dozen of the pterosaurs peeled off from the main group and landed in the center of the village—for all the grace of their flight, the landings were awkward as they stumbled and nearly fell, their short legs pumping and the membranes of their huge wings flapping noisily.

They gathered around the glowing stones, and Aaron felt a stabbing of fear in his own chest. "No . . ." he said.

The Gairk were boiling out of their shelters and caves now, some of them hurriedly strapping on armor, others bare-skinned as they swung their *broaii*. The Mutata were awake as well; Aaron could see Fergie rushing toward the Floating Stones.

The squadron of pterosaurs in the air had made another circuit of the encampment and now began what looked like a strafing run, coming in low and fast over the river. They stabbed at the Gairk and Mutata with their savage, thin beaks or raked them with the long, curved claws on their rear feet, their targets always the throats or eyes or softer underbellies of their victims. High-pitched screams of animal rage came from their throats as they slashed, then their wings cupped air, beating mightily as they rose again, their long, spiked tails swinging behind. Two of the Gairk had gone down, clutching at their faces; one of the pterosaurs, a wingbone shattered, flapped helplessly in the dirt. As Aaron watched, the nearest Gairk brought his *broaii* down on the creature's head. It flopped once more and went still.

"Saorods!" Jennifer's fingers clutched at Aaron's shoulder.

"Yeah, that's what the guard-lizards called them."

"We've met them before. One of them nearly killed me."

The others were up now, crowding around the entrance to the cave. The guard-lizards hissed at them, but their attention was mostly on the commotion below. "Those things are after the temporal machinery. Look!" Travis pointed at the saorods who had landed near the Floating Stones. One of them had taken one of the smaller pieces in the claws of its feet. Cawing like an immense crow, the creature tried to take off with the glowing fragment. Aaron thought for a moment that it wasn't going to make it as it half hopped across the clearing, but at last the saorod took to the air. Two of the saorods had taken hold of another fragment; together, they were bearing it off when Fergie threw his spear, catching one of them in its muscular chest. The creature tumbled out of the sky; its companion dropped the piece of temporal machinery rather than be dragged down with it. As Fergie charged the group near the Floating Stones, more saorods arrived, as Klaido led a squadron of Gairk to help Fergie.

In a few moments, a full-scale battle was raging. The guard-lizards drawn by the furor, went scampering angrily off to help. "Now's our chance!" Eckels said. "Let's get out of here!" He began running upslope, away from the combat and toward the beckoning pass out of the valley.

Peter began to push past Aaron to follow, but Aaron stopped him with a hand on his chest. Mundo crowded behind, while Jennifer and Travis looked at Aaron expectantly. "That's not the way back," he told Peter. "Now's our chance, yes, but it's down there."

Peter stared at Aaron's restraining hand, then the redhead glanced up at Aaron belligerently. "What do you mean?"

"I mean that if we lose those pieces, we lose Green Town forever. You want to stay here for the rest of your life?" Aaron and Peter locked gazes. Once they'd been able to look at each other and know instantly what the other was thinking. Now Aaron wasn't sure what he glimpsed behind those green, hard eyes that glared unblinkingly back at him. Aaron dropped his hand. "We don't have time to argue, Peter. You do whatever you think you need to do. That goes for everyone," Aaron said, glancing at Mundo, Travis, and—more gently—Jennifer. "But make up your minds now."

Aaron took a deep breath, then began running toward the swirling chaos below.

The saorods outnumbered the Gairk and Mutata. Already, they'd plucked up nearly all the pieces of temporal fragments. Like a flock of clumsy dragons, they were trying to bear them away as the Gairk and Mutata pursued them. Other saorods continued to swoop down, striking and rising again—at least those who were not swatted out of the sky by the vicious *broaii* of the Gairk and the flashing spears of the Mutata. The ground around the Floating Stones was stained with bright, wet splashes of blood; the badly injured or dead—Gairk, Mutata, and saorod—lay there in the golden light of dawn as the locus of the fighting moved to the edges of the encampment. That made it easy enough for Aaron to reach the Floating Stones. He stooped down once to pick up a Mutata spear—the Mutata who had borne the weapon would never need it again, Aaron saw; a saorod had torn its throat open.

Jennifer came up behind him, breathing hard from the run. "Now what?" she asked.

"See if they've left any of the pieces," he said. "Look around . . ."

The others had followed, Aaron noted. All of them—even Eckels, who was shaking his head. Aaron began looking for the telltale glow of the temporal fragments among the remnants of the battle. The fighting still continued not a hundred yards away, and Aaron knew that all it would take was for one of the Gairk or Mutata to look in their direction.

"Here!" Jennifer called. She was holding aloft a twisted hunk of glowing metal tubing. Her face suddenly went pale as she saw Aaron raise the spear toward her threateningly as he cocked his arm back. "Aaron!" she shouted.

"Duck!" he said, and threw the spear.

The pterosaur that had swooped in low behind Jennifer suddenly found that its prey had disappeared. Instead, it met the implacable tip of Aaron's weapon. The blade slashed up through hollow chest bones and through the vital organs inside: the saorod crumpled as if hit by an invisible fist and fell, dead before it hit the ground.

Jennifer crawled out from underneath one leathery sail of wing, still holding the tubing. "I'm glad you know a duck from a saorod," she said shakily. "Here, I assume you wanted this."

"Yeah. Hope this works."

"It's only one piece, Aaron," Travis said. "There were three or four embedded in each piece of path."

"I know. I'm gambling that we don't need all the pieces to reestablish the link." Aaron took the radiant scrap from Jennifer. He recognized it as a fragment that he and Travis had taken from the Nipponjin path. Going to the Green Town roadway, Aaron slid quickly underneath and jammed the tubing into the explosion-blackened underside until it stuck. He scrambled back to his feet quickly. None of the Gairk had noticed them yet, and the battle with the saorods was still raging.

"Hey, Travis, I think it's going to work," he said. He pointed to the sky.

A quick wall of clouds rushed in from the east. Lightning flickered bright tongues. For a moment, the roll of thunder drowned out the clashing of *broaii* and spear nearby.

"Everyone aboard for Green Town," Aaron said, and hopped onto the Floating Stone.

He fell into cold and darkness.

6

The Chosen Path

Aaron realized that he wasn't quite in total darkness. It took a few seconds for his eyes to adjust to the darkness, then he realized with a disappointing shock where he was.

Torches guttered along whitewashed walls. Ornate paper screens brushed with delicate ink paintings lined the dais on which this side of the broken path was placed. A trio of red-robed priests was staring up at him in amazement as he stepped off the roadway. Two of the priests were Asian; the other had the high cheekbones and ruddy complexion of an American Indian. On the back wall was a large painting, set over the *shoji* door to the temple. The rendition was crude, but the image was recognizably Mundo, arrayed as the Monkey King.

Wonderful, Aaron thought. *Of all of us, it's Mundo who managed to get famous.*

Aaron was back in the world of the Nipponjin. The temple had been rebuilt since he'd last seen it—which told him that far more time had passed here than had passed back in the Mutata world—but it was arguably the same place. The roadway which had once led to Green

Town now ended in another alternate history. *It's the piece of temporal material I used*, Aaron realized. *It's the fragment of machinery that determines where the link goes, not the roadway itself.*

Aaron glanced back at the roadway, expecting Jennifer, Peter, and the others to come through, but the white plastic remained empty as seconds passed and the priests stared at this apparition in their temple.

"*Ohio gozaimas*," he said. That was about the limit of the Japanese he remembered except for various phrases from his aikido classes. He couldn't quite recall if the greeting translated as "good morning," "good afternoon," or "good evening," but it was all that came to mind, and Aaron doubted that reciting the names of aikido techniques would win many points. "Otomo-san?" he said hopefully. The priests just watched him, fear and wonder in their eyes. "Don't just stare. You should know that name: Otomo. Is Otomo here? Come *on* Jen, I really need someone who speaks the lingo."

But Jennifer didn't arrive. Aaron took a deep breath, worried. They should have been right behind him. . . .

The priests seemed to have recovered from their shock. One of them spat out a stream of high-velocity Japanese at Aaron. He smiled back, shrugging. The priest didn't seem thrilled with the response. The man frowned and said something to his Amerind companion, who bowed low and quickly left the temple. "Otomo-san?" Aaron said hopefully. He looked at the roadway again. Still no one.

The temple door slid open, and out of the darkness came several samurai. Aaron didn't recognize the standards they bore on their armored chests—they weren't Lord Akira's samurai, and Aaron wondered what that meant. If some other *daimyo* now held the territory, they couldn't count on a friendly reception.

Definitely couldn't count on it, he realized, as the samurai drew their *katanas* as one. The foremost of the group stepped forward and grunted something. Aaron bowed; that seemed to be the safest response. More grunting and gesturing—they were telling Aaron to step down from the dais. Aaron shook his head. "Not a chance," he said. No reinforcements seemed to be coming through the roadway, and Aaron had absolutely no desire to be trapped here again.

Any decision was made for Aaron then. With a fierce *kiai*, the samurai rushed him.

Aaron made a leap for the roadway, praying that it still worked.

"Aaron!" Jennifer and the rest had seen something very strange. Aaron had stepped onto the roadway; they'd seen him flicker out of existence, then almost instantaneously return, this time jumping quickly off the roadway with a desperate glance behind him. Without a word to any of them, he rolled and scrambled underneath the roadway, digging frantically for the temporal key.

"Aaron, what—" Jennifer stopped. With a guttural cry, a samurai waving a sword was materializing on the roadway, as if he were striding through a doorway. At the same time, Aaron yanked the scrap of glowing metal free.

The samurai screamed. The sparkling gleam of the transfer faded as if someone had hit a switch. Trapped halfway between the worlds, the samurai tumbled forward. At least, about half of him did. The other half simply wasn't there anymore.

The man was dead before he hit the ground.

"Gr-*oss*," Peter said.

Aaron crawled out from under the roadway, carefully avoiding the gory mess that had spilled over the front. He quickly explained what had happened, trying not to glance back at the cloven body of the samurai.

"I learned something," he said. "The Floating Stones aren't connected to any particular location, but the temporal machinery *is*. The bottom line is that we need at least some of the Green Town mechanism if we want to go back there." Aaron looked eastward, where the clearing ended and the river entered tangled jungle. Among the cycads and ferns, the saorod were flying away as Gairk and Mutata pursued.

"And they all went that-a-way," Aaron said.

It wasn't too difficult to follow the saorods back to the gateway to their world. They simply listened for the sound of the running battle, staying to the cover of the ferns and being careful to keep downwind of the Gairk. A fifteen-minute trek brought them to another clearing farther downriver. There, a piece of the broken roadway was wedged a few feet up between two of the fern-trees. A trio of slain Gairk was sprawled at the trunks, evidently the ones set to guard the roadway.

Around the clearing, the battle was nearly over. The saorods with their stolen treasure of temporal material had already gone through; only the last few saorods who remained to harry the pursuing Gairk and Mutata remained, and they landed on the roadway as Aaron and the others arrived, cawing hoarse triumph as their forms sparked and disappeared. Klaido swung his *broaii* at the last of them, the deadly head of the weapon slicing through air as the saorod vanished. Fergie and Struth stood with the group of Mutata, watching the OColi Nakia as she glared at the roadway.

OColi Nakia, her coloration bright with fury, called the others to her as Jennifer gave a whispered translation to the six of them huddled in the undergrowth. "We go back," she said with a significant glance at the Mutata. "This is the All-Ancestor's sign to us. I don't need the *zhiotae* to translate this. It is clear enough to me, but then I'm not a blind helpless creature like the OColi Mutata Raajek."

"Should we set guards around this Floating Stone?" Klaido asked his OColi.

Nakia bellowed irritation. She swung her *broaii* at the nearest cycad and shattered it, the dark blades scything through the thick trunk as if it were paper. "No. The saorods have what they want. They've never returned sooner than a hand of days. Let the guarding wait; we have our dead to Give. We go back. Now."

With that, she turned violently, her spiked tail armor shivering the trees that held the roadway. She crashed noisily back toward the Gairk *jhaka* as Klaido, Fergie, Struth, and the other Mutata followed. The remaining Gairk grabbed the bodies of their fallen and hauled them unceremoniously away. Aaron waited until silence settled over the clearing, then crept cautiously out of cover.

"What now?" Peter asked. "I don't know about you people, but I want to put some distance between me and those lizards. They ain't gonna be happy campers when they find out we're gone."

"And our little diplomat isn't going to be able to talk her way around them this time, either," Eckels added. Aaron didn't care for the way the man's sullen gaze lingered on Jennifer.

"I see two choices," Travis said. "One—we stay here, get as far away as possible from our dinosaur friends, and try to do the best we can for as long as we can." The effort of speaking after their run cost Travis. He was racked briefly by a series of coughs.

"And your second choice?" Mundo asked Travis after the spasm had passed. "Pardon me if the idea of living the rest of my life with you people isn't my idea of paradise. In fact, it's more my idea of the opposite."

Travis gave Mundo a long glance. "The keys to all the roadways we know about went through there." He pointed at the saorod path. "We go after them."

"That's suicide," Eckels said.

Travis shrugged. "Then stay here."

"Anything's better than following a washed-up guide like you."

"Hey, we wouldn't have this mess at *all* if you'd followed my directions in the first place, Eckels."

"*Stop* it, both of you," Jennifer said. "We don't have time to argue. Pete's right—the Gairk will be after us in no time. We need to decide *now*."

"I'm going through the path," Aaron said without hesitation. "That's where Green Town went. I'm going after it."

"Me, too," Jennifer said. She took Aaron's hand.

"The time machine's here," Eckels protested. "We can live off this land—I did. You don't have any idea what it's going to be like through there."

"Then stay," Aaron told him. "I won't—in fact, I can't—force you or anyone else to go with me. Stay here if that's what you think's best. But if you're going to go, you go now."

With that, Aaron smiled at Jennifer. He took her hand. Together, they started walking toward the saorod section of the path. After a moment, Travis and Mundo followed. Peter shrugged at Eckels and fell in behind. Finally Eckels, with a wordless sigh, followed as well.

They hadn't taken more than a few steps when Struth came out from the shadows under the ferns. The Mutata stopped where they could see her, staring at the humans. Her low brass voice called to them.

"Hey, the lizard says she wants to go too," Mundo said.

"It's a trap," Eckels said. "You can't trust the lizards. She's going to delay us so the rest can catch us."

"Jenny?" Aaron asked.

"Give me a second." Jennifer released Aaron's hand and went to Struth. She spoke with her for a few moments, then came back to Aaron. "Struth says there's nothing here for her. Raajek's changed. She still believes that somehow we might be able to change things back. She wants to help. Aaron, I believe her."

"That's good enough for me," Aaron said. Through the screen of greenery, they all heard a distant uproar on the breeze that swayed the fronds, like a dozen brass bands all playing a different song—a shrill and angry cacophony. "Sounds like they've figured out we're gone. Tell Struth she can come along if she wants, but we're going now."

Aaron took Jennifer's hand again. "Ready?"

Her answer was unhesitating. She smiled at him, and her confidence eased the boiling in his stomach. "Before we go—" he began.

"Hush." Jennifer gently touched his lips with her fingertip. "I already know."

Aaron grinned. He nodded to Travis.

Aaron and Jennifer ran to the path, jumped onto it, and were gone.

SStragh waited until the humans and Mundo had all vanished. She stood next to the path, gazing at the familiar shape of her world and trying to remember it all. The All-Ancestor seemed to call within her, saying *You will never see this again*. SStragh was just stepping onto the path when Klaido burst through the line of ferns, *broaii* in hand. "Mutata!" the Gairk screamed, saliva frothing at its mouth. "Your OColi orders you to return!"

Old shackles of habit and instinct forced her to stop. SStragh turned, compelled by the spoken order and the scent of musky superiority from Klaido. She started to step away, then forced herself to halt with a shudder. "*Yeie*," she said. "The OColihi is broken. I no longer listen to my OColi."

That brought forth pure rage in Klaido. The Gairk brought his hand back and flung his *broaii* across the clearing. The weapon hurtled end over end, the aim utterly true.

But SStragh had jumped onto the path. The *broaii* whistled through empty air.

7

Dogfight in the Sky

"*Whoaa!*"

Aaron stumbled and nearly fell as Jennifer pulled him quickly back.

It would have been a long, long drop.

The two stepped off the hovering path onto a landscape stretched and pulled vertically, all sharp edges and stone. They stood on a precarious ledge midway up a craggy cliff of rose and ocher rock like something torn from the cover of a pulp magazine depiction of another planet.

A hot, swirling wind buffeted them, making Aaron squint with its ferocity, and there was a hint of sulphur in the air. The cliff ran in a jagged curve above them and into the distance on either side, its still-distant summit pocked with steeples of fissured stone like a thousand Gothic towers jammed together. Across a fog-wrapped chasm as deep and wide as two Grand Canyons set side by side, the far wall of this crack in the world loomed, a broken and shattered plain ripped from the earth by a god and set on edge, its roots lost in mists and its serrated peaks stabbing impossible heights.

There, wheeling in the inky blue sky like ancient visions of dragons, were the pterosaurs. Both Aaron and Jennifer were stunned to silence by the vision before them. A sound behind them finally pulled their gaze away from the awe-inspiring vista.

Travis and Mundo had appeared on the roadway, which here was snagged between two massive boulders of quartz-pocked granite. They both had the momentum given them by their leap onto the Dinosaur World end of the gateway. Aaron caught Mundo before the creature took the extra steps that would have taken him over the edge; Jennifer aided Travis, who stumbled and nearly fell. "Thanks," Travis said. "How long you two been here?"

"Not long," Aaron answered. "Time must be running at close to the same speed here."

Mundo gaped at the vision in front of him. "Excuse me for complaining, boss, but this does *not* qualify as an improvement," he muttered. He seemed to frown, as if listening for voices inside his head. "Another dead world like yours—every creature all alone and separate. Let's go back while we have a chance. Right now."

Peter and Eckels came through then. The ledge was getting crowded. Aaron noticed that all of them with the exception of Mundo were keeping the cliff wall close to their backs, staying as far away as possible from the crumbling edge of their perch. "This is great, Aaron," Peter said. "We're going mountain climbing without any equipment. Just great."

Aaron didn't answer—frankly, most of him wanted to echo his friend's pessimism. "Where's Struth?" Jennifer asked Peter.

"I don't know," Peter answered. He'd put his back against the cliff wall, staying as far away from the edge as he could. "She was right behind us when we left. You want the damn lizard, go back and get her. *I'm* just as happy not to have her and her big, clumsy body here, to tell you the truth. I doubt that cliff climbing is going to be one of her skills."

"Hey," Mundo said. "Look. They're *fighting*."

Aaron turned to see the ape pointing at the sky above the vast canyon, his fur tousled by the invisible fingers of the wind. Mundo was right, Aaron saw after a few moments. There were two squadrons of the saorods banking and turning like gigantic bats. One of them was the group who had evidently just come from the Mutata world. Aaron could see the glow of the temporal material clutched in the feet of several of them. Those carrying the glowing stones and pieces of machinery were being protected by a sheltering wing of their companions as they made for the distant, opposite cliff wall.

The second group, their skin a delicate yellow-brown compared to the azure blues of the other saorods, had just come over the top of the cliff where Aaron and the others stood. The browns came down out of the sun like jet fighters. Their tactics were simple enough: above the other group, they folded their wings and plummeted feetfirst like aerial, sentient bombs, shredding the delicate skin of their victim's wings with their claws as they passed before opening their own wings again and rising once more. Had the blues been less vigilant, the strategy might well have worked to perfection, but just before the attack came, the blue formation suddenly split and scattered. Still, as Aaron watched, the first wave sent two blues pinwheeling out of the sky like broken kites, their wing membranes flapping as uselessly as rags tied on a thrown stick.

They disappeared into foggy depths.

Alert, the protecting blues regrouped around their burdened convoy. Tactics altered as they watched. Now that the blues were aware of their danger, the conflict became a strange, chaotic dogfight that spread out over the sky. Two saorods would meet virtually head-on, screaming and clawing at each other in a tangle of wings as they both fell, each trying to rip the thin sails of flesh between the wingbones or to inflict a deadly wound on the muscular body.

Beak and claw snapped and tore as the saorod combatants dropped, and then suddenly they would break free of each other, their wings beating desperately as each tried to regain altitude. The two might meet again far above for another round of deadly combat, or they would find yet another opponent—sometimes, only one of them would rise again while the other would continue to fall, screeching helplessly until at last it struck unseen rocks far, far below.

The air in front of Aaron and the others was full of swooping, banking, diving saorods. They could see that the blues outnumbered the browns. Having withstood the initial surprise of the browns' attack, the blues' superiority of numbers showed. Often, it was two blues attacking a single brown; whenever that happened, only the blues would glide away again, majestic and fierce, already seeking their next victim.

Abruptly, as if a silent retreat had been called, it was over. The remaining browns wheeled and turned, diving quickly into the concealing mists below. The blues pursued for a moment, then returned with high, piercing screeches of triumph.

And Struth arrived.

The Mutata seemed to be off-balance as she appeared. She tried to take a step and her foot found only air. Her thick tail whipped about as she flailed for balance, hooting loudly. Aaron grabbed quickly for Struth's outstretched hands; Jennifer put her arms around the Mutata's neck and Peter turned to block the dinosaur like a football lineman. Mundo howled; Travis and Eckels ducked out of the way of the wildly flapping tail. Struth went down, but her momentum rolled them all toward the edge. Aaron dug his sneakers into the rocks desperately, listening to the sound as pebbles shot over the edge of the precipice and into oblivion. "Hang on!" he shouted, "Peter, Jenny . . ."

They came to a skidding, scraping halt a few feet from the edge. Peter's feet were hanging over emptiness, and Aaron could feel the wind at his back. Peter scrambled furiously back onto the ledge in a wild panic. "That's it," he said, his voice breaking with emotion. "I'm going back, Aaron. I hate this. That lizard almost killed me just now. Mundo, Eckels, you with me?"

Peter started grimly toward the path. Behind him, Struth hooted something as she lay on the rocks. "Peter," Jennifer called, still clutching Struth. "She says Klaido's there waiting, maybe others. That's who she was running from."

"That's not the worst." Mundo was pointing at the saorods. The commotion on the ledge hadn't escaped their attention. Several of the pterosaurs had turned around and were obviously heading toward them. "I think this is what you people call between a rock and a hard place," he said. As Struth was pulled back by Aaron and Jennifer, the saorods circled above them.

And dived.

The saorods came in like bombers on a strafing run, low and fast. There was no place to hide, no room on the ledge in which to scatter and run. Aaron watched helplessly as the lead pterosaur arrowed toward Jennifer. She cowered, covering her head with her hands, but the creature came right at her. A strong clawed foot closed around her arm, another grasped a handful of clothing. As Aaron stared in horror, the saorod's wing cupped air mightily and the creature and Jennifer both disappeared over the edge.

"Jenny!" he cried, trying to run after her, wanting at least to see what was happening even if there was nothing he could do. He didn't make it. Aaron was struck from behind, a blow that sent him sprawling. Then saorod claws dug into his biceps and he was half-dragged, half-lifted himself. He struggled to get free, then suddenly stopped as he realized that he was about to go over the edge himself.

Involuntarily, he screamed.

8

The Guardians of the Stones

It was as if Aaron had reached the top of the world's largest roller coaster and gone careening over the summit. There was that same terrifying moment of hesitation and balance as they hung over nothingness. Then the saorod and Aaron dropped headfirst like twin stones, plummeting faster and faster. Aaron's stomach was somewhere in his throat and the wind battered his face, tearing away the scream. Walls of stone rushed by, dangerously close, then the cool, wet fog enveloped them. Aaron was certain that they would smash into the unseen rocks at the bottom. He wouldn't even see his death coming. He was blind and helpless.

Then Aaron's insides were tossed violently as the saorod came out of its dive with a sharp looping upward turn. Now it was Aaron who clutched at the pterosaur's feet in desperation, trying to hang on.

The wings began a desperate, steady beat as the creature tried to climb out of the strands of low cloud, but Aaron could tell that it was struggling with the burden of

Aaron's additional weight. He couldn't see Jennifer. He glanced behind—the others must have been treated the same: through the fleeting gray-white wisps of vapor, he could see Peter and Mundo, each being hauled like a salmon in the claws of an eagle.

They weren't going to make it, Aaron realized. Despite the saorod's best efforts, they were losing altitude again, falling deeper into the fog once more. Aaron was certain he knew what would happen in a few moments: the claws would open, the beak would stab down to force Aaron to let go, and he would fall.

As the thought filled him with despair, Aaron felt a quick nausea in his stomach as he and the saorod suddenly shot upward. *An updraft!* Aaron exulted. *That's what it was looking for down here. . . .* The heat from the hidden landscape below scoured Aaron as the saorod turned, staying within the funnel of the draft and using it to circle upward. They came out of the mist into sunlight once more, still using the updraft's lift, until they were higher than the ledge. Aaron had a good view of the vista. They were nearer the far side of the canyon now, and Aaron could see a jagged vertical mouth of darkness there, a slit in the rock into which several saorods were entering. Below, a saorod with Peter hanging on desperately below came out of the fog. *I wonder how Pete's enjoying his ride. He won't even get on a roller coaster.*

Aaron's saorod canted over, banking out of the updraft. They glided gently down, heading directly toward the cave mouth themselves, the saorod guiding them with slow, careful thrusts of its wings.

They slid from bright sunlight to darkness, and as Aaron's eyes tried desperately to adjust to the rapid drop in illumination, he saw that the entrance opened into a vast open well of a cavern which opened several stories above and below them, noisy with the harsh cries of the saorods and—surprisingly—lit by hundreds of lanterns—large, flat stones jutting out from the walls on which were heaped piles of moss. The moss glowed a strange, cold blue-green, far brighter than any bioluminescence Aaron had ever seen. Other lanterns, suspended from the ceiling of the immense space by long strands of vines, swayed and moved in the vagrant breezes within the cavern, illuminating airy galleries and openings. This was a city, Aaron realized, and if he had not believed so before, he knew now that the saorods were sentient.

Like humans, like the Mutata or Gairk, they must be tool users.

They were aiming toward a long gallery about a third of the way down from the top of the cave and far back from the cavern mouth. They crossed over the edge, the saorod coming in faster than Aaron would have liked, and Aaron found himself running along broken ground as the saorod suddenly released its grip on him. Aaron stumbled and went down heavily as the saorod landed clumsily several yards farther on.

Aaron lay there for a few seconds, trying to catch the breath which the slab of rock under his stomach had knocked from him. Nothing seemed to be broken, though his knee was throbbing and he felt like he'd scraped most of the skin from his arms. He'd hit the side of his head on an outcropping; Aaron touched the area gingerly, working his jaw tentatively.

"Aaron?"

"Jenny!" Aaron sat up, stretching his neck. Jennifer was standing against the wall across the gallery from him. "They need to work on those landings. You okay?"

"Yes." Jennifer ran quickly to Aaron as he stood up cautiously. They hugged, Aaron simply reveling in the smell of her hair as they held each other close. Jennifer pulled away reluctantly. "Where are the others?"

Aaron looked out over the unprotected edge of their space. They could see four more saorods coming in, bearing Peter, Eckels, Travis, and Mundo. They were unceremoniously deposited nearby in the same manner. The group quickly huddled together well back from the edge.

"Where's Struth?" Jennifer asked.

"Think about it," Peter told her. "These things had enough trouble with us. The lizard's gotta weigh, what, four or five times what we do? They ain't gonna pick her up without a flying derrick. The last I saw, they were dive-bombing her on the ledge."

"Who's worried about her anyway?" Eckels said, with a dark glance at Jennifer. "We have our own problems. Take a look over there."

They had been placed on a long, deep balcony that curved around the perimeter of the cavern. They could look out over the enormous open shaft of the cave and see other shelves of rock like their own, some higher, others lower down on the flanks of stone. The saorods who had brought them here had gathered at the back, where an overhanging stone roof led back into indistinct shadows. A wind blew out from behind them, and they could see the dark opening of a cave corridor leading farther back into the cliff. A mound of the radiant moss was set there in front of a massive, polished slab of quartz.

Standing in this crude lamp's glow was another saorod.

He stood like a ten-foot-tall Bela Lugosi posing for a Dracula poster, his wings wrapped about him like a leathery cloak. As he realized that they were watching, he spread his wings wide in display. The skin between the elongated fingerbones that made up his wings shimmered in the light of the lamp, mottled blue shot through with specks of orange and gold, while his body was covered with a fine down of feathery brown hair. His long beak was a pale yellow, snaggled with small sharp teeth and coming to a tearing hook at the end like that of a sea gull. The eyes, set on either side of the narrow head, were large and golden brown, the pupils jet black. The skull was high with a thick, hairless crest, the exposed skin there a brilliant, deep scarlet. Around his neck, trapped in a tiny, delicate wooden cage attached to a leathern thong, was a cylindrical fragment of the temporal material, gleaming against the down of the saorod's chest.

The saorod spoke to them. Rather, he hissed and sputtered, sounding vaguely like a teakettle about to boil over. His speech was energetic but short, and when it was over, he stared at them expectantly.

"I love the way his tongue waggles when he talks. Too bad none of us speak saorod," Peter said.

"He said: I' am Salisos: the Wings of Truth, the Claws That Strike from the Sun, and the Keeper of Burning Stones' He also asked for our own names and titles."

Everyone looked at Mundo, who shrugged innocently back at them. "You people have short memories. I'm the mind skimmer, remember?"

"Oh, I remember," Aaron said. "In the Japanese world . . ." Aaron also remembered how Mundo had tried to use his knowledge to his own advantage. There, at least, they had Jennifer to double-check Mundo's translations. In this situation, they would have to trust Mundo, and Aaron wasn't certain that was entirely smart. It didn't seem, though, that they had much choice. "So can you talk back to this Keeper of Burning Stones?" Aaron asked.

"I can try. It'll be like speaking Mutata—this body just isn't built for it, so I'm not going to be very good at it. But I've picked up enough of the vocabulary from him to try." Mundo looked at Aaron blandly. "And you're right. You *will* have to trust me."

Aaron ignored that. "Jenny, you're quick with languages. Was any of what he said like Mutata?"

Jennifer shook her head. "Not even slightly. Sorry, Aaron."

Mundo grinned.

"Right," Aaron said with little enthusiasm. "Just remember how you managed to foul things up before, Mundo."

"I am your humble servant and will speak only the words you give me in your vast wisdom," Mundo told him. "So what do you want me to say, Oh Leader?"

"Introduce Aaron as 'Oz, the Great and Powerful,'" Peter interjected. He met Aaron's glare challengingly. "Would you rather be 'Dorothy, the Small and Meek,'?" He gave a sarcastic, angry laugh.

"Peter—"

"Hey, don't give me a lecture, *friend*. I don't remember electing you dictator here, but it looks like you're taking over. Fine, go ahead. But as soon as I can, I'm out of this little kingdom."

Later. Deal with this later. Pete's just mad that's all. Mad and scared. The past has been ripped away from all of us— everything we thought we were, everything we were going to be. Not only that, but he doesn't like enclosed spaces and now he's stuck in a cave. Tomorrow he'll have forgotten he said anything.

Aaron swallowed the retort he wanted to make. He glanced at Salisos, who was watching them patiently, his head cocked to one side like a gigantic parakeet.

"Tell him our names," Aaron told Mundo. "And tell him that we don't use titles, not where we come from."

"You're the boss," Mundo said. The ape turned to Salisos and uttered a halting stream of sibilant words. The saorods gathered behind Salisos all chattered among themselves, while Salisos seemed to meditate on what he'd just been told. Finally, Salisos spoke again.

"He says that not having titles is ridiculous. How can we tell who is important without titles? He also wants to know why we unimportant creatures have come here."

Aaron pointed at Salisos's necklace. "Tell him we've come for the glowing stones," he told Mundo. "Tell him . . ."

Aaron hesitated as inspiration suddenly came to him. "Tell him that we are the Guardians of the Stones, Mundo. Tell him that's our title and our task—to guard these Burning Stones."

Mundo shrugged, his dark eyes regarding Aaron blandly. "I certainly hope he likes hearing that," Mundo said, and turned back to Salisos. A sibilant barrage of words came from the ape's throat.

Salisos hissed in response, his wings fluttering wide, and his reptilian eyes glared down at them. He uttered a single word and then launched himself over the edge of gallery into the vast central space of the cave. They watched Salisos spiral downward like a gigantic toy glider before finding an updraft and rising well above them. He disappeared into an upper chamber.

"What'd he say?" Peter asked Mundo.

"He said: 'Follow me,' " Mundo answered. He grinned at them. "So who's first?" he asked.

His question was answered as the saorods who had brought them here advanced. Mundo was grabbed first, then each of the humans, as they were hauled away like so much extra baggage.

9

The Cave of Bones

The saorods screamed as they dived out of the sky. SStragh howled back her own defiance.

SStragh thrust her spear at the first attacker, sinking the black stone blade deep in the creature's chest. The impact nearly stunned her as the saorod flapped its wings and tried to bite at SStragh, who held the creature at bay with the spear's shaft. But the spear was suddenly too heavy to hold with the saorod's weight on the end, and the dying creature's struggles tore the weapon from her hands. Saorod and spear went tumbling down the sheer cliffs into cloud.

SStragh had no time to contemplate her fleeting victory. More of the creatures were coming, and SStragh cast about in vain for a new weapon. The saorods were obviously *iado*, since they were not going to follow the rules of *ciosie*, but that was hardly a comfort—it was just as easy to be killed by an unintelligent animal as by any other. SStragh ducked under the claws of an incoming saorod, who wheeled quickly away from the narrow ledge, its wingtip scraping rock as it turned.

That gave SStragh an idea. The cliff above her leaned in slightly. She moved all the way to the rear of the ledge behind the Floating Stone, pressing her spinal frill flat against the rocks. The next saorod tried to claw her, but it was unable to reach SStragh, nearly colliding with the cliff before it banked sharply away.

The next one landed near the Floating Stone. It snarled at SStragh, but she could see that the saorods didn't move well on the ground. The creature hissed and spat, the long dangerous beak slashing, but it couldn't use its claws and the wings were a definite liability. The ledge itself was narrow and short enough that only one of the creatures could comfortably land on it at any one time. As the saorod came close to SStragh, she made a quick half-turn with her hips, her thick, heavy tail whipping through the air with the motion and sending the saorod, broken-winged, careening over the edge to its death.

The others, shrieking, wheeled through the air in front of SStragh, but they'd seen what had happened with their companions and had realized that SStragh was in too entrenched a position. They swirled around in front of her, making futile passes, then evidently decided that this contest had to be declared a draw. One by one, they peeled out of formation, moving out over the canyon toward the far cliffs.

In a few minutes, SStragh was alone except for one saorod watching her from far above. SStragh hooted sadly as she stepped cautiously forward.

Jhenini and the other humans were gone. She could not climb up or down from the ledge—she simply wasn't built for that. SStragh had no way out. Between the two boulders that held it in place, the Floating Stone mocked her with its empty promise. SStragh had rejected the

OColihi and by now both Gairk and Mutata would have stripped her of her name. She could be considered *iado* herself, something to be killed on sight. Behind or in front, there was only death.

No way out.

SStragh turned in angry desperation. Her tail struck the Floating Stone a glancing blow and she glanced back to see it bob slightly.

She stared. Thoughts that were not of the OColihi nudged her, an inspiration that had no grounding in her Ancient Path of instinct and cultural habit.

Something original. Something—she thought—almost *human*.

SStragh prodded the edge of the Floating Stone with her hand. It rocked, scraping against the granite fingers gripping it. She could maneuver it free, she realized: a twist there, a push, and it would come out of where it was lodged.

And when it did, it would *float*, like its identical twin on the other side. SStragh *hmmmed* softly to herself, crooning a low note through her nasal horn. She moved around the Floating Stone, hunkering down carefully so that she could look underneath it. Yes, there were two glowing shapes, two pieces of *mahcheenery*, as Jhenini and the others called them, half-embedded in the charred underside of the path. She tugged at one of them; it came loose reluctantly. The other piece was more difficult; SStragh almost gave up before it suddenly fell to the ground with a strange ringing *clang*.

SStragh snorted and backed away. Then, taking a long breath, she jumped on top of the Floating Stone. She went . . . nowhere. Stepping down again, she began tugging and pulling and prying the Floating Stone loose from its mooring. That took several minutes and required far more effort than she expected, but at last the Floating Stone was free, hovering effortlessly a foot or so above the broken ground of the ledge. Again SStragh stepped onto the path, this time bouncing experimentally—the path held her weight and stayed above the ground. Nothing she did caused it to sink.

Climbing down again, SStragh pushed the stone toward the back of the ledge—it moved sluggishly in response, but it moved. SStragh moved it as close to the wall as she could, then hopped up on the bone white perch. She lowered herself so that she gripped the sides of the Floating Stone with her hands.

With all her strength, she kicked out with one back leg, pushing herself off the cliff wall like a swimmer kicking off a pool wall. The path, with SStragh hanging on desperately, went skimming over the edge onto empty air.

Where it dropped like the stone it was.

The six of them were dumped into an airy cave where long, narrow, vertical shafts let in filtered sunlight. The glow illuminated a tangled wonderland of tented white arches. For several seconds, Aaron didn't realize what he was seeing. It was Jennifer who first understood.

"Bones!" she cried, and the scene suddenly snapped into focus for Aaron.

They were looking on a graveyard of fragile kites. The skeletal remains of the huge saorods knit fairy caverns in space. Tatters of translucent flesh hung stretched on the frames of bones, like paper on the kites of Aaron's childhood, snared in the fingers of autumn trees. There were thousands of the bodies here, leading back into unguessed depths beyond the ledge. The ground beneath their feet was dusted with the flour of ancient bones; the sun wove shadows through skyscraper skeletons. A multitude of empty-socketed eyes stared at them from bleached white skulls, a horde of saorod jaws gaped in unhinged amazement at the sight of themselves, and in the silence of the cavern, a breeze sighed through the xylophone expanse of rib cages like the ghost of their collective breaths. Each of the skeletons looked as though it had been posed in death, even though the weight of the bones above had crushed those lower down: wings outspread as if in display, the heads up and claws out as if ready to grasp something.

Small wraiths skittered through the tomb: rats glaring at this intrusion into their world. They scampered along the tightrope curve of high wingbones, glancing down with their naked tails wriggling, and then leaping acrobatically away to disappear into the maze of death.

"The saorods must have been using this cave for generations," Jennifer said softly.

"Smells like it, too," Peter answered. Like Jennifer, he whispered; none of them seemed to care to interrupt the slumber of the corpses here. Aaron had to admit that Peter was right; there was an undeniable scent of corruption in the air here, the scent of death.

Their escorts weren't quite as awed by the scene. They roughly pushed the humans forward. "Hey, no need to shove," Eckels said, and his saorod hissed at him like an angry cobra, the long mouth opening wide to show the double rows of needled teeth. "Okay, I'm going, I'm going."

They were herded along the edges of the piled bones. Aaron nudged Peter and pointed upward as they walked. "That's a recent one up there," he whispered. "See—it hasn't lost much flesh yet. You can still see the colors on the wings."

"Yeah," Peter answered sullenly. "It was dropped in from the shafts. So what?"

Aaron forced himself not to respond in anger. Somehow, their little group needed to work as a team and end their bickering, or they were going to be in worse trouble than they already were. Peter, whom Aaron had once called a friend, was the best one with whom to start. "Let's remember these shafts, Peter. At least that'd be a way out without having to learn how to fly. What do you think?"

Peter eyed the steep, long fissures in the roof of the cavern. "Better than flying, sure, but they still aren't going to be my first choice."

"We need to think of something, and I'm fresh out of thoughts right at the moment. You remember when you, I, and Kenny got lost down by Big Bend Pond? You were the one who came up with the idea of following the water downstream until we hit the Mill Greek. We'd *still* be wandering around up there if you hadn't thought of that."

"Yeah? Well, you should have asked me about *this* before we ended up jumping into this place," Peter retorted, but his tone was less harsh than it might have been, and he shrugged. "I'll keep my eyes open," he said at last.

"Thanks, Peter," Aaron said, and smiled at his friend. "We'd all appreciate it."

Peter nodded. The frown on his lips seemed cemented in place, but he didn't say anything. Aaron decided he would take any victory at the moment, no matter how small. *Leadership lesson number one*, he thought. *Nothing comes easy, and nothing comes quick.*

They were herded by their ground-clumsy saorod escorts toward the center of the cavern. There, very near the edge overlooking the great central cavern, Salisos stood before seven saorod skeletons set apart from the chaotic mass of the others.

These seven had been placed upright, their huge arm and fingerbones spread out in mock flight as their long beaks opened in silent shouts. The great sails of their wings had been replaced by painted leather stitched around the bones—Aaron didn't care to wonder about the origin of the mummified flesh that adorned them. Their eyes were polished agate pebbles, gleaming in the dusty beams of sunlight and the glow of the moss baskets. The corpses were taller than Salisos by a head, their wingspans wider, and the knurled bones of their chests told Aaron's practiced eyes that huge bands of muscles had once been attached there. They would have been truly fearsome creatures in life, these seven.

Piled before them like an offering were fragments of glowing metal and stone: the shattered pieces of Eckels's time machine's temporal mechanism. "That one's from the Green Town piece," Travis whispered to Aaron. "You see it?"

"Yeah," Aaron answered. "So's the one on the right, and the big one's from the Japanese world. When we leave, we have to make sure that we get them first."

"You expect the Travis the Great Hunter to help you?" Eckels commented behind them. "Fat chance."

Travis turned to glare at Eckels, who backed away a careful step. Jennifer came up to stand next to Aaron as Salisos began speaking to them.

"These are the Seven," Salisos said, with Mundo translating for the group. "The first to find the Hollow Mountain and the first to bear pups here, the first to live here and the first to die. Their spirits remain, watching over the Family and guiding us in our battles with rival Families. Because of them, we alone of all Families have been able to secure the Burning Stones. If you are indeed the Guardians of the Stones, then you have done a poor job."

"That's why we came here," Aaron said. "To ask that you return them."

Salisos threw his head back, his narrow beak wide as he cawed in what must have been saorod laughter. "Wingless, clawless, and yet you think because you ask, we'd return the stones which cost the lives of so many of us?"

"Why are the Burning Stones so important to you?" Jennifer asked Salisos.

"Because the Burning Stones open the gateways," Salisos replied, looking at Jennifer. "Because when anyone walks a world-path, the storms come."

Aaron felt himself taking a deep involuntary breath of shock with the words. "You *know* that removing the, uhh, 'Burning Stones' closes the path?"

Salisos regarded Aaron with bright, angry eyes. "You think us stupid, Guardian? We are not. Yes, we know that. We know that when we first went through the gateway that appeared here, the first storm came, bearing chaos and destruction rather than rain. We know that storms come more and more often, even when we are not using our gateway. We know that in the world of wingless lizards, there are several of these gateways. And we know that if the Burning Stones are removed, the gateways no longer work."

Salisos brought his wings in, wrapping them around him as if he were cold. "And we believe one other thing: once all the Burning Stones are found and removed, the storms will end."

Behind Aaron, there was a harsh call far out in the air of the central cavern. Aaron turned to see a saorod climbing the thermals toward them from the distant entrance well below. The creature made the usual stumbling landing on the ledge near Salisos, recovered its dignity with a rustling of wings, and bowed to the leader. The saorod began speaking rapidly and urgently to Salisos, who suddenly gave a sharp cry of anger. Salisos began barking orders to the other saorods. "Mundo, what's going on?" Aaron asked.

"It's Struth," Mundo said. "It seems Jennifer's little Mutata friend killed a couple of the saorods, dismantled the path, threw the Burning Stones into the canyon, and then went over the edge herself, carrying the path. Interesting form of suicide, don't you think?"

"Oh, no!" Jennifer cried. "Struth—"

"Forget the lizard," Eckels said. "She doesn't matter. The *path*'s the important thing. With the path and the right piece of temporal material, we could get out of here."

"You've never cared about anyone but yourself," Travis shot back at the man. "That's your trouble, Eckels. I've never seen such a self-absorbed, egotistical fool—"

A spasm of coughing stopped Travis's tirade, and Salisos put an abrupt end to any confrontation between Travis and Eckels, even as Jennifer put her arm around Travis worriedly and Aaron stepped between the safari guide and Eckels.

"Now we know you, Guardians," Salisos said. "We know your treachery and your evil. You've come to steal back the stones. You are the heralds of more storms and more destruction."

"You've got the wrong idea," Aaron said desperately, but Mundo had no chance to translate before Salisos spoke again.

"We will find the stones the wingless lizard has thrown away. We will recover the gateway. And then we will deal with you as we have dealt with all the storm heralds."

With that Salisos moved aside, and they saw that behind him lay a human corpse: battered and broken, but still recognizable. "Lord Akira!" Jennifer cried. It was indeed the Nipponjin prince; they all knew the thin features of the face and the designs of his armor. Salisos crouched and leapt out into the emptiness of the main cavern. His wings beat with two mighty thrusts, and then he glided in a slow spiral downward toward the entrance of the caverns. Aaron, Jennifer, and the others moved close to the edge to watch. The other saorods on the ledge had joined their leader; more were taking flight from the balconies and ledges lower down. With sharp cries, they swayed and banked—a cloud, a moving shadow. In a few moments, they were gone.

Leaving the humans alone on the ledge.

"I guess they didn't exactly need to lock us up," Jennifer said, leaning out over the vast depths of the cavern. Aaron felt vertigo himself, watching Jennifer at the edge, and he was glad when she moved back.

Aaron looked up at the crevices above them, where blue sky showed mockingly. "What do you think?" he asked. "If we can climb up these bones and get to the roof. . . well, we might be able to chimney up. The walls look like they'd have plenty of handholds."

The others broke into argument. "I'm not climbing up there. . . ." ". . . You want to stay here and be killed . . .?" ". . . Travis isn't going to be able to climb . . ." ". . . It still leaves us a mountain to climb down . . ."

But Aaron noticed that Peter had gone to Lord Akira's corpse. Peter stared down at it for several seconds, then moved his gaze to the imposing figures of the Seven. Peter ran contemplative figures through his red hair, scowling. He tugged at the nearest wing, rocking the huge saorod corpse on its stubby legs.

"Peter?" Aaron said.

"Just a sec." Peter was stripping two of the leather ties from Akira's armor and lacing them between the saorod's legs above the claws. Peter tested his knots and then stood up.

"Give me a hand, would you, Aaron?"

Together, Aaron and Peter each took hold of a wing. They walked the saorod body toward the edge of their balcony. The corpse was far lighter than Aaron would have thought from its size: a dried-out husk. It couldn't have weighed more than twenty pounds. "What are you thinking, Peter?" Aaron asked when they set the saorod down again.

"I did some hang gliding last summer out at the Bluffs," Peter answered. "Here's my chance to try it again."

"Peter—" Jennifer began, but the redhead cut her off with a wave of his hand.

"No," he said to Jennifer. "Look, I haven't exactly been your best friend so far on this little adventure, and it's obvious that if anyone's in charge here, it's Aaron and you. Frankly, I don't think we have a prayer of coming out of this—things are just too fouled up. But if we *are* going to get out of here, we aren't going to do it by climbing. No one else seems to have a better idea. So . . ." Peter grinned at them, a flash of the old Peter, the impulsive kid they remembered from Green Town. "There's only one way to find out if this is gonna work."

With that, Peter grabbed hold of the saorod's claws, lifted the corpse above his head, placed his head and shoulders between the creature's legs, and pushed off from the ledge before any of them could protest.

"*Geeee-RONimo!*" he yelled.

10

Frequent Flyers

SStragh heard someone screaming: a thin, high, word-less wail of distress that sounded like nothing she had ever heard before. It was the cry of someone in mortal terror.

She was surprised to find the horrible sound coming from her own throat.

SStragh had thought that the Floating Stone would continue to hover once she'd left the ledge. She'd expect-ed to sail across the gap on the vessel of the Floating Stone or—at the very worst—to float gracefully down to the canyon floor like a dead *ginjai* leaf in the dry season.

She hadn't expected to go into free-fall.

The wind nearly tore her grasp loose from the Floating Stone. SStragh held on with all her considerable strength as if she were intending to mold her hands into the slick white surface, knowing that even this gesture was useless and she was going to die, crushed against the stones that must wait somewhere in the white mist below. The frag-ment of path planed wildly back and forth, taking her out from the cliff wall and then bringing her dangerously back toward the craggy outcroppings, knives of stone that threatened to rip her open as they blurred past her.

Though they weren't blurring quite as much, she noticed suddenly.

SStragh realized that her breakneck descent had slowed. At the same time, she could feel the Floating Stone growing decidedly warm beneath her desperate grip. Before she could decide what this meant, the stone tilted underneath her again and banked away from the wall, accelerating downward once more. SStragh fought with the aeroplaning piece of plastic, trying to move closer to the wall of the canyon yet again as she prayed to the All-Ancestor for help.

Geedo! As she approached the cliff, she could feel the Floating Stone brake and seem to grab at the rocks, as if the air had turned gelid. SStragh forced the Floating Stone to stay near the rocks, the plastic shuddering under her hands. She could feel the surface growing warm again, even as the cliff wall changed from a racing gray blur to a more defined sequence of stones and crevices, still moving "upward" far too quickly for comfort. SStragh clung to falling path, trying to hug it to her and keep it from gliding away from the cliff again.

She also felt the Floating Stone growing increasingly hot as she continued to plummet, though she was falling at a far slower rate now. The heat built up under her fingers, and SStragh groaned. Her fingers were burning, and every fiber in her screamed that she must let go.

With a cry, SStragh allowed the Floating Stone to cant over and fall away from the cliff. The wind began to tear at her again as she fell free once more, but at least the stone cooled. She was falling into the mist now, a warm, gray-white wetness enveloping her. She reveled in its wet chill, but only for an instant.

You don't know how far down this goes, she thought frantically. *You don't have a choice. Follow the cliff and you may cook your fingers right down to the bone, but you also might survive the fall. Out here, you don't have a chance.*

With a moan that seemed to come from her tingling fingertips, SStragh leaned to one side, bringing the Floating Stone back toward the broken wall. She immediately began to slow once more. The Floating Stone quickly heated up as it absorbed the energy of her fall. SStragh tried to ignore the pain, as her very skin seemed to blister and burn under her grasp. She allowed herself to scream, anything as long as she continued to hold on—as the Floating Stone slowed almost to a feather's fall, as the mist hissed and steamed around the falling path slicing through it.

A jolt nearly threw SStragh off her perch; her body slammed agonizingly against the griddle of the path. The Floating Stone canted over sharply, SStragh's heavy body sliding until she was half-off the path. A huge outcropping of jagged granite slid past her to the left. Another jolt: SStragh was thrown just as violently to the right.

The cliff was no longer sheer, SStragh realized. She was reaching the very roots of the canyon, where old rockfalls spread out like a stone skirt over the foot of the cliff. Through the mist, she caught a quick glimpse of the canyon floor—lush greenery and a meandering river, still far below her. The sight gave SStragh a quick vertigo that made her forget the heat of the Floating Stone momentarily. Then the sight was wiped away as another outcropping sent her careening backward. SStragh fought for control of her wild vehicle, the plastic now searingly hot under her fingertips.

But she was falling at a more moderate pace now, sliding through the bottom of the mist toward the jungle below, the Floating Stone bumping and tossing like an out-of-control roller coaster down the flattening slope of the cliffside. The tops of trees were coming closer so that SStragh could see the individual fronds, and the Floating Stone was coasting, moving easily down the rocky slope like an eggling sliding down a sand dune on the Nesting Grounds. SStragh thought for an instant that she was going to make it, that she would simply come to a halt on the ground . . .

. . . when the Floating Stone moved up and then sharply down as it went over a lip of stone. SStragh was flipped head over tail. Her blistered and burnt fingers lost their grip and a great deal of skin. The Floating Stone went one way, SStragh another. SStragh was truly flying now, tumbling out of control and picking up speed again.

She crashed into the treetops like a scaly meteorite. The branches held her for an instant, then gave with a *crack*! SStragh thudded down from branch to branch, and finally landed with an *oomph* in a muddy, shallow swamp below. Dirty water cascaded as the breath went entirely out of her; the Floating Stone wheeled end over end behind her a few seconds later, hitting the water a dozen feet away, the water hissing and sputtering angrily as it contacted the scorching surface. A few seconds later, the stone came bobbing up to hover several inches above the water's surface.

SStragh, on her back, mud and filmy strings of algae covering her, looked from the dripping Floating Stone up to the broken canopy of green above her, where she could see the immense flank of the cliff ascending in impossible heights to the clouds above.

No one should have survived that fall, she told herself. *No one*.

But she had.

SStragh blinked. The pain in her hands and along her belly where she'd touched the Floating Stone was real enough, as was the taste of the filthy water in her mouth and the smell of this world.

SStragh lifted her head and gave a loud cry of triumph. The call of her victory echoed through the misty forest.

"Peter!" Aaron cried as his friend launched himself from the ledge. He was certain that he was about to witness the impetuous redhead tumble to his death to the unseen rocks in the darkness below.

For a few seconds, that almost seemed to be the case. The corpse of the saorod twisted in Peter's hands, nose down. The air went out of the wings as Peter tumbled, then he managed to bring the head up. Wind caught leather wings with a sound like sheets snapping in a sharp breeze, and Peter was gliding now, not falling.

"All right!" Peter exclaimed, and banked left. He caught the thermals rising from below and spiraled upward until he was as high as the ledge once again. He continued up one more turn, then tilted out of the updraft. He came in toward them at a rush, landing with his feet pumping as Aaron, Jennifer, and Travis caught him.

All of them, the stiff body of the saorod included, ended in a jumble of legs and arms. Peter was laughing and whooping as he disentangled himself from the pile. "Yes! Now that was fun! Come on—we can all get out of here if we hurry."

Mundo was looking dubiously at Peter. "Flying," he said with utter seriousness, "is for the birds." Aaron, Peter, and Jennifer all burst into laughter at that. Mundo wrin-kled his snout at the grinning trio. "I don't see what's so funny."

"It's okay, Mundo," Aaron said. "I guess you can't be expected to know human clichés. Peter . . ." Aaron shook his head as he looked at his friend. "That was a crazy stunt."

"It'll work better than trying to climb out of here. Even if we managed to get all the way to the top of those crevices without killing ourselves, then we're stuck on the top of a mountain with no way down. Now we can ride all the way down to the bottom." Peter looked at Jennifer, the grin fading and an odd look crossing his light eyes. "That's where the pathway's gone, anyway, if what they said about Struth is true. We gotta find that, first of all."

Jennifer, reminded suddenly of Struth, shivered. She seemed to withdraw into herself for a moment, then spoke with a harsh voice that surprised both Peter and Aaron. "All right, then. Let's get on with this. What do we need to do, Peter?"

"We'll each need to rig something to hold on to—your arms are going to get awfully tired on a long flight, and we don't want anyone accidentally letting go. The laces from Akira's armor should work even better if we can jury-rig bars across the legs to hang on to . . ."

Under Peter's direction, each of them chose one of the Seven and began work. Several minutes later, all of them were lined up along the ledge. A piece of temporal mate-rial was laced to each of the saorods' legs, lending their faces a strange green glow.

"Travis," Jennifer called. "Are you going to be able to hold on?" Travis smiled at her, winding the leather strap tight around his wrist and knotting it with his teeth.

"Worry about yourself, not me, Jenny," he said. "I'll manage. Let's just get out of here, quickly. Peter, do you have any helpful hints for us novices?"

"Don't try to do anything fancy," Peter told them. "Put the head down too much and you'll go into a dive that'll tear you right off when you try to pull out; too high and you're going to stall. Same thing with turning: bank too hard and you're going to be in trouble. We're way above the entrance to the caverns—just head for the opening. Once we're through, get away from the cliff and continue to spiral down. The problem's going to be speed—the landing could be really rough if you're going too fast. I'm not sure how aerodynamic all of our winged friends here are going to be."

"What if mine's not aerodynamic at all?" Mundo asked. "How am I going to know?"

"Oh, you'll know," Peter said. "Believe me. You'll know very quickly. One way or the other."

Mundo started to protest again, but Aaron interrupted the ape. "Everyone try to stay together as much as you can." He looked down the line of grim faces, each grasping the legs of a saorod, and he gave them the best grin he could muster. "And I gotta tell you—you all look pretty silly if you ask me."

The remark didn't break the tension as much as he'd hoped, but it did net him a few wan smiles from Jennifer and Travis. Mundo didn't look happy at all, and Eckels was his usual sour self. *Nothing you can do about it. All you can do now is see if fate and luck are on your side.*

"Okay," Aaron said. "Let's go. Peter? You've done this before; why don't you take the lead?"

Peter kicked away from the ledge, followed by Jennifer. One by one the others followed. Aaron watched each of them anxiously, but with Peter's example in front of them, everyone seemed to be mostly under control, despite some alarming initial wobbles. In a ragged line, they began the slow, circling descent toward the cave entrance. Aaron, with a last look back at the saorod graveyard, nodded to the lone standing remnant of the Seven.

"Thanks," he told the mute, mummified creature. "I hope your friends get returned to you eventually. We're really on the same side in this."

Aaron crouched, took a deep breath, and kicked himself out over empty space.

His stomach migrated to his throat. There was a horrible, momentary sensation of falling, and then the wings *whoomped* above him and he was gliding. His friends were now well below him and to the left; Aaron let the left wing drop slightly and the well of the cavern did a slow pirouette around him as he turned. Aaron laughed: in relief, in joy, in the sheer rapture of flying. "This is *great*," he said aloud, not caring that no one was there to hear him.

But there *was* an answer.

There was a sharp cry behind him, and a sudden wind buffeted him. The dark shape of a saorod streaked past him, the claws extended and the long beak open in surprise.

11

Swept Away

SStragh found herself in a gray world.

Soft tendrils of mist wound through the trunks of tall trees and the delicate fronds of gigantic ferns. The roots of the trees plunged into swampy water, with hillocks of earth humping out of the dark water here and there. Where SStragh could see through the tops of the trees, the cliff wall reared up into the bottom of low, thick clouds. Only a wan, diffuse light filtered down through the perpetual overcast of this world.

SStragh's body ached. Puffy blisters had risen all over her hands; she could barely close her fingers. Her entire belly was red with the burn; more blisters adorned the spaces between her scales. Her head pounded and she was cut and scraped everywhere from her fall through the foliage. When she lifted her tail to walk, the long muscles along her back ached; she couldn't easily move the tail as she walked and that affected her balance. A long cut had opened up on her right foot and an annoying cloudlet of tiny insects hovered around the bloody wound.

She might be alive—and she certainly thanked the All-Ancestor for that small miracle—but that didn't mean she had to feel good.

SStragh settled onto a grassy hillock near the Floating Stone. *What now?* Her idea had seemed so clear up on the ledge, but since it had turned into a near-disaster, she found herself distrusting her sudden inventiveness.

Still, she *had* survived the experience, and the Floating Stone was still needed if she was ever going to return to her own world. Instinctive need merged with this new way of thinking into which she'd fallen, this OChiihi.

SStragh looked around the hillock. A thick, coiling vine had choked dead a small tree near her, and then had died itself. SStragh closed tender fingers around the brown, dry tree and pulled. Blisters broke and she sounded a low, throbbing, mournful note involuntarily through her nasal horn, but she held the grip as vine and trunk came loose from the wet earth. Ignoring the throbbing pain as much as she could, SStragh splashed back into the water and pulled herself up onto the Floating Stone. The pathway had already cooled, though the white surface was now brownish gray, as if the heat had discolored the material. It held her—that was all that mattered.

Using the tree trunk as a crude oar, SStragh poled herself forward on the Floating Stone, moving on her strange gondola through the meandering bayou.

The saorod's beak gaped wide as it noticed Aaron hanging underneath the body of one of the Seven. The surprise sent it into a brief stall as it flapped its wings desperately. The saorod cawed again, looking more at its ancestor than at Aaron, as if expecting an answer from the corpse for its unexpected flight from the ledge of death.

I should have known they'd leave lookouts, Aaron thought. *It was too easy.*

"Nothing to worry about. He's just taking me out for a ride," Aaron said, knowing the creature couldn't understand him. The saorod screeched again, looping around them in evident confusion. On the next pass, it saw the others ahead of Aaron, and the saorod folded its wings to plummet toward them, streaking through the formation with a cry. "Hey, folks, we've got company!" Aaron shouted at his friends. "Just hang on and keep going."

As if we had a choice, he added to himself.

The saorod, to Aaron's surprise, didn't attack. Aaron wondered if that was due to the presence of the saorod ancestors. *You'd hesitate if someone were using King Tut's body as a shield. You wouldn't want to destroy it. You'd wait, too—especially when you know that we've got to hit ground at some point.*

The saorod evidently felt the same way, as it circled once more around their loose formation and then—wings pumping—darted out from the cavern through the entrance fissure. "That's going to be trouble for us!" Travis called back to Aaron. "You can bet that it's going to tell Salisos and the others."

"Unfortunately, you're probably right," Aaron called back. "But we can't do anything about it. How's everyone doing?"

"My arms are beginning to ache," Jennifer said. "Otherwise I'm okay." The others responded with the same sentiments.

"Once we're out, I think we should come down as fast as we can," Peter said.

"I agree," Aaron answered. "You keep the lead. Everyone follow Peter and do what he does. If Salisos and his friends show up, we'll deal with that then. And hang on; once we're out of here, it's an awfully long fall."

Peter banked sharply right, slipping between the vertical lips of stone and out into open air. One by one, the others followed him. Aaron blinked as sunlight glared in his dark-adjusted eyes; he sneezed once involuntarily. Squinting, he tried to find Salisos or the saorod who had gone after the Keeper of Burning Stones—he saw nothing ahead or below him, but the widespread wings of the saorod he held blocked his view above. Peter was arrowing quickly down toward the cloud tops below.

Aaron followed. Even though his arms were beginning to tire from gripping the bone he'd lashed between the saorod's legs, he found the experience to be exhilarating. The wind tousling his hair, the warm sunlight and ocean blue sky, the rugged burnt umber and gold beauty of the canyon walls—deeper and wider than the Grand Canyon—between which he flew, the vastness of the space around him and the silence except for the sound of the leathery sails above him: all this was a wonder that made it difficult for him not to shout his pleasure.

This must be how the Seven must have felt the first time they saw this place. No wonder they chose to live here. How wonderful . . .

An updraft from the clouds below lifted him suddenly and he *did* laugh, feeling the wings billow and carry him upward. Then he was out of the current and sliding gracefully downward again. It would be easy to circle around and find the column of rising air again, to ride it up and up until he was above the rim of the canyon, so that he could see the glittering panorama of this world. So easy, riding the wings of one of the Seven again.

Reluctantly, Aaron let himself continue downward in the path of his companions. Peter and Jennifer had disappeared into the filmy embrace of the mist; Mundo was just entering the fringes of the clouds, with Eckels and Travis close behind. Aaron angled his saorod's head down to increase the angle of descent. Once they were all in the mist, at least they'd be hidden from Salisos. Aaron remembered that during the battle with the browns, both groups had avoided entering the mist. Somewhere down there was the hidden bottom of the canyon—another unknown, but at least they knew that down there somewhere was the fragment of path that led back to the Mutata World—and, if Aaron's experience with the piece from the Nipponjin world held true— would also lead back to Green Town once they put in place the piece of temporal material he held.

Despite the fact that when he'd last seen "Green Town" it hadn't been there, Aaron still held out hope that this time it would be different. Even if it was no better than the odd Green Town with Captain Michaels and the Compound, well, at least they could *live* there. At least it was something halfway familiar.

Eckels and Mundo had disappeared into the gray-white cotton candy froth of the mist; Travis was just about to enter the topmost layer. Aaron took a last, lingering look around.

And he saw the saorods to his left, a V-formation of them like an arrow in the sky pointed in their direction, coming hard and fast from the cliff wall where the Floating Stone had once been. Salisos was at the point, and from the faint cry that came to Aaron, it was obvious that he was enraged. Aaron tilted his saorod's head down further to hasten his descent, hoping that he might lose his pursuers in the clouds.

As the clouds closed in around him, blanketing him in their cool wetness, Aaron saw Salisos heading directly toward him.

SStragh poled herself through fog-wrapped tunnels between the trees. She had no idea how much time passed. The sun had been not long past zenith when she'd taken her wild ride down the cliff, but here under the clouds only a pale, directionless ghost of the sun filtered through. The Mutata rarely worried about time intervals of less than half a day or longer than a few breaths, but here there was no sense of time at all.

Nor was there a sense of direction. Like most of the Mutata, SStragh always had an instinctive knowledge of where magnetic north resided, a sense resonating in her head. But here there were no references to align with that. She might know where north was, but without knowledge of what was around her, it was very little help. She poled in the general direction of south, the direction in which the saorod had taken Jhenini and the rest.

For lack of anything else to do, she counted the pole strokes.

Far too many strokes later, SStragh came out from the meandering swamp to a long, narrow lake. For some time, she'd been hearing periodic sounds, a wet roaring as if the earth were in pain. Here, it was warmer. Across the lake was a bare island, which looked as if it had been sprinkled with the *parak* powder that made sweetgruel. As SStragh glided out into the open, the source of the strange sound and the powdery appearance was revealed. A geyser exploded into action on the island, sending a cascade of white, steamy water splashing and gurgling into the lake. The mists boiled above the island, swirling in chaotic air currents. Through the boiling mist over the island, SStragh caught glimpses of blue sky.

The water was deeper here. SStragh used her makeshift pole to bring the Floating Stone to a halt before it became impossible to guide it. Another geyser vented foaming steam while SStragh pondered. As the last fountain of water from the eruption subsided, SStragh glimpsed something through the mist: a saorod, one even larger than the ones who had attacked her on the ledge.

SStragh honked in dismay. She tried to pole herself back into the cover of the trees, but the mud of the lake bottom was treacherous and the pole slid without moving the Floating Stone. She pushed again, and this time the Floating Stone began to move slowly backward. The saorod had descended beneath the mist now, coming in fast toward the island, and a second one was following it. SStragh noted something peculiar about the creatures. She squinted in the twilight overcast. There was something hanging beneath each of them.

"Struth! You're alive!"

The faint words, shouted in her own language from the second saorod, made SStragh start. She suddenly realized that the forms beneath each saorod were humans: *Peetah and Jhenini*. SStragh wondered how they'd managed to tame the saorods.

The great winged lizards were coming down quickly; SStragh realized that they were going to land on the island. She plunged the pole back into the water, shoving herself as hard as possible in that direction. As the Floating Stone moved at its ponderous pace toward them, SStragh watched them land.

The saorods didn't flap their wings to slow down at all. Instead, they continued to coast downward at breakneck speed. As they approached the land, Peetah and Jhenini started running. Even so, they were unable to keep their footing on the treacherous ground. Both of them went tumbling head over heels. The strangest thing was that the saorods made no effort to save themselves. Wings still extended, they too went crashing into the ground. SStragh saw a broken wing go tumbling away.

"Jhenini!" SStragh called.

"I'm all right. I think so, anyway." Jhenini was getting to her feet. Her clothing was covered in the crumbly *parak* of the island's surface; she made a futile attempt to brush away the worst of the dirt. "A little bumped and bruised."

Peetah was getting up also. Jhenini and he conversed for a moment in their own language, hugging each other, and then both—strangely to SStragh—looked upward.

The saorods who had carried them, also strangely, were motionless: one with its beak half-buried in the ground and its tail in the air, the other on its back. As SStragh puzzled over this, trying to push the the Floating Stone more quickly to the island, two more saorods glided down through the cloud cover, with Eckels and Mundo dangling below.

SStragh decided then that nothing humans did would ever surprise her again.

Aaron lost sight of the pursuing saorods as soon as the clouds closed in over his head. He could catch only fleeting glimpses of Travis's saorod, just ahead of him in the limited visibility of the mist. The dirty white blanket was wet, as well. Water was beading on his shirt and making him wish that he had windshield wipers for his eyes. Aaron peered ahead desperately. He had no idea how far above the ground he was—the last thing he wanted now was to have a tree come flying out of the fog and swat him out of the sky.

"Travis!" he yelled.

"Aaron?" came a reply from somewhere below and ahead. "You okay?"

"At the moment. We have Salisos and some friends right behind us, though. Can you see the ground yet?"

"Not yet."

There was nothing else to say, nothing to do. Aaron felt helpless as he fell slowly through the cloud banks, trying to keep Travis in sight through the damp soup. He craned his head back, trying to see behind him, but the mist had closed in behind. There was nothing behind or ahead but gray. Aaron prayed that Salisos would lose them in the fog, or that there'd at least be time to run for cover before the saorods came after them.

The mist cleared like frost on a heated windshield. Aaron was looking down from maybe a hundred feet or so above the level of the trees below, and he was dropping fast. The ground below seemed to be mostly swamp, and ahead of him was a long lake. Travis was well ahead of him, angling his saorod toward an island on the lake. Aaron could make out figures on the island: Jennifer, Peter, Mundo, and Eckels. The sight of them (and especially, Jennifer) safe caused a flood of relief to go through Aaron, relaxing a tension he hadn't known he was holding.

A small, irregular white raft was about to land on the island, and on the raft was another familiar sight: *Struth*. With the recognition came another shock—the raft had to be Struth's Floating Stone, Eckels's path. Aaron glanced down once at the emerald gleam lashed to his waist. For the first time since they'd come to this world,

Aaron had a sense that they were in control of their destiny. All the pieces had come together: the Floating Stone, the fragment of temporal machinery that would open the gateway to Green Town. Aaron felt more optimism than he had in . . . well, now that he thought about it, "days" wasn't exactly right. Moving about through timelines caused one to lose any perception that time was anything so steady, dependable, and comfortable as the concept of days and hours and minutes.

Travis had landed, and now Aaron was coming in himself, his legs nearly brushing the tops of the trees bordering the lake. The island seemed to be covered with fumeroles. Whitish deposits centered around small mounds dusted the darker earth, and steam wafted from a few of the holes. As Aaron approached, one of the mounds suddenly gushed water and steam, scattering the small band of humans nearby. Aaron veered away from the small eruption, and then found the ground approaching fast. He tried to hit running, but he was moving too fast. Aaron released the saorod and dropped into a roll. The body of the saorod went crashing to the ground somewhere nearby as Aaron shook his head and took a quick inventory of arms and legs.

Aaron rose to find himself in the rushing and very welcome embrace of Jennifer. "Safe and sound," Aaron said. "Peter, that was truly excellent. Really grand."

Peter couldn't quite keep the pleased grin from his face, though he tried. "You're not the only one with good ideas," he said, and Aaron couldn't help noticing that at least some of Peter's attention was on the arm Aaron had around Jennifer's shoulder. Aaron decided that the best course was to ignore the challenge in Peter's tone and words. "I never thought I was," he said as neutrally as possible. "Thanks."

Peter nodded.

Struth came paddling up to the rocky shore, Travis and Mundo helping the Mutata push and pull the Floating Stone over to the others. Struth gave a plaintive bellow and snort, her scent spicy, her spinal frill engorged and colored a deep aquamarine. Jennifer laughed. "We thought you were dead, too," she told the dinosaur, and rubbed the long nasal horn, scratching the thin skin there. She noticed Struth's hands then and gave a short gasp. "Look, she's burned," she told Aaron. "Those blisters . . . I'll need to wrap those."

"We haven't got time." It was Eckels who answered. "Look!"

Eckels was pointing off into the distance, well out over the lake. A squadron of saorods had appeared, dropping out of the low overcast and into the open air. They had evidently sighted the island and the humans. They could hear the calls of the saorods and see their wings thrusting as they came quickly toward them.

"We've got to go through the path," Aaron said, unlashing the piece of temporal machinery from himself.

"Back to the Gairk?" Peter said. "No way. I'll take my chances here."

"Back to Green Town," Aaron told him. "That's where this piece of machinery's linked. Remember? It's the fragments of the temporal mechanism that are anchored to their timelines, not the path. And this piece"—he hefted it up in his hand—"is linked to home." He glanced at the onrushing saorods and—strangely—grinned. "And it looks like *someone's* going through," he said.

"Time storm," Travis breathed. They could all see it now: a sullen black wall of cloud racing just behind the saorods. The thunderheads had formed in an instant, and now the snake tongues of yellow lightning flickered in the darkness, illuminating fleeting visions of other worlds and other times. An ice mountain, the tumbled front wall of a glacier, formed in the middle of the lake and was gone; a truncated skyscraper leaned precariously over the swampy shoreline, its ledges full of Gothic frills and fearsome gargoyles, and strangely clothed people who looked more feline than human peered out from iron grillwork windows at the saorod streaking past in the time storm's rising winds; then the skyscraper too was gone and in the distance well beyond the tree line the top of a ziggurat smoldered like a man-made volcano.

"C'mon," Aaron shouted to Peter through the cannoning thunder, and dived underneath the Floating Stone. Peter wriggled under after him. "We gotta jam this in here somewhere," Aaron told him.

"Is one piece gonna do it? I mean, each one of us has a piece or two."

"One *has* to be enough—I'm not sure who has another Green Town fragment and it's too late to go looking now. Here, push on this end . . . See if you can wedge it under that tear . . ."

The two grunted as they tried to force the mechanism into the blackened, rough undersurface. "You'll feel it if we make the right contact," Aaron said. "You'll get a tingle, like a shock."

Aaron pushed at the glowing mechanism, and the knob of roadway they were trying to fit it under broke off, the piece of luminescent machinery falling heavily to the ground, nearly crushing Aaron's fingers. The small fragment of roadway he'd cracked off, still floating, went streaking off in the wind, tumbling end over end. "*Aaron!*" Jennifer called as Aaron and Peter fumbled for the mechanism.

"I've got it—" Peter called.

They heard the hoarse cry of the saorods through the wail of the wind, far too near, and the Floating Stone tilted abruptly as something heavy hit it from above. The underside struck Aaron in the head and scraped along Peter's back. Lightning flared close by, further blinding Aaron, and the wind gusted wildly, sending Peter sprawling. A saorod went tumbling out of control past them— Aaron couldn't see if it was one of the corpses of the Seven or a live one—and the Floating Stone, tilted up, dipped even more, and then caught in the wind like a sail.

It went spiraling off over the lake to snag itself like an errant kite in the trees on the far side.

"No!" Aaron shouted into the gale. The others were shouting too. The storm front loomed over them like a nightmare monster, having tossed Salisos and the other saorods contemptuously away.

Lightning flared, blindingly, but there was no thunder.

Instead, the storm was gone and the air was still.

A hot sun sweltered above them in blue sky. They were still standing on their island, but only a small portion of it remained—a neat, clean, precise circle that was set in the midst of a lush tropical jungle. Aaron could see the leaves of the bushes and palm trees around them sliced off as if by a cosmic knife, in a column all the way up to where the open sky beckoned. They could hear birdcalls, the shrill sound of monkeys shrieking, and the smell of flowers and moist earth was powerful. Aaron took a quick count of heads. Everyone was with them, though Mundo and Struth were standing dangerously close to the arc where the crusty ground of the island met the black earth of the jungle.

Wherever they were, it wasn't the saorod world any-more.

"Stay together!" Aaron warned everyone. "Mundo, move closer to the center; Jennifer, tell Struth the same thing. Only the very last lightning strike of the time storms leaves behind anything permanent, remember? We've been shifted to another world, but if the time storm's still going on back where we were, it should take us right back as long as we stay in the circle."

They waited. The jungle was loud around them.

Nothing happened. After a minute, Aaron let out a long breath. He looked at Jennifer, at Peter, at Travis. Finally, the time safari guide shrugged at Aaron.

"Doesn't look like we're going back, people," Travis said.

12

A Man of Stele

"This is just fabulous," Peter groaned. "It wasn't bad enough that we had overgrown bats angry at us where we were, Gairk waiting for us in Lizard Land, and God knows what nonsense going on in Green Town. Now we're *totally* lost."

"Peter . . ." Jennifer cautioned, but the redhead gestured wildly at the lush tropical foliage around them.

"I mean it, Jen. We don't know where we are, or *when* we are, and even worse, whether there's any way back. You don't think that's cause for some alarm?"

"It's not *my* world," Mundo commented disconsolately. "Like all the rest, it's silent. I can't *be* any of these creatures . . ."

"Okay, okay," Aaron said as everyone seemed to begin talking at once. To be honest, he felt as pessimistic as Peter, but this hardly seemed to be the time to admit it. "We're not getting anywhere complaining about things. We're here, so let's concentrate on that. We still have the pieces of temporal machinery, right? If there's a piece of the path in this world, then we can use it to get us back. That's something."

153

"*If* there's a piece," Eckels said morosely. "If someone knows where it is. And if it's not across an ocean or up a mountain or guarded by an army."

"Quit your bellyaching, Eckels," Travis grunted. "That's all we ever get from you. Just shut up."

"Hey, you know what, I'm tired of your attitude, Travis," Eckels retorted. "I hired and fired people just like you every day back home, and I don't have to listen to you now. This is hopeless, and telling me to shut up when I point it out doesn't change anything."

"You just going to lie down and die, then?" Travis asked. He glared at the man, taking a step toward him. "I'll be glad to lend you a hand getting there."

Eckels started to answer back, but Jennifer stepped between the two. "Travis, please," she said. "Why don't you come with me; I want to check your bandages. I could use your help with Struth, too." Jennifer took Travis's arm and pulled him away while the man continued to glare at Eckels. "Please."

"Everyone," Aaron said. "Look. We have the saorod's Burning Stones. It's warm here so we we're not going to freeze, it's not raining, and so far nothing's attacked us. We could have landed in places a lot worse—in fact, Travis and I have seen a few. Let's start concentrating on what we're going to do. Our best asset is us. We can't afford to lose any person here. No one," he said force-fully, looking at Travis and Eckels, and then at Mundo, who was watching the confrontation from just outside the circle.

"I think we ought to plan on sleeping here tonight—on this patch of ground," he continued. "Maybe we're stuck in another time differential situation. That next lightning strike back in the saorod world might be hours away here even though it's only a few seconds there." He caught Mundo's eye. "And if you're not standing here when that happens, you'll be marooned," he added.

At Aaron's words, Mundo sidled silently onto the gray segment of the island. The thought also seemed to have put a temporary truce on the constant battle between Travis and Eckels, and if Peter didn't look happy . . . well, Peter rarely looked happy anymore. *If we're lucky, we'll wake up back in the saorod world, where we can get the Floating Stone again and get out fast.*

If we're lucky . . .

Luck wasn't listening.

They endured a long, moonless night. Once the sun went down, the air seemed to cool rapidly. Aaron and Mundo made a series of quick, frantic dashes out into the fringes of the jungle to gather deadwood for a fire; Peter still had his lighter. The crackle of flame made the chill bearable. Occasional eyes reflected firelight back at them from the darkness of the jungle, and the land around them was, if anything, louder by night than by day, with insects, birds, frogs, and a hundred other assorted animal calls.

Definitely not a prehistoric world, Aaron realized. The only lizards here seemed to be the little ones venturing out from cover to skitter quickly across this patch of alien landscape in their world.

No one seemed to sleep well. Travis had set up a tentative guard rotation, but it wasn't needed—there was always someone awake. Dawn, fingers of misty light streaking through the fronds of the palms, found everyone irritable, tired, and hungry.

"Now what?" Peter grumbled. "It doesn't look like we're going back the way we came." He glared at the encircling landscape as if it were a personal affront. "Some home *this* is."

"If it's going to be home, we'd better find out more about it," Aaron suggested. "Those look like coconut palms over there; they're probably as good a breakfast as we're likely to get. Then let's head north—unless someone has a better idea." No one seemed inclined to disagree. After getting themselves ready, the band set off with Aaron and Travis on point and Struth bringing up the rear.

They quickly found that movement through the dense foliage of tropical broad-leaved evergreens wasn't easy. The underbrush was thick and the leaves of the plants were stiff and unyielding. The ground was soft underfoot, and as the sun rose, so did the tropical heat and the land below them, as they found themselves toiling up inclines and scrambling down steep embankments. It was difficult to keep their footing or to continue moving in a consistent direction. Aaron called a halt to rig slings from thin vines for the pieces of temporal machinery they carried—causing another brief argument over whether they should continue to drag the heavy, glowing metal with them. They continued on, and soon they were all sweating, clouds of flies and small biting insects rising to the feast.

As the sun reached the midway point in its climb toward the zenith, they came to a fast-running creek in a small clearing. Over the tops of the trees, they could see more of the basic topography. They were on the southern flanks of a mountain, one of several in a range that seemed to move from northwest to southeast. There was a long, dark blue smudge on the horizon just over the treetops to the southwest.

"That's the ocean," Travis confirmed to Aaron, "or a damn big lake."

An argument immediately broke out among the party, Eckels insisting that they should head toward the water. "People always build along the water," he said. "Why keep heading inland? We could follow the shoreline."

"That's a good twenty or thirty miles away," Aaron answered. "You're talking at least three or four days hacking through this stuff. The higher we get, the more the jungle's going to thin out, and the better we'll be able to see more of what's around."

"Yeah? Well, I think that's stupid. I say we should talk about it, take a vote."

"No," Aaron said. He barked out the word, startling himself. He sounded like Otomo back in Nipponjin, snapping a command to an insolent underling. Aaron wondered at himself, at the changes that had been wrought in him since the day—ages ago, it seemed—when he and Jennifer had first seen the dinosaur eggs in the woods. The "old" Aaron would never have been so assertive.

When did you decide you had to be the leader? Peter's right—no one elected you president. For a moment, self-doubt threatened to take Aaron, but he shook his head again, realizing that the morale of the group was fragile at best. Right or wrong, if he allowed them to question his decision now, they'd flounder or collapse. "I said north," he told Eckels, "and that's where we're heading, at least until we can see that there's a better choice to be made."

Eckels shook his head, still muttering, but Travis was already making his way upslope past the creek. "Come on," Aaron said, and followed. He didn't dare look behind. He could hear Jennifer padding after him, but no one else. As he approached the edge of the jungle and started up a rocky outcropping in the wake of Travis, he heard Peter make a sound of disgust.

When he glanced quickly over his shoulder, Peter and Mundo were already hurrying after Jennifer. Eckels was still standing, hands on hips, but Aaron knew the man would follow. Eckels wasn't someone to strike out on his own. Aaron had won this round, at least.

And by noon, he'd been repaid for the effort.

Travis broke through a screen of brush and stopped, staring. "What's up?" Aaron asked.

"Take a look," the man said, stepping aside.

Just ahead of them, angling off to the northeast and farther into the mountains, was a wide path carved out of the jungle. The foliage was beaten down by the passage of many feet. "It's been used enough, but not constantly," Travis said. He knelt on the path, looking up and down it with a practiced eye. "See—here and there the ground's actually bare, so there's traffic through here with some regularity. No ruts, though—so no wheeled traffic. I'm not surprised at that in these mountains."

Travis got to his feet, groaning softly under his breath and holding his side. Aaron glanced at Jennifer; she shook her head. Travis crouched beside one of the bare patches, studying the dirt. "A couple hoofprints," he said. "Small ones, like a donkey or mule, and not shod. Those are deep—I'd say they were probably pack animals, because there are also prints from sandals, even a few bare footprints."

"People, you mean?" Peter asked. "*Our* kind of people? Human?"

"Yes," Travis said. He managed a smile. "Five toes and all."

"All *right*," Peter said. "Break out the champagne. That's one mark in the good column. What are you doing now, Travis?"

Travis had placed one of his feet alongside one of the footprints. "They're smaller," he said.

"What's that mean?"

"Either this was a caravan of thirteen-year-olds, or these people are significantly shorter than us. That could mean lots of things—an undernourished culture, a race of shorter people, or maybe we've kicked back into your past or my past—even a few centuries would do it." Travis shrugged. "We'll find out," he said.

Aaron suspected the man was exactly right about that. "We're going to need shelter and food," Aaron said. "I think we should follow the path." He looked at the others. Jennifer nodded, Peter shrugged. Mundo didn't give any indication at all and Eckels was studiously ignoring him entirely. Struth simply looked bewildered.

"Which way are most of the footprints going?" Aaron asked Travis, who pointed to the right, up the flank of the mountain.

"Figures it'd be uphill," Peter commented. "Well, if we're going to go, let's do it."

Several hundred yards up the winding trail, they came to a sharp bend where crude stairs had been cut into the rock to ascend a particularly steep section. At the foot of the stairs, a carved stone column had been erected.

"It's beautiful," Jennifer said, going up to the sculpture and touching it wonderingly. Ten feet high, painted in shades of reds and ochers, the column depicted a huge, grimacing face adorned with an intricately carved and elaborate headdress. Below the face were several blocks of squarish carvings, again very detailed. They could see representations of a serpent, of feathers, of what seemed to be fabulous monsters and faces.

"Glyphs," Peter said. Everyone turned to look at him. "Hey, I might not have been the 'A' student Aaron and Jenny were, but I know some things, too. We were studying early Mesoamerica in school last semester. That looks like the Mayan or Aztec writing we were shown. It fits, too—the tropical setting, the mountains. This is a marker of some kind."

"That makes the hoofprints we saw more interesting," Travis commented.

"How so?"

"In the history of *my* world, at least, there weren't any horses in the New World until the Europeans brought them over."

"That's right," Jennifer said. "After Columbus."

"After who?" both Travis and Eckels echoed.

"Christopher Columbus?" Jennifer said. "Discovered America? 'In fourteen hundred and ninety-two, Columbus sailed the ocean blue'?"

Travis shook his head. "Diego Velasquez was the first to sail west from Europe—1507. He established New Madrid on the Floridian peninsula; it's still the biggest city in North America. Every school kid knows that, but I've never heard of any Columbus."

"That's why you'd never heard of Illinois, either, way back when we first found you," Aaron said. "So we *are* from parallel timelines. Evidently we share a lot of common history, but somewhere things diverged." Aaron looked at Eckels. *Or maybe someone stepped on other world-changing butterflies*, he thought.

"Columbus or Velasquez, what's the difference?" Peter interjected. "What you're saying is that if this is Mexico, there's been contact with Europe. Fine. But we're not going to find out when and where we are by standing here. For once I agree with Aaron. Let's keep going."

With a last glance back at the impassive stone face, they continued up the mountainside. Jennifer moved close to Aaron. "I remember something else about both the Aztec and the Mayans," she said to him softly.

"What's that?"

"They both sacrificed their captives to their gods. Aaron, I think we should be very careful."

13

The Tale of Ilhuicamina

As they climbed, the tropical vegetation gave way to forest mixed with conifers, evergreens, and a few hardwoods. The air was cooler and thinner. Travis doggedly continued on point, but he was moving slower and with obvious effort. He was coughing again, and Jennifer stayed close to him with a worried look on her face. Peter wasn't much better, pained by the wound he'd taken from Gray Raven, and he'd never really had the time and rest to recover from the loss of blood. Struth never complained, but Aaron knew the Mutata couldn't use her blistered hands while scrambling up the steep trail, and the burns must have ached tremendously.

Aaron called for frequent rest stops—no one objected. Now high up in the mountains, they'd yet to meet anyone on the path, which zigzagged in relentless switchbacks toward the peak. Through the occasional break in the trees, they could look out over the rain forest covering the coastal plain, fading into the blue distance where the land met the sea to the southwest.

The sun had nearly fallen behind the peaks to the west when they reached a point where the trail slid behind the mountain and began to descend again. There, from an open glade, they could look out over another valley. Halfway down the mountain's far side was a village.

Surrounded by wide terraces of cleared and planted ground spreading like a mantle around the shoulder of the mountain, several gleaming white buildings with thatched roofs faced a large open courtyard paved with light stone. Other smaller groupings of structures were scattered nearby down the mountainside. The main plaza opened to the north, and there a paved boulevard swept up the mountain to a stepped, flat-topped pyramid that mirrored the angular mountains around it. The plaster that covered the walls and stones of the stairway leading up to the summit was painted a bright red, while lines of other colors adorned the detailed carvings on the faces of each of the pyramid's layers. At the top of the edifice a temple had been erected, the lintels and columns of the doors swirling with hieroglyphic carvings, the entrance itself looking like the wide-gaping face of some monster. The entrance to the temple and its roof were blackened, as if a large fire had recently burned there.

There was activity all over the village: children chasing each other through the plaza area, women sitting in groups in the shadow of the buildings with reddish-colored, large bowls set before them, tending pots set over open fires or working on looms. Several dogs were lying curled in the sunlight or begging near the women preparing food; a gray burro munched hay in a stall just off the plaza. Behind one of the larger buildings overlooking a terrace garden, a group of young boys was being instructed by an older man who held a bow and arrow in his hands. The children were universally naked; the adults wore loincloths wrapped around their hips with folds draping over the front and rear. Some sported cotton capes dyed in geometric patterns of blue and orange; the man addressing the boys was adorned with an elaborate feathered head-piece and, in addition to the loincloth, wore a quilted short-sleeved jacket. The people were copperskinned, with dark hair oiled and cut. "I think your guess about where and when we are might be right," Jennifer said to Peter.

"Yeah," Peter said back to her, staring down at the small town spread out before them. "Now I'm wishing I'd studied a bit harder than I did. I hope you remember more than I did."

"I wonder how they're going to react when we walk in?" Aaron said.

"They'll call us *ix-tz'ul*," Mundo said. "Foreigners."

Everyone looked at Mundo. "That's what *he's* thinking," Mundo said, pointing toward the brush to the left of the path.

Where Mundo pointed, a small boy emerged shyly from cover, staring at the group—and especially Mundo and Struth—with wide, dark eyes.

"As receptions go, this is definitely the best we've had recently," Jennifer commented.

No one could disagree. Their arrivals in other timelines had certainly been more immediately threatening. As a contrast, the townsfolk had welcomed them with wonderment. They'd marveled at the appearance of the humans, gasped as Mundo—with his amazingly quick grasp of language—answered them in their own tongue, and gaped in undisguised awe at Struth. The glowing pieces of greenish metal the strangers carried in their vine slings had caused them to exclaim loudly among themselves. "You have to admit that we're probably the most unusual group of travelers they've ever seen," Aaron said.

They'd been escorted into the town by a growing escort of children and townsfolk. With Mundo translating, they'd made it known that they were travelers, and that they were seeking food and shelter for the evening. That had brought about a bustle and scurry as fires were lit, maize ground into flour, and water fetched. The arrival of the group seemed to have given the villagers an excuse for a festival.

As evening spread its soft blue mantle over the mountains and the sunlight lent a last departing touch of gold to the highest peaks, an impromptu feast began. Fruit was offered, and hot corn mush spiced with chili and chocolate. A deer was roasted over a charcoal pit, and there were various vegetables and a constant variety of maize dishes, as well as steamed freshwater snails from the nearby river. They were given sweet honey mead in clay cups, and an old man offered them *pulque*, a drink made from the fermented juice of the maguey plant—after a polite sip of the bitter, strong stuff, only Travis continued to drink it.

They were entertained, as well. Several of the townsfolk sang songs, accompanied by clay whistles and wooden flutes, and there was a constant chatter from the conversations around them. The children were constantly darting through the crowd to touch Struth, who seemed amused by the attention.

"Has it given blood—is that why its hands are covered? Is it a god?" asked the children wonderingly. "Or a *cipactli*?—that's an alligator," Mundo translated for Jennifer, who laughed and shook her head at the child who'd spoken. The little boy stroked Struth's side once more and ran off to his mother.

"I like this place," Aaron said to Jennifer and Peter. He reached over to a brown and ocher glazed platter for another piece of corn flour cake. He nodded to one of the women seated on the plaza stones just across from them. She smiled back.

"I like it just because it's the first place where we haven't been immediately considered to be someone's enemy," Peter commented. "That's a nice change, if you ask me."

"I don't know. There's at least a couple of people who don't look real thrilled with us," Jennifer told Peter and Aaron. "Over there; you see them?"

Peter and Aaron looked out beyond the bonfire that burned in the middle of the plaza. Two men stood at the edge of the light near a wellspring, staring in toward them. Firelight played over ridged faces almost as mountainous as the hidden landscape around them. Jennifer recognized one as the man who was teaching the children archery earlier. Along with his feathered headdress, he wore a cape with an intricate pattern of blue squares, each with a white dot inside. The other man was dressed more simply, a white loincloth under a red and yellow cloak. His craggy mouth was set in a frown—the expression looked very comfortable there.

"I've been watching them," Jennifer said. "Everyone seems to treat them with respect, but they don't laugh or joke with them as they do with the others."

"They're probably the head honchos," Peter said. "Ask Mundo to find out. Hey, Mundo!"

Peter didn't have the chance to ask. Noticing the attention of the trio, the two men came through the crowd toward them. They strode through the throng with the heedless grace of people accustomed to having others move aside for them. The villagers gathered around Jennifer and the others vanished quietly, and they found themselves alone with the two while the celebration—judiciously—moved farther down the plaza.

"Hello," Aaron said. "Mundo, why don't you handle the introductions."

The men listened gravely as Mundo gave each of their names, their flintlike gazes going one by one to each of their faces. The man in red and yellow especially held Jennifer's eyes. When it was her turn to be introduced, she felt as if the man were penetrating to her very soul, reading her private thoughts and feelings. His face revealed nothing of what he thought himself. Jennifer felt only a strange sense of nakedness, as if he had held aside a cloak in her mind. Then the moment was gone as Mundo spoke Travis's name and the man's gaze moved aside.

"I am Ilhuicamina," the one with the headdress said after Mundo had given all their names. "I govern this *alteptl*—this village—for the Huey Tlatoani, the great King Cuauhtemoc Acamapichtli, who rules in Tenochtitlán over all the Mexica. And this—he gestured to the other man—"is Tezozomoc. He is the priest of our temple." Ilhuicamina paused, looking at them. "Tezozomoc has been troubled ever since the omen yesterday, and since you have come, the significance seems even stronger. We must ask—are you Spaniards?"

"No," Aaron answered simply, hoping it was the answer Ilhuicamina was looking for. "We're not from Spain."

Ilhuicamina gave an audible sigh of relief, but Tezozomoc's face never relaxed.

"I did not think so," Ilhuicamina said. "You do not speak the language of the ship-lords among yourselves, and Spaniards did not have hair of red flame, or yellow hair like the excrement of the sun. The Spaniards did not dress as you do. The Spaniards did not have serpent gods walking with them or white-haired, giant monkeys who speak the language of Nahuatl." He looked long at the pieces of temporal machinery piled near their group. "The Spaniards also did not have sacred glowing greenstones."

"You speak of the Spaniards as if they're gone," Jennifer said, hoping to draw their attention away from the temporal machinery.

"They *are* gone," Ilhuicamina answered, and he could not suppress the slow smile as he said the words. "Over fifty *xiuhpohualli*—the years of the sun—have passed since the army of the ship-lords was destroyed, and they have not troubled us since."

Jennifer looked at Peter and Aaron with raised eyebrows. "That's not the way *our* history went," she said. "Travis, Eckels? How about in yours?"

Travis shook his head. "We may not have known about your Columbus person, but Hernán Cortés is famous enough. His army defeated the Mayan *Ahua* Can-Ek in 1521."

"Mayans? Can-Ek? Don't you mean the Aztecs and Montezuma?"

"Never heard of the Aztecs or this Monty person," Travis said. "More minor differences in our pasts, I suppose. But look—Ilhuicamina's ears just perked up."

"I hear the name Cortés. I hear you speak of Motecuhzoma Xocoyotzin." Ilhuicamina nodded. "My father was there. That is a tale I know . . ."

My father (Ilhuicamina told them, as Mundo translated his words), was called Tizoc. For several generations, my family has been *pipiltin*, nobolity, and Tizoc, like his father before him, served under Motecuhzoma's banner in Tenochtitlán. Many times, as fathers do when their sons ask them about their youth, Tizoc would tell me of the times of the Spaniards, sharing his memories. I enjoyed those times, until Tizoc's soul was called and he was lost to me.

I remember my father's voice, though. It was deep and rough, like the sound of stones tumbling in a river. . . . But I wander from my story. I was telling you about when the Spaniards came.

My father would always tell me first of the many signs that preceded the coming of the ship-lords, signs not unlike the one we witnessed here last night. The omens began in the sun-year preceding the coming of Cortés, and all the Mexica witnessed them. Even the southern tribes who place tree-stones on their altars spoke of visions in the sky. Tizoc was proud that he himself had a two-headed dog born in his household, which he promptly sacrificed to Xiuhtecuhtli, and there were many stillbirths among the Mexica that year. The rainy season was dry. The mountain Popocatepetl vented dark smoke during the month of Tlacaxipehualiztli, so much smoke that the city was like night even at the height of day, disturbing the rites of the Flayed Men.

Everyone knew that something waited to happen. Tizoc said that no one was greatly surprised when word came to the city that strange folk had come to our land, for we knew that the very gods had stirred with their coming.

The ship-lord Cortés landed on the shores of Ilhuica tl, the Heavenly Water. He had with him over two thousand soldiers with bright suits of metal and long knives. They could not speak Nahuatl, but they had brought some of our southern cousins who knew both our language and Spanish. They had their arquebuses and their cannons with fire demons who could throw round stones great distances, through walls or through the cotton armor of a Mexica warrior. The *tlatoani* of the city nearest to Cortés sent a peace delegation to the ship-lord, but Cortés fought with them. The black priests with the Spaniards refused to let the delegation practice their rites, and when they made the proper sacrifices anyway, the black priests went howling to Cortés. This madman, this blasphemer of the gods, ordered the delegation killed, and he took the daughter of the *tlatoani* captive for his own uses.

Tizoc told me how none of them could believe the vanity, pride, and cruelty of this man Cortés. Motecuhzoma sent his own delegation to Cortés, asking for either proper tribute or for a date on which our warriors could meet with those of Cortés for the necessary battle. Tizoc, my father, asked to go with the delegation, but Motecuhzoma would not let him go. It must have been that the gods wished my father to live, since Cortés slew that delegation also, and declared that it was Motecuhzoma who owed tribute and not the Spaniards.

My father was among the counselors Motecuhzoma now called to him. Tizoc advised Motecuhzoma to march immediately upon the Spaniards, but in his wisdom Motecuhzoma decided to wait, to watch the signs the gods would bring, and see if Cortés would come to understand his errors. The priests let blood—*chalchiuh-atl*, the precious water—piercing themselves over and over with the spines of stingrays. There were a hundred sacrifices of captive warriors made to Tlaloc and Huitzilopochtlio from the Great Temple.

Cortés—the abomination, the fool—gathered the Spanish army together to march on Tenochtitlán itself. Tizoc would always laugh at that part of the story. Tie would lean back and drink his *pulque*, looking at the sky and shaking his head.

"Can you believe that, Ilhuicamina?" he would say. "There was a madness in the man. He and his black priests mocked the gods, threw down their images, and destroyed the temples, took our greenstones and stole the gold metal that is the sun's. There could only be one answer to that. Only one answer."

My father was right. Cortés had so angered the gods that they rose up against him: Tizoc, who brought the reports to Motecuhzoma, witnessed it. I wish . . . I wish I could give you the words as he spoke them. I wish you could listen to his voice, for it spoke so vividly of the march of Cortés.

They must have been a vision, this army of the Spaniards, a sea of glinting metal tossing the light of the sun back into the sky. They unfurled their strange banners, and Cortés waved his long knife at the mountains and motioned his army forward. Cortés, like the other ship-lords with him, rode upon a horse, which none of us had ever seen before. Behind the army came captives they had pressed into service, and the animals they called donkeys and burros—like the one we have here in our village—carried their cloth houses and supplies. They moved on our land like shining ants, leaving behind a trail of destruction. As they passed our towns and villages, some of the Mexica warriors challenged them, but spears and stone knives were no match for swords and guns, and the Spaniards did not fight honorably. For them, it was slaughter, and Motecuhzoma sent word that no more challenges were to be offered.

But the gods were watching the sacrifices of our priests, and they tasted the blood Motecuhzoma offered them. The gods sent a punishment to Cortés and his people. First the earth trembled, shaking even the stones of Tenochtitlán. The army of the Spaniards was in the mountains. Boulders fell on them like rain, killing many of them and driving off their horses and other beasts— the horses, donkeys, and burros we now have are the off-spring of those who ran away in panic. Tizoc, my father, was later gifted with one of the recaptured horses by Motecuhzoma himself. He used to tell us that it was Cortés's horse itself, but I don't believe that. That was the *pulque* talking.

The gods also sent a sickness to the Spaniards. Boils and pustules erupted on the faces and hands of the sol-diers, and their skin turned dark underneath the sores. The soldiers became ill; they could not eat and a fever burned like fire on their brows. When the pustules reached the trunk of the body, they died—screaming in pain and madness. The Spaniards were even more afraid because the sickness did not touch the Mexica, even those who were with Cortés. Of the two thousand sol-diers who left with Cortés, only six hundred reached the shores of the great lake, where the city of Tenochtitlán waited on its island. The Spaniards we took captive later told us that Cortés shivered when he first looked upon Tenochtitlán, with her white causeways linking her to the land of the Valley, with her shining temples and palaces, and the double-staired Great Temple set in her very center.

Motecuhzoma sent a force to meet Cortés there on the shore, and a great battle was fought. The feathers of the Mexica war helms seethed like a great wind blowing across the forest, and the backpieces of the armor towered above their faces, causing a coldness to grip the hearts of the enemy. The sound of them was like jaguars roaring, like mountains falling, and none of them cared that they might find *xochimiquiztli*, the death of battle, waiting for them on the bright metal of the Spaniards' long knives. My father himself took two Spaniards captive, but Cortés . . . he did not capture those he defeated. He killed them there, spilling their blood uselessly on the ground. Tizoc told me that Motecuhzoma had hoped that Cortés would at last turn back when he saw the might of Tenoehtitlán coming upon him, but Cortés had been blinded by the gods so that his defeat would be even more terrible.

And it was terrible.

The warriors—and my father—fell upon the Spaniards. Even weakened by sickness, even outnumbered, the army of Cortés killed three Mexica to every Spaniard who was captured or killed, and they made their way across the bridges into the city itself. Motecuhzoma sent down a storm of javelins and spears and arrows, though many of the bolts simply fell from their armor like rain off the back of a tortoise. Tizoc claimed that for a time, even he was afraid that Cortés would yet be stronger than Motecuhzoma, for the Spanish cannons sounded like thunder and tore holes in the palace where the *tla-toani* stood watching the battle, and the guns of the Spaniards killed our warriors before they could even strike a blow.

But the Spaniards, who had made their way deep into the city, finally turned and retreated down the main

causeway out of the range of arrows. There, Motecuhzoma could see the lords of the Spaniards gathering
around Cortés as they planned another assault.

Tizoc said that on that day he could feel the energy of
the earth concentrated in the city. Motecuhzoma felt it
too, my father told me, and so the ruler called to the
priests. The day demanded sanctification, the day
demanded that our energy be focused and channeled to
ensure our victory. Motecuhzoma ordered that the shell-
horns be sounded from the platform of the Great Temple,
that whistles blow and trumpets sound.

The priests brought out all the Spanish soldiers captured in the weeks of Cortés's march. In the sight of
Cortés and his soldiers, the captives were marched up the
stairs of the Great Temple to the sanctuary of
Huitzilopochtlio.

The priests gave the Spaniards fans to hold, set plumes
on their heads, and made them dance the creation dance
while the priests chanted and pierced themselves, pulling
bark paper strips through the wounds so that the blood
would flow well. My father was there, and when the ritual
of the dance was finished, he himself helped the priests
lay the captives down on the *techcatl*, the sacred stone.
Then the priests used their *tecpatl*, the ceremonial flint
knives, to cut the living hearts from the sacrifices, holding them up to the sky before placing them in the eagle
vessel, the *cuauxicalli*. My father rolled the bodies down
the stairs for the attendants. He said that the stairs ran
red before they were done.

The rich, bright blood, given there at the world's very
center, fed the gods and their energy revitalized us. When
Motecuhzoma gave the command, the Mexica warriors
came down like a hammer upon a stone to scatter the

Spanish troops, who fled wailing and crying from the city. Tizoc and the others harried Cortés all the way back to the sea, and Cortés fled to his ships with only a bare hundred left of the thousands who had come.

Afterward, Motecuhzoma rewarded Tizoc by proclaiming him a *calpixque*, a tribute collector. During his travels, my father came here. As he told it, when he saw this village, thunder sounded from the sky even though there were no clouds, and he knew that the gods called him from the mountains to say that he should stay here, so he obeyed. I think it was because he also met the woman who would be my mother.

In time, I was born, and he told me all this.

As to the Spaniards, Cortés himself became ill with the gods' sickness, and we learned that he died on his way back across the great water to his homeland. The gods' sickness found its way to the cities the Spaniards had established around the Ilhuica Atl, and in fear they went into their ships, all of them, and left.

They have not troubled us since.

14

Meetings and Summons

Ilhuicamina's eyes glowed in the light of the bonfire as he ended his story. Whirling sparks danced their way to the stars, and the mountains were a silent, hidden darkness around them.

Jennifer found that Ilhuicamina's tale had raised goose pimples on her arms despite the warmth of the evening. She could all too vividly imagine the chests of the captives sliced open on the altar of the pyramid so that the priests could pluck out their hearts, and the stones of the temple stairs running wet with their bright blood. She knew that cultures had different mores and different rites. Jennifer had no doubt Ilhuicamina would find some of their customs just as incomprehensible. Yet she watched Ilhuicamina's face as he spoke, and the calm with which he related the tale of death and the casual way he'd spoken of the sacrifice of the captives unsettled her.

She realized that she was in a world where life was not necessarily sacred, where beliefs demanded blood and death, where myth and reality were bound together in a complex web and the boundaries between the two were not always clear. The realization made the noisy celebration in the village around them seem somehow surreal, made her supper turn to ashes in her stomach.

She glanced at Struth, sitting on her haunches in the nocturnal half slumber of the Mutata. The dinosaur's eyes were still open, but unfocused. One of the village children was sleeping propped up against Struth's side. It was a strangely gentle scene, a seeming contradiction of what she'd just heard.

Funny . . . I'll bet Struth understands these people better than I do. In some ways, they're more like the Mutata than me.

As Ilhuicamina finished speaking, Jennifer looked at Peter and Aaron. The three of them had drawn together during the story, as if unconsciously seeking the company of someone familiar. Peter shrugged, grimacing as the motion pulled at the gunshot wound on his shoulder. "Man, talk about Montezuma's revenge . . . That's not exactly the way our history books have it, is it?"

"Not for Eckels and me, either," Travis said, nearby. He swallowed the last of his *pulque*.

"I don't understand *any* of it," Mundo said. "I'd say the primary occupation of humans seems to be figuring out creative ways to kill each other. And you do it very well. Congratulations."

Then Tezozomoc, the priest, spoke suddenly and Mundo rushed to translate. "There are signs now," he told them. His voice was gruff and low. "Signs just as there were in Ilhuicamina's father's time. Only now the omens are worse. The dry vision-storms come—every day, sometimes. We have heard that the temple of Texococo vanished during one of the storms, and in its place was a barren desert like the one our ancestors came from.

A bird of metal fell from the sky and struck the mountain of Iztac Cihuatl. The gods show dreams that even the common people can see, dreams that come while we are awake. They plague us with strange sights, with monsters that sometimes walk out of the visions into this world. The signs worsen with each month—I have been told that the main road from Tenochtitlán to the coast has been broken by a new lake, a salt lake as round as the moon. At first these things occurred rarely, but now . . ."

Tezozomoc shook his head. "Now there is disorder and chaos everywhere: here, as well as in the realm of the gods. The walls of the world are broken."

The man leaned over the fire toward them, his face lit from below by the flames. "Yesterday, as the sun set in Cihuatlampa, yet another storm came bearing its visions. I watched the thunderheads form over the mountain as I stood in front of Tlaloc's temple, and I saw the first stroke of lightning descend from boiling, black clouds. The bolt struck the temple, blinding me and sending me sprawling. When I could see again, the roof of the temple was on fire, but the wind came and blew away the burning thatch, gusting so hard that the embers that were left couldn't catch. I knew this was a sign: a temple burning, and then miraculously saved. Tlaloc was telling me that he was sending someone to save us, someone to put the walls back in place. And you came."

Tezozomoc kicked at one of the logs with a sandaled toe and more sparks flared. He plucked something under the wrapping about his waist. Jennifer could see it, glinting in the firelight between Tezozomoc's forefinger and thumb: a flake of obsidian. The priest reached up with his other hand, grasping his earlobe and stretching it out. With a sudden motion, he nicked the lobe with the razor edge of the glassy stone; Jennifer hissed with a sudden, sympathetic intake of breath, but Tezozomoc's face was entirely stoic.

Blood welled thick in the cut, and Tezozomoc held a strip of paper to his ear. The dark liquid spread along the fibers of the paper. When the piece was saturated, Tezozomoc tossed it into the fire. The paper hissed and steamed and finally curled into ash that floated up and away as they watched. Jennifer found that she'd been holding her breath. She looked again at the priest, who ignored the blood still flowing sluggishly down the side of his neck. He was staring at the rising ash, and there was satisfaction on his face.

"You came," Tezozomoc said. "I know that you have stepped out of a vision-storm. You have come from Tlaloc."

"No," Aaron said quickly. "We didn't. Sorry to disappoint you, but you've misinterpreted your vision."

Mundo didn't translate that. "I don't think that's something we should tell this guy," Mundo said. "If he wants to think we're messengers of the gods, let's let him believe it." The ape looked at the others for confirmation. Eckels nodded; Travis merely watched, still holding the empty cup of *pulque*.

"Tell him what I said, Mundo," Aaron insisted. "Word for word."

"It's a mistake, Aaron."

"Tell him."

Mundo wrinkled his snout, but he turned to Tezozomoc and spat out a stream of Nahuatl. The priest seemed amused.

"Even those chosen might not realize it," Tezozomoc replied. "Didn't you come here from the storm? Don't you carry sacred greenstones, strangely carved, which glow like stars in the night?"

"Yes," Aaron said. "I guess so. But we came here entirely by accident. We saw no gods, and we don't have any celestial messages."

The priest only smiled when Mundo translated that, a gesture that touched the corners of his mouth and then fled. "I don't think he bought that," Aaron muttered.

"Ask him if he's seen a Floating Stone or other 'greenstones' like ours," Jennifer told Mundo. "If they've seen all these 'signs,' maybe they have a piece of the roadway, too."

As Mundo translated, Jennifer watched the faces of the two Aztec leaders. Ilhuicamina simply shrugged and shook his head—Floating Stones were obviously not something in the village leader's experience. Tezozomoc, however . . . In the firelight, it was difficult to tell, but Jennifer thought that the lines of the Tezozomoc's face tightened as Mundo asked the question, as if some interior curtain had been drawn more tightly around the man's emotions.

"They would know of Floating Stones in Tenochtitlán," Tezozomoc said curtly. He seemed to be looking at something beyond them. A moment later, the priest nodded slightly to each of them, and said something to Mundo, who replied at some length. Finally Tezozomoc gestured to Ilhuicamina and the two men left the plaza, disappearing into the night.

"Well, that was certainly abrupt. . . . What'd he say to you at the end, Mundo?" Jennifer asked as the villagers gathered around their fire again. "And what'd you say to him?"

"Oh, that?" Mundo answered. He grinned at all of them. "Nothing. He just thanked me for translating, that's all. Said I did a great job—for a monkey."

Mundo scampered away before Jennifer could ask any-thing else, taking the hands of one of the young women of the village and dancing with her to the music of a flute and drum as people clapped and began cavorting with them. "Do you believe him?" Aaron asked Jennifer, watching the firelight gleam from Mundo's hair as he capered around the plaza to the laughter of the villagers.

"After what happened in Nipponjin?" Jennifer an-swered. She leaned back against Aaron, enjoying the feel of his arms around her but shaking her head. "No. I could have sworn I heard Mundo say something about Tlaloc. But I don't know what we can do about it right now."

Morning was gorgeous. A mist wreathed the trees on the mountainside while the rising sun, still hidden behind the eastern slopes, speared the broken clouds overhead with dusty brilliance. Brightly colored birds flitted through the trees, and a river splashed and foamed over rocks as it cascaded down the steep slope toward the val-ley. The village was glittering white, a diamond in an emerald setting framed by the ordered terraces. At dawn, the villagers were already up and about their daily tasks. They nodded and smiled at Jennifer as she passed.

She and the others had spent the night in one of the single-room dwellings, in the compound of Ilhuicamina's family. Jennifer had awakened with the light, hearing the bright sound of voices outside. Struth was missing, but the others, Mundo included, were still asleep. She'd got-ten up and gone looking for the dinosaur.

She wasn't hard to spot. The Mutata was standing near one of the limestone walls at the edge of the plaza. A crowd of children surrounded her, giggling everytime Struth would bend down to speak to them.

"Jhenini," Struth called, seeing her. "Your egglings are not much different than ours—too curious for their own good. They will not leave me alone."

Jennifer grinned. "You're definitely a novelty," she said. "Just don't step on any of them."

Struth managed to look offended at that, snorting once through her nasal horn, a trombone bleat that sent the children scurrying away momentarily. Some of them hid behind Jennifer, and she hugged them to her. "I would not step on the egglings," Struth said seriously, her scent musky and her stance indicating that she was offended.

"Struth, that was a . . ." Jennifer stopped, realizing that she didn't know any words for "joke" in the Mutata language. With what she knew of the OColihi, she suspected that the term didn't exist. "Well, let's try 'an intentional untruth meant to amuse, not offend.' Long-winded, but accurate enough. I'm sorry. Here, let me see your hands . . ."

Struth snorted again, but her stance relaxed. She extended her hands. Jennifer unwrapped the bandages she'd placed around the burns. She grimaced when the flesh was exposed. The blisters were huge and both hands were swollen, though there didn't seem to be any obvious infection. "I'll clean this up in a bit," she told Struth. "I want to get some new bandages on this."

Struth gave the wriggle that was a Mutata shrug as Jennifer rewrapped the hands. "This is a *jhaka* that even Mutata would like," the Mutata said. "A very pleasing place, though colder than my world."

"Yes, it's very pretty here," Jennifer agreed. She rumpled the hair of a child who tugged at her hand and let her gaze travel around the village once more. The pyramid temple farther up the steep flank of the mountain caught her, and with it came a reminder of the beliefs

that lay under the pastoral scene. She could see
Tezozomoc on the platform there, kneeling with his arms
extended and his eyes cast skyward. Behind him, the dark
vestiges of the lightning strike on the temple stained the
stones. Struth noticed her attention, and her scent under-
went an alteration.

"What did the stone-faces say last night?" Struth asked.

"Stone-faces? You mean Ilhuicamina and Tezozomoc?"
Jennifer gave Struth a synopsis of what they'd been told.
Struth listened attentively, though she watched Tezo-
zomoc on the temple platform rather than Jennifer. She
nodded at Jennifer's description of the sacrifices at the
Great Temple.

"You seem distressed by that, and I don't know why,"
Struth said. "It was what their OColihi needed."

"My OColihi says that killing is wrong, Struth," Jennifer answered, almost angrily.

Struth looked puzzled. "Then you don't follow your
path very well," she answered, "since I have seen you kill
a saorod, and your males have also killed. There is nothing wrong in the stone-faces' OColihi, Jhenini. Their way
is not *evil*; it is just different. You can't judge them by
your own standards—that is the mistake you have made
with the Mutata, too."

Jennifer had no ready answer. She shook her head,
stroking Struth's spinal crest affectionately. "You'll make
a good OTsio one day, Struth," she said. "I even know
you're right. Sort of, anyway."

On the summit of the pyramid, the feathered plumes
of Tezozomoc's headdress glinted brightly as the sun's rays
touched the temple with gold. The priest rose and shouted something to the sunrise before going into the temple.
"We try to understand," Jennifer said, "but it isn't easy."

"I know," Struth told her. "It is not easy for me, either. At least you have companions."

Struth said it so sadly and with such a scent of musk that Jennifer hugged the Mutata's neck. "Poor Struth," she said. "We'll find a way to get you back. We will."

"I hope so, Jhenini," Struth answered. "I do hope so."

"Here's the way I see things," Aaron said. "If anyone has a different thought, let's hear it, but it seems pretty apparent that Peter was right. We're in a timeline very similar to our own—in fact, it might be ours or Travis's changed a little. Judging by what Ilhuicamina told us, the year is 1570 or thereabouts, and we're in Mexico."

"Which in both my world *and* yours," Travis interjected, "should be under the control of Spain at this point."

Aaron, Travis, Jennifer, Peter, and Eckels sat in the shade of their house on the plaza. A midday meal had been brought to them—more corn dishes and vegetables—and they'd been left alone. Struth, after tasting the offerings, had made a face and told Jennifer that she was going to forage for something edible in the forest. Mundo had been missing when Jennifer returned to the house with Struth; no one knew where the ape had gone. "Who cares anyway?" Aaron had said, but he knew that he, at least, did. He didn't trust Mundo, and yet Mundo was also their only communications link. Without Mundo, talking with Ilhuicamina, Tezozomoc, and the others would be difficult at best.

And you also feel responsible for him. Admit it—you feel guilty because Mundo wouldn't be here at all if it weren't for you.

"That's what worries me," Aaron said in answer to Travis's comment. "Ilhuicamina says it's been half a century since anyone *saw* a foreigner around here, yet this should be the time frame for all sorts of exploration in the New World: the Spanish, the English, the French, the Portuguese. There should have been *some* contact with Europe even if the Spanish are out of the picture . . ."

"It's the disease," Jennifer said. Having done what she could for Struth's burns earlier, she was now cleaning Peter's shoulder with water she'd boiled to make sterile. She rinsed out the washcloth and began wrapping the shoulder. "I'll bet on it. Ilhuicamina said that Cortés lost half his army to a plague before he got to the Aztec capital, an infection that didn't touch the Aztecs. In *our* world, it was the other way around. One of the residents in the hospital did a research paper on the subject. He said that something like ninety-five percent of the Native American population died in the first two centuries after Columbus arrived—for no other reason than the diseases the Europeans brought over, like smallpox and influenza. What if . . ."

Jennifer stopped and took a breath. "What if the opposite happened here? What if the first explorers took *back* a virus? No one in Europe would have an immunity to it. As crowded and dirty as most of the cities were at that time, the disease would spread quickly through the cities, with infected travelers spreading it even farther . . ."

"If most or even half of the population of Europe died, they wouldn't have the resources or the energy to send expeditions back here. Not for a long time, anyway," Aaron finished for her. "My God, I hate to say it, but that fits, Jenny. And *that* means that a Floating Stone in Europe or Asia would be unreachable."

"Why should one be there anyway?" Eckels said. "You said that the path to Nipponjin led right back to the same place you'd lived."

"That one did, yes, but the canyon in the saorod world never existed in any Illinois past, and I don't think that Struth's valley is Illinois, either. I think your little temporal explosion threw the pieces through space as well as time."

"I hate to be Mr. Doom-and-Gloom again, but everyone seems to keep forgetting that there may not *be* a Floating Stone here," Peter interjected.

"The Gairk caught an Aztec warrior," Jennifer said.

"What?"

"Yes. I'd forgotten—it seems so long ago. It was right after we'd been captured, and there was so much strangeness going on that I really didn't pay a lot of attention. But they'd killed a man who was dressed like Ilhuicamina: feathered headdress, the loincloth, a cloak with geometric patterns, a jade necklace, skin the same color. He might have come from one of the storms, but . . ." Jennifer stopped, shading her eyes against the sun as she looked out to the plaza. "Ilhuicamina's on his way over now, and Mundo's with him."

"Wonderful," Peter muttered. "He's sucking up to the person in charge again. We all remember *that* trick."

"What trick?" Mundo asked as he approached.

"You have really good hearing too," Peter said. Mundo gave him the wide-lipped leer that was the closest the ape's face could come to a smile.

"I'm glad you're impressed with my abilities. I've been talking with Ilhuicamina and Tezozomoc for us," Mundo said.

"I'll just bet," Peter said. "And you have our best interests at heart, too, don't you?"

"Always," Mundo replied smugly. "Aaron said that we all need each other. Just doing my part."

"So what did your 'part' consist of this morning?" Jennifer asked the ape.

"Tezozomoc is certain that we're the ones his gods sent to fix things. I've convinced him that to do anything, we need to find a Floating Stone—and he knows where one is. He didn't say so, but I could hear some of what he was thinking. Tezozomoc knows more than he's saying, but he *did* tell me that he's willing to help."

Mundo smiled again, showing his pointed teeth. "All it will require is a little sacrifice on our part."

15

Giving Blood

Standing on the platform at the top of the pyramid, they could look out over the village to see the forest reclaim its hold on mountains just beyond the terraced fields. A mountain stream tumbled its white water down into the valley under the shade of the conifers, and they could follow the wandering curve of the trail they'd followed into the village as it snaked over the far ridge to disappear in the east.

But the panorama held far less interest than the area in front of the temple itself. No amount of scrubbing of the flags near the flat-topped, narrow stone at the top of the long stairs could hide the bloodstains lurking in the pores of the limestone, and the brown-red hue of the eagle-shaped receptacle near the stone gave an ominous hint of the block's purpose. Jennifer shuddered, just looking at it.

Tezozomoc came from the shadowed interior of the temple as, panting from the effort, they reached the top of the long stairs. The priest wore a simple white tunic, the left sleeve of which was saturated with blood dripping from the cloth. Jennifer gave a gasp and started to move toward the man, but Tezozomoc held up his hand. The sleeve fell back, revealing a long, deep cut. He held a small ceramic bowl under his elbow, catching the red droplets that fell from the wound.

Tezozomoc began to chant, a low droning that continued as he placed the bowl on the sacrificial altar. He ignored the presence of the others, his gaze outward but unseeing. Blood continued to flow freely from the unbound cut.

"He's in shock," Jennifer whispered. She'd seen a hundred patients coming into the emergency room with the same glazed stare, bleeding freely because of car wrecks or fights or falls, and not yet feeling the pain from their injuries because the body's natural defense was to remove them from the reality of the situation. A tiny splinter in the finger might send a kid into a howling fit, but the same child could come in with a broken arm, the shattered bone poking through the skin, and sit there silently sniffing. "Look at his eyes," Jennifer told them. "He might even be hallucinating from blood loss. I have to do something." Jennifer started forward, but Travis held her back, his hand on her shoulder.

"No," he said. "You can't. This is his world and his customs. Let him do what he needs to do."

"That's not just a scratch, Travis. He's really laid himself open. He could die if he doesn't take care of it." Jennifer looked to Aaron for support.

"We all could die, at any time," Aaron said. "I'm sorry, Jen, but Travis is right. It's his choice. His religion."

Tezozomoc paid no attention to their debate. He continued chanting, pouring the thick liquid from the ceramic bowl into the stone eagle. Ilhuicamina took the bowl from Tezozomoc when he was done, and disappeared into the temple. Tezozomoc continued to chant. Jennifer could tell that some of them, Eckels especially, were getting restless. "This is creepy," the man said. "Let's get the h—"

He didn't finish the statement. With a hoarse, guttural cry, Tezozomoc suddenly brought his hands down and tipped the eagle bowl over the stone, its gory contents splashing over the gray rock. Tezozomoc bent down, staring at the patterns intently. He seemed to listen to unheard voices, cocking his head slightly. Finally, he straightened. Ilhuicamina came from the temple with another bowl filled with a greenish pulp and several strips of white cloth. He offered the bowl to Tezozomoc, who slathered the ugly poultice on the cut and then began to bind his own arm with the cloths.

"Here, let me," Jennifer said. "Mundo, ask him if I can help."

Mundo spoke quickly to Tezozomoc, who simply grunted, glared at Jennifer for a moment, and then continued to wrap the wound. "I'd say that means no," Mundo said. "And no brownie points for asking, either."

"Thanks, I'd figured that out."

Tezozomoc finished binding his arm, pulling the final knot tight with his teeth. He stood swaying slightly, but Ilhuicamina didn't move to steady the priest. Tezozomoc took a deep breath and brought his chin up as he looked at the group before him. At Aaron.

"I need your blood," he said. "To know what you must do, you must give it."

"What?" Aaron asked him. "A scratch, a few drops? You want me to slice my arm open like you just did?"

"Yes," Tezozomoc replied calmly. "As I did."

When Aaron didn't immediately reply, Jennifer spoke hurriedly, pulling Aaron around so he looked at her.

"Listen to me," she said urgently. "No. You *can't* do that. First, it's not needed—there's no reason for it. It may be their rite, but it's not ours. Second, it's dangerous. It'd be bad enough at home, where we could go to a doctor and sew it up. Here, it's just stupid. If you don't bleed to death in the first place, you're going to be scarred for life at best. If you get an infection in the cut, and given the sanitary conditions around here, I'd say that's a probability, you're going to die. We don't have antibiotics, we don't even have aspirin. Aaron . . ."

Jennifer stopped, taking a long breath as she gazed at him. "Please. I just found you again. I don't want to lose you."

Aaron smiled at her and hugged her. "I hear you," he whispered into her ear as they embraced. "I don't want to lose you either." Letting her go, he turned back to Tezozomoc. "No," he said. "I'm sorry."

Tezozomoc looked as if that was the answer he'd expected. "You will," he told them. "If not now, then later."

"I doubt it."

"Sometimes the gods give you no choice." Tezozomoc almost, *almost* smiled. "You have the warrior's look, and the warrior's burden. All of you. I have seen it. You will each be called upon to make your own sacrifices before you can mend what has been broken."

"What do you mean—you've *seen* it?"

Tezozomoc only shook his head. "You will not give me the *chalchiuh-atl*, the blood, I need. That is your choice—for the moment. As to what I have seen . . ." He paused, looking out over the landscape, his eyes narrowed against the sun.

"I have seen my death," he said. "I know what Huehueteotl, God of Fire and God of Time, has ordained for me. I will take you to Tenochtitlán, and there you will give whatever is asked of you. You will do it because there, and only there, will you learn of your Floating Stone."

"It still sounded like a threat to me," Peter said.

They were a day into their journey to Tenochtitlán. Tezozomoc led the way, along with a dozen young warriors from the village. The presence of the men didn't make any of them feel comfortable, but there had been very little dissension among the group regarding the trip. It seemed obvious that if they wanted to find their way back to their various homes, then they had little choice. Still, Aaron wished they weren't quite so outnumbered and defenseless. It didn't escape any of them how Tezozomoc positioned the travelers in the middle of the group, with warriors both ahead and behind.

They walked along an ill-defined trail that led ever higher among the mountains. The last vestiges of the tropical foliage still remained, but they were scarcer now as they walked through evergreen glades. Most of them wore serapes given to them by the villagers. The air cooled and became thinner as they went higher. Steep vistas of rock clothed in emerald green seemed to greet them at every turn of the trail. This was a gorgeous land, if a harsh one. One of the gifts that had been given to them by Ilhuicamina on leaving had been paper made of some fig bark, a brush, and ink. Aaron—who had always enjoyed drawing and painting—had gladly taken the chance to sketch some of the scenery around them.

"Threat or not," Aaron said, "I'll admit that they've treated us well enough so far."

"So far," repeated Peter. "Looks like the only one *really* enjoying the trek is Mundo." He nodded toward the front of the file strung along the trail, where Mundo walked alongside Tezozomoc, talking animatedly with the priest. "I wish I knew what he was saying."

"You and me both. Maybe I should find out. Keep an eye on Travis, would you? He's not going to say anything, but he's really hurting."

Aaron moved forward until he trudged alongside the priest. Mundo gave him a sharp-toothed smile that didn't seem to quite make it to the rest of his face. "Hey, boss," the ape said. "Nice day for a walk, ain't it?"

"Lovely. I'd like to talk to Tezozomoc."

"No problem. I live to translate." Mundo's voice sounded cheery, but again there was nothing in his expression to match the jocular tone.

"Great. By the way, what have you two been chatting about all this time?"

"Oh, the weather, the sights, how the kids are doing, sports. You know, the usual stuff."

"Mundo—"

Mundo raised his hands in mock innocence. "Honest, Aaron. Just small talk. He's asked about us, but I haven't told him a thing. He's real curious about the temporal machinery we're carrying though—the 'fiery greenstones,' he calls them. He's *real* interested in them."

Aaron glanced at Tezozomoc, who was watching them with a stern face. "Enough to, say, kill us for them?"

Mundo shrugged, then looked almost comically conspiratorial. "I don't think so. Well, maybe . . . He . . . he was talking real strange there for awhile, but I think I calmed him down. A good thing, I guess, when he's got all those warriors along, right? I'm looking out for us. Don't worry about a thing."

"Uh-huh." Aaron had deliberately been thinking about the men along with them, to see if Mundo was doing his mind-skimming trick, and it seemed he was. Aaron set himself to humming a song by U2—*let's see what Mundo makes of that*—and looked ahead. The trail curved upward around an outsloping rim of rock. New mountains peered around the shoulders of those surrounding them, well out into the blue distance. To the southeast, a plume of smoke drifted away from the peak of a smoldering volcano, and an eagle—its wings outstretched like feathery hands—circled slowly in the north ahead of them. Otherwise, the land was empty, untouched, and lonely. "Mundo, how about asking Tezozomoc about this Huehueteotl character."

Mundo spoke briefly to Tezozomoc, who continued walking for several paces, his sandaled feet raising dust along the trail. "What more is there to tell you?" Tezozomoc asked at last. "You have seen the storms; you have ridden them yourselves. I have seen visions from our own past, and I have seen that which must be the future. This tells me that Huehueteotl, the eldest of the gods, he who controls time itself, stirs in his caves far below the Great Temple. That is why we must go there."

"Is there a Floating Stone at the Great Temple?"

Again, Tezozomoc didn't answer for a long time. "Tell me first why you carry the carved greenstones that have fire captured inside, Aaron," Tezozomoc said. "Tell me why this Floating Stone is so important to you."

Mundo looked at Aaron after he'd finished translating and commented. "I don't think I'd tell him that," the ape said. "He seems a little fanatical on the subject."

"He knows where there's a piece of the pathway," Aaron said to Mundo. "I'm sure of it. Otherwise he wouldn't be evading like this. Tell Tezozomoc that the greenstones are part of the magic of the Floating Stones. Tell him that the Floating Stones are causing the vision-storms and that we've come to end them."

"Isn't that a little dangerous, bluffing like that?" Mundo protested. "Especially after you've already denied that you're sent from his gods. I think—"

"Don't think. Just tell him what I said," Aaron interrupted, and then regretted his irritation. "Listen, Mundo. I'm sorry, I know what you're thinking—"

"I don't *think*," Mundo answered curtly. "I just *translate*."

With that, Mundo turned to Tezozomoc and spoke in rapid-fire Aztec. *That was real smart*, Aaron berated himself as Mundo spoke. *You just insulted the only person who can communicate with these people. Good move, Cofield. . . .*

Tezozomoc answered, but Mundo didn't translate. Instead, he replied, a brief back-and-forth exchange. At last Tezozomoc grunted something and looked away, continuing his stolid pace upward along the trail. "What was all that about, Mundo?"

Mundo sniffed. "Tezozomoc said that you have to trust him."

"Mundo, that doesn't even come close to answering what I told him."

Mundo wrinkled his nose and bared his teeth. "That's what he said," the ape snarled. "And you have to trust *me*, too, don't you?"

The setting sun painted the valleys with long purple shadows even though they were still in sunlight themselves. They had come to a high meadow where deer grazed and birds flitted from the widely spaced piñon pines to their nests in rocky crevices. A small stone structure was there, the roof flat and thatched—a traveler's way station, Mundo told them. Tezozomoc called to his companions, and they swung their packs from their shoulders and placed them in the one-room building. Someone started a fire, another began mixing corn flour with water from a nearby spring to make small cakes. Jennifer went to where the meadow grass bearded the edge of a precipice and looked out over the landscape.

She could see for miles. The air was crystalline and sharp; well across the valley, each branch of the fir-covered slopes seemed visible. A chill seemed to be coming from the shadowed land below, and Jennifer was glad for the serape she wore. She heard footsteps behind her. "Pretty, isn't it?" Aaron said. His hands went around her waist and she leaned back against him, her hands over his.

"Mmm-hmm," she murmured. "We're staying here tonight?"

"That's what it looks like."

"Good. I think Travis has been going on pure will-power for the last hour or so. I'm really worried about him. And poor Struth—she may be entirely coldblooded, but she doesn't like the chill up here at all."

"You're always worried about everyone else."

"Keeps me from worrying about *me*."

"I guess."

His voice sounded so sad to her that she turned to him, hugging him fiercely. "We'll get out of this," she told him. "I know it looks bad now, but we'll find a way."

"You promise, right?" he answered, mockingly, and Jennifer took his head between her hands.

"Yes, I do," she told him. "I know it. Somewhere, somehow, we'll figure this mess out."

"I hope so, Jen. I do. But right now . . ."

"Right now, we do what we can. And right now, I think the best thing to do is sit here and watch the sun set. At least that's one thing constant in all of this, as much as everything else has changed. No matter how history has been twisted and distorted, that one simple thing goes on."

"Jen—"

"Shhh." She put a finger to his lips. "Watch with me . . ."

Leaning against him, feeling his comforting warmth on her back, they watched the slow interplay of shadow and sun as darkness climbed the ridges and hills and the fire-touched flanks of the clouds faded to sullen red and then extinguished themselves in the blue night.

The soft rumble of thunder reverberated among the stones, like the sound of a temple falling to rubble in the distance. Tezozomoc stood where the young couple had watched the day end. The dark-haired one had tried to stay awake after they had eaten, obviously distrustful of all the Mexica, but he had finally fallen asleep. Tezozomoc had not eaten himself, following the *nezahualiztli*, the fasting. His stomach rumbled, thinking of it. The old warrior, the one called Travis, had watched after the boy's eyes had closed, but even he had eventually fallen to exhaustion. It had been tempting, watching them all sleeping and unaware. His warriors had looked to him, but Tezozomoc had only shaken his head.

He had slept, too, until the faint sound of the god-storm called him. He had walked from the wayhouse to see that a quick storm had covered the western mountains, though the dome of the sky was dusted with stars above them. Now he watched the bright tongues of lightning lick the floor of the valley below, and he could see in those distant flashes the visions of the gods appearing for a few instants, to be annihilated in the next flash. He could plainly see strange buildings and odd vistas flicker into brief life as the storm moved rapidly across the valley. Tezozomoc wished he were closer, so that he could see the strange beings that sometimes lived within the storms, so that he might be able to interpret the signs the gods sent.

The talking monkey creature was awake as well. Tezozomoc saw the white fur from the corner of his eye. "Ahh, a time storm," Mundo said.

"Every day they come," Tezozomoc said. "They become larger each time, and they leave their spoor behind. The gods are angry, and they are threatening to destroy this land."

"Yes, you're right, of course, Tezozomoc," Mundo said. The creature had a voice of oil and mint. "As always. Unless . . ."

"Unless?"

"Unless you do as I have asked, great Tezozomoc. Mundo knows the secrets of the fiery greenstones, too, and he will give you their magic so that you may have what you've lost. It will be yours. All yours—for just a small price."

Tezozomoc watched as the storm passed beyond a ridge and was lost from view. He could see the stuttering strobe of the lightning continuing.

"I hear you, Mundo," he said. He turned. Mundo's wizened, dark face looked up at him from within its ruffle of snowy fur. "I hear you."

16

Into the City

Aaron awoke the next morning with a start, his heart hammering. For a moment he thought that he'd simply fallen asleep for a moment and was ready to continue his vigil, but then realized that bright sunlight was streaming through the blankets that served as a door for the way-house, and that everyone was up and moving about. Tezozomoc himself was still sleeping, bundled in the corner. Aaron rubbed his eyes and yawned.

"We were *all* asleep," Travis said. Aaron looked to where the man was sitting up under a rough cotton blanket. Travis shrugged. "I was worried about that, too," he said. "But nothing happened."

"I still don't trust them."

"Good. Neither do I. Let's keep an eye out, but I have to admit that they had a chance to do anything they wanted last night, and they didn't."

"Maybe the signs weren't right. The stars weren't in the right place."

Travis grinned, his heavily stubbled cheeks creasing. "And here I thought you were the optimist of the group, Aaron." He threw the covers aside and, groaning, got to his feet. The man moved slowly, hunched over—much the way Grandpa Carl used to move in the morning. The memory brought back the sound of Carl's voice. "*Gotta warm these old joints up first, boy. All the oil's gone out of 'em. . . .*"

Aaron blinked. The pain of his grandfather's death was as keen as ever, a rip in his soul strangely sharper even than the loss of his parents. Aaron still couldn't believe that his parents were really gone, but then he hadn't seen them as he'd seen Grandpa Carl's body. The remembrance of the twisted, mutated Green Town he'd left seemingly only a few weeks before made him angry and determined again to fix things.

Somehow.

"I can smell breakfast, though," Travis said, stretching tentatively. "And I am definitely hungry. Let's get some food, kid. I have the feeling we have a long walk ahead of us."

Travis was more right about that than Aaron liked. The party moved steadily north and east through the mountains until they came to a high plateau of rolling, forested hills studded with the crowns of slumbering volcanoes. Most nights they stopped in other Aztec villages, where they were greeted with reserved curiosity. The people seemed awed by both Struth and Mundo. They crowded around them, Struth enduring their attentions patiently while Mundo took every opportunity to show off for them, regaling them with long tales. Aaron suspected those stories featured Mundo as the hero—though Mundo always hedged when asked to translate.

The rest of them were treated with courtesy but also a certain guarded aloofness. Aaron was never quite certain if that was because he and Jennifer and the others reminded the Aztecs of the hated Cortés, or because they were so obviously under the guardianship of Tezozomoc. Aaron noticed that Tezozomoc was accorded a wary respect. The village priests greeted him with the attitude of someone welcoming a visitor on a higher social level, and the warriors who had come with Tezozomoc always kept their weapons within easy reach.

"Looks like they don't quite trust each other, either," Travis commented to Aaron.

"Then let's hope Tezozomoc's on the right side," Aaron said. "And that Mundo's saying all the right things."

Travis glanced at Mundo, as always stationed alongside Tezozomoc. "I'm sure he's saying all the right things to put *himself* in the best position," Travis answered. "Whether it'll do *us* any good or not, well . . ." He left the statement unfinished.

They continued on each morning, halting only when the sun disappeared behind the flanks of the western peaks. The thin air made Aaron call to Tezozomoc for frequent halts so that they could rest and recover their strength. Jennifer and Travis, with the help of one of Tezozomoc's warriors, spent the time learning what they could of the language; Aaron tried to do the same, but became frustrated with his slowness, especially in comparison to Jennifer's quick facility with the language. Struth—wearing a doubled serape over her for warmth—was never far from Jennifer's side. The dinosaur seemed morose and oddly quiet. Aaron wondered whether it was the cold, the loneliness, or both. Peter and Eckels seemed to have drifted back into their uneasy companionship.

Peter thinks that, like Eckels, he's an outcast in the group.

Aaron tried to spend time with Peter, to act as mediator between Travis and Eckels, to try anything to knit their little band together. Nothing seemed to have much effect.

Finally, twelve days after the expedition had left the village, they came over the ridge of a hill to see a series of interconnected lakes spread out in the valley below. "Look at *that*!" Jennifer cried alongside Aaron.

"Tenochtitlán," Tezozomoc said softly.

"It's a floating city!"

Tenochtitlán certainly appeared to be that. The city blanketed an island in the nearest lake, and was connected to the mainland with a series of stone bridges. Canals laced the city, each of them running alongside a broad thoroughfare. The streets, the walls of the buildings, the palaces and temples—they were all an aching white, as if they were freshly scrubbed, polished, and painted. Tenochtitlán gleamed like a jewel, a pearl melted from the sun and set down to float on blue waters.

Odd little floating islands rimmed the main island, with mud and wattle huts built on them. They could see workers tending gardens on these islands, and a multitude of canoes and rafts moved slowly through the majestic waters. The city itself was a bustle of activity, with people moving through the streets and Crowded around the markets. Tenochtitlán was a metropolis, with thousands upon thousands of people living within its boundaries.

But even here, Aaron noted, the time storms had left their mark. Off to one side, in its own cylindrical space that sliced open the Aztec buildings in unrelenting curves, stood a tall cone of white, lumpy material, with openings inset at odd angles. Aaron remembered seeing something very like it before.

As did Struth, who suddenly hooted mournfully. Aaron remembered then—this was a Mutata dwelling, snatched from its own world and plunked down here. It looked very much out of place in the midst of the geometric Aztec architecture, like a child's misshapen sand castle in the middle of Manhattan skyscrapers.

In the utter center of the city very near the Mutata building, a huge pyramid had been erected. The four main roads of Tenochtitlán, entering from the cardinal points of the compass, arrowed in to that immense structure. Great stairs ascended the west face of the pyramid, and at the summit were set two temples. Tezozomoc pointed to it and spoke. "That is the Great Temple," he said as Mundo translated. "And that is where we will go."

"Why there?" Aaron asked. "Does someone there know about the Floating Stones?"

"Be patient," Tezozomoc told him, and he looked at Aaron oddly. "You, most of all, must be patient."

Tezozomoc turned away and started down the hill toward the beckoning city. "What the heck did that mean?" Aaron asked.

Peter shrugged. "I have the feeling we'll find out," he answered.

As they approached the main causeway into Tenochtitlán, they began to attract the attention of the inhabitants. By the time they reached the stone-flagged roadway, there was a reception committee awaiting them. The head of the group was a tall warrior, wearing what Mundo told them was the *cuexte-catl*, or higher-caste armor. A high, ornate backplate towered over the man's head, which sported a conical pointed hat, rosette, and cotton flaps over the ears. A brightly colored, padded tunic covered his wide, muscular torso, and a shield with the same geometric designs was on his arm. He also wore leggings dyed in the same colors.

He stood grim-faced in the center of the bridge approach before a quartet of similarly attired warriors, his spear at his side. His dark-eyed gaze flitted from Tezozomoc to the humans, and then peered more closely at Mundo and—especially—Struth. Aaron grabbed Mundo by the arm and whispered to him: "You stay with us. Translate. I want to know what's going on."

Tezozomoc and the warrior were already in the middle of what seemed to be a heated conversation. "Mr. Pectorals there—his name's Acayacatl, by the way—doesn't seem to want to let us in," Mundo told them. "The big lizard seems to be what's especially bothering him. He's telling Tezozomoc that we're going to have to camp outside until someone higher up gives permission. Tezozomoc is arguing that he doesn't need permission, and that if Acayacatl wants to interfere with the business of a priest of Tlaloc, then the consequences are on his head."

It didn't appear that Acayacatl was too worried about his head. He stalked up to Tezozomoc, glared at him silently for a moment, then pushed past the priest to stand before Struth. Jennifer moved quickly to interpose herself between Struth and Acayacatl. "Jen . . ." Aaron began warningly, but Acayacatl stared down the end of his nose at Jennifer and barked out a command, gesturing her aside with his spear. The order was clear enough, and from the ice in Jennifer's stare, she understood perfectly.

"I'm not moving," Jennifer said back to the man in his own language, and if Aaron didn't understand her words, her body language told him what she'd just answered.

"Jennifer," he said again, but then Acayacatl, with a grunt, shoved Jennifer aside with his shield. She went tumbling to the ground with a cry. The next few seconds were chaotic. Aaron was never quite sure exactly what happened. Tezozomoc was bellowing something, and Aaron was just about to hurl himself at Acayacatl even though a small, sane voice inside him was telling him how stupid that was. Acayacatl himself, paying no attention at all to Jennifer or the rest of them, prodded Struth with his spear. Struth batted it aside, honking in irritation, and Acayacatl brought the spear back as if to thrust it into Struth's chest. Struth honked again, her spinal frill rising under the crude serape, fully engorged and brightly colored. She rose up, angry, and Acayacatl took a step back.

But only a step. He suddenly yelled and lunged for Struth, spear foremost.

He never made it. Struth, with an acrobatic grace that utterly surprised Aaron, spun at the same time. Her tail, a heavy blur with the added momentum of her pirouette, slammed into the onrushing Acayacatl, lifting the man entirely off his feet. Acayacatl, with a screech, went flying off the bridge and into the lake, his spear shattered and his shield broken, his hat and backpiece pinwheeling away in opposite directions. Water and mud cascaded as he landed on his back in the shallows.

As everyone watched, stunned into inaction, Struth took two huge steps toward the shore, leaned down toward where Acayacatl was thrashing frantically, and—her nostrils flaring—gave him a loud, fluttering raspberry from her nasal horn. The Mutata helped Jennifer to her feet and—with an almost comically offended dignity—strode across the causeway toward Tenochtitlán, pushing through the other astounded guards.

Tezozomoc glanced from Struth to Acayacatl, who had finally regained his feet, adorned with mud and festooned with strands of algae. A wide, slow grin moved across the weathered face of the priest, erupting finally into a long, unfettered laugh as Acayacatl stamped and fumed in the mud.

Still laughing, Tezozomoc gestured to his warriors, to Aaron, Jennifer, and the rest. Accompanied by the sound of his amusement, they entered the city.

17

The Sacrifice

They were given an apartment in a lavish palace on the grounds surrounding the Great Temple. The pretense, at least, was that they were honored guests, free to come and go as they pleased, but all of them noted that guards were placed prominently near the front and back entrances to their room, and that whenever any of them went outside, someone followed at a judicious distance.

Not that they were given much time to explore— Struth especially had wanted to explore the Mutata building. But they had entered Tenochtitlán during the late afternoon, and by the time Tezozomoc had escorted them to the Great Temple and made his obeisance to the head priest there—a man named Techtopec, they were told—it was nearly evening. Food was brought to them by an attentive cadre of what were either servants or slaves, as was clothing and water to cleanse themselves. By the time they were rested, fed, and dressed, the sun had gone down and the servants had lit the oil lamps that hung from the beams and started a delightful, roaring fire in the open fireplace in the center of the room.

It was full dark when Tezozomoc came to get them, the stars gleaming hard and bright in the cold, high sky.

"Follow me," he said.

"Where are we going?" Aaron asked.

"Follow me," Tezozomoc repeated. "This is not the time to ask questions. But you, especially, Aaron, need to see. Come."

They started to gather up their packs which held the pieces of temporal machinery they'd collected from the saorods, but Tezozomoc shook his head. "The bright greenstones should stay here," he said.

Aaron looked at the man. "They are . . . *sacred* to us," he told him. "We can't afford to lose them."

"They will be safe here," Tezozomoc told him. "No one will touch them. That is my promise."

Aaron studied the impassive, dark face of the priest. He wanted to trust the man. *If he wanted the greenstones, he had lots of opportunity to take them on the way here*, he reminded himself. "All right," he said. "On your promise."

Putting on the woven slippers they'd been given, they followed. Tezozomoc led them out into the courtyard of the palace, where birds flitted through the hanging gardens, and out the massive wooden gate of the edifice.

There, the plaza before the steps of the pyramid was packed with people and ablaze with the light of thousands of torches. The onlookers were singing, an insistent and rhythmic chant accompanied by drums and flutes. Tezozomoc strode into their midst and the crowd parted around them, all the while continuing to sing as they closed in again around the strange procession of Aaron, Peter, and Jennifer, Travis and Eckels, Struth and Mundo. Half-propelled by the chanting throngs, they moved toward the base of the pyramid, where a double line of white-robed acolytes held torches, forming an aisle of fire leading to the summit.

Far above, on the platform where the twin temples stood, a huge bonfire blazed between the two main buildings, crackling and tossing a fountain of wild, twirling sparks into the night sky. Braziers burned at the corners where the platform met the sharply sloping sides of the structure.

As they approached the steps, they could see—on both sides—a low balcony just before the steps, where the carved and painted figures of serpents writhed. There were smaller temples to the north and south of the westward-facing pyramid: the one to the north decorated with a multitude of carved eagles, the smaller one to the south painted bright red. Tezozomoc led them forward until they stopped at the bottom of the stairs, and the crowd closed in around them, their coppery skin ablaze with sweat and the ruddy light of the torches.

There they stood, as the thousands moved around them, as the celebration swirled everywhere they looked.

The drums hammered out their insistent beat, louder and faster, and the singing became more raucous and wilder in response. Aaron could feel his heart falling into the cadence, captive, pounding unbidden against the ribbed bars of his chest. By the look on the faces of Jennifer and the others, the same spell had fallen on them. The chant, the song, was intoxicating and magical, and each of them found that he had been snared by its power. None of them was immune: not Aaron, not Jennifer, not Peter, not Travis or Eckels or the two nonhumans among them.

Aaron thought that he dreamed. The images around him had a surreal quality, and everything seemed blurred, as if his eyes could not focus.

He grinned, unbidden.

They all found themselves breathing in time to the song, swaying with the crowd and sometimes humming under their breath as if they wanted to join in with the rising and falling melody. The chanting rhythms seemed to have the greatest effect on Mundo and Struth. Mundo began to dance in time, his long, white arms waving as he capered, and those around them laughed and clapped in response, giving the ape room for his gyrations. One of the women took Mundo's hand and danced with him, her other hand lifting the hem of her long skirt as they cavorted.

Struth was humming as she watched Mundo, a low drone like a muttering tuba. Her head was cocked, as if listening intently to some interior call, and she suddenly vented a long, loud trumpet blast that rang echoing around the square. The beat faltered for a moment, then cheers arose from around them. The drummers looked down, grinned, and bent their heads as they flailed and punished the stretched skin of their drumheads.

Then, in an instant, it all stopped. The enchantment was broken. Aaron shook his head, trying to clear away the fogginess.

The people in the square went silent; the drummers panted, their chests heaving, the flautists licked dry lips. Up on the platform, a single drum tolled, a slow beat: *toom, toom, toom*. With each strike of the mallet against the drumhead, Aaron's heart jumped.

Tezozomoc motioned to them again. To the beat of the drum, he began striding up the wide steps of the pyramid, moving along the lane of torches. Aaron looked at Jennifer, all the gaiety gone out of him. He felt empty, suddenly. Drained—as if the chant had pulled all the energy from him. Tezozomoc glanced back once, his gaze commanding: *follow*, it said wordlessly.

"What else can we do?" Jennifer asked.

Reluctantly, Aaron started up the steep stairs, the others following.

Tezozomoc gestured as they came to a platform just below the summit. There, the sculpture of a jaguar crouched. Aaron's group clustered around the statue. Tezozomoc nodded and continued walking toward the platform at the utter top of the pyramid. There, he stopped, facing toward the open doors of the temples. The lone drummer continued the monotonous, slow tolling.

A man stepped out from the temple door, and the crowd immediately erupted into acclamation: *"Cuauhtemoc Acamapichtli!"* they shouted. "Cuauhtemoc . . . That's the man Ilhuicamina said was the emperor here," Jennifer said. Cuauhtemoc was tall and muscular, and around his neck was a wide necklace of carved jade: faces and snarling beast's, with a central pendant of a man. The emperor was adorned with a quetzal-feather cloak, the fabric checked with small blue squares at the center of which was a white dot.

Alongside him was another man, evidently a trusted personal guard or retainer, and seeing him caused Aaron to shiver: it was Acayacatl, the warrior whom Struth had so unceremoniously dumped into the lake that afternoon. The warrior kept his gaze stoically outward, but Aaron saw that Acayacatl glanced down once at them, and there was no kindness in his eyes at all.

After Cuauhtemoc had stationed himself near the northern edge of the platform, a priest stepped out solemnly from the northern temple structures. He was dressed all in gleaming white that caught the glow of the torches, and he had on his head an ornate, plumed hat. "That has to be Techtopec, the high priest," Aaron ventured.

Flanking Techtopec were two processional lines of other priests or acolytes. A man—bare-chested and wearing only a white loincloth—walked directly behind the priest, between the two lines. Techtopec and Tezozomoc moved to the south end of the platform, facing the emperor Cuauhtemoc Acamapichtli; for the first time, Aaron saw what was behind the man and between the line of priests.

A Floating Stone.

Aaron heard the collective intake of breath from those around him.

The piece was jagged like all the others they'd seen, perhaps a little larger, its pristine surface marred by the smoke and soot of the temporal explosion that had sent it careening into this world. The acolytes pushed the shattered roadway forward until it hovered at the edge of the platform alongside an eagle-shaped pedestal, easily visible to the crowds below. They could hear the shouts of affirmation from the thousands of throats, like a tidal roar.

From their vantage point slightly below the stone, they could clearly see the charred underside. There was nothing there, no gleaming fragments of temporal machinery. "They've disabled it," Travis whispered to the others. "They've figured it out."

They soon found out how right that was. Two of the acolytes came forward with a large jade box. They bowed before Tezozomoc and Techtopec, who lifted the lid of the box and brought out a necklace. He placed the string of cowry shells and greenstones around his neck, gestured the acolytes away, and spread his hands to the crowd below.

Against his white tunic now gleamed a green, twisted piece of metal, radiant with its own light. The undersea glow, brighter even than the firelight, illuminated the priest's face from below. "I wonder where that one goes?" Peter commented. "Back to Lizard World?"

"I don't think so," Jennifer answered. "We'd have seen lots of the Aztecs then. The Gairk claimed that the one they killed came from a time storm."

While the drum continued its steady, unchanging beat, Techtopec signaled to his acolytes. Two of them stepped forward and grasped the bare-chested man by the arms. They escorted him forward, and laid the man, faceup, on the Floating Stone. Several more acolytes moved into position, so that the man was firmly held by two acolytes at each of his limbs, though the man had not struggled at all.

"I don't like this," Jennifer said uneasily, and Aaron took her hand, squeezing gently.

It comforted him as much as it did Jennifer.

Tezozomoc had taken a flask and poured the liquid contents into a receptacle on the eagle pedestal. Someone had brought a lamp out from the southern temple. Tezozomoc took it and touched the guttering wick to the pedestal, which burst immediately into flame. Now Tezozomoc gave the flask of oil to Techtopec, who poured it over the chest of the man on the Floating Stone. As Jennifer's fingers tightened around Aaron's hand, the priest took the temple lamp from the acolyte and—as Tezozomoc had done with the eagle vessel—touched the wick to the oil.

Flames rushed over the man's body, dripping down the sides of the Floating Stone. The acolytes bore down on

the man's arms and legs, but though he thrashed involuntarily, he never cried out. He stared up at the priest,
and there was—almost—a smile on his face.

From within his robe, Techtopec brought out a knife
with a dull flint blade. He held it over the Floating Stone
and the victim held there. The drumming stopped. There
was silence.

"Let the blood purify the flame!" the priest cried, and
plunged his knife into the man's chest.

It wasn't like the movies, wasn't like television. Aaron,
Jennifer, and Peter had seen scenes of human sacrifice
before in adventure films and historical dramas. Such
things, or at least the threat of them, were a staple, a
cliché and they'd always been antiseptic and safe. The
director would focus on the victim's drawn, frantic face,
then on the poised knife. The knife would suddenly slash
down out of the picture and there would be the sound of
the deathblow, or the camera would pull back to a distant
shot. If the hero hadn't managed to intervene at the last
moment to save the victim (nearly always a woman if the
hero was successful), they might have seen the knife
withdrawn, covered with stage blood, but it was somehow
clean, somehow distant, and fast.

This . . . well, this was none of those. Like the reality
of being shot, Aaron realized, this was altogether different
than something on the screen.

This was true.

The very sound the blade met as it struck the man was
horrible. The victim grunted and arched his back as the
acolytes bore down on his limbs. Tendons stood out on
the man's neck as he struggled, determined to be silent in
his agony. Techtopec dug in deeper with the blade, the
point sliding between ribs, and blood fountained and

pulsed as arteries were severed. Almost black in the fire-light, the liquid splattered wildly over the priest's hand, face, and tunic, over the acolytes, over Tezozomoc, spilling over the Floating Stone and to the flags below. The amount of blood seemed impossible, and Techtopec was still slashing, enlarging the wound he'd made. The victim groaned once and fell back; at the same time, the priest bore down hard on the knife and they heard the sickening *crack* of ribs breaking.

Techtopec let the knife drop and plunged his hand into the chest.

He brought forth the still-pulsing heart, lifting the gory trophy high in display: as the crowd below sighed, as the acolytes stared in wonder, as Eckels was loudly and suddenly sick behind Aaron. Jennifer had averted her face, but Aaron found that though he wanted desperately to do the same, he could not. The sight horrified and sickened him, but the sheer terror of it also held him.

As Techtopec held up the heart, his arm coated to the elbow in thick red, the acolytes took the body and heaved it up and off the Floating Stone, tossing it contemptuously away toward the stairs. Like a broken, discarded rag doll, it flopped and rolled heavily down the stones, passing within a few feet of Aaron. Jennifer gasped beside him, and Travis cursed wordlessly. They watched the victim's remains tumble bloodily all the way to the distant plaza, leaving the stairs stained with its passage.

Techtopec took a step away from the Floating Stone and deposited the heart in the flaming receptacle of the eagle's pillar. The flames hissed and sputtered around the offering, and the smell drifting down from the platform made Aaron's stomach turn over. His vision was blurring again, edged with fog as if trying to put the blur of a dream between himself and the world. He wanted to be sick himself, and suddenly his stomach lurched. One hand on the statue of the jaguar, he retched helplessly, feeling Jennifer's comforting hand on his back. When he could look up again, the Emperor Cuauhtemoc and Tezozomoc had both moved to the eagle vessel. Cuauhtemoc plunged his hand into the flaming depths of the vessel, bringing out a small heap of glowing ashes.

Although Aaron knew that the ash must be searing Cuauhtemoc's flesh, the emperor made a slow and dignified salute to the crowds with this fire before placing it carefully in a bowl held by Tezozomoc. The priest blew carefully on the glowing embers Cuauhtemoc had given him, then nodded to an acolyte. The flames in the four braziers set in the corners of the platform were extinguished. Tezozomoc, walking slowly, went to each of them in turn and rekindled the flame with the embers in his bowl. When he had finished, he placed the bowl on the Floating Stone.

"The fire is purified!" Cuauhtemoc proclaimed in a loud voice. "Let the new fire be taken throughout Tenochtitlán!" As the crowds cheered, runners went to each of the braziers and lit torches, which were borne quickly down the stairs. People pushed forward as the torches reached the ground, rolling their own torches on the ground to snuff out the flames, and then touching them to the runners' torches to relight them. The runners, torches held high, fanned out in four directions from the pyramid plaza to the cheers of the multitudes.

As Aaron and the others watched, the new fire began to move slowly out into the city. The drums and flutes began their song once more, and the chanting rose loud.

It seemed far less enthralling now.

As Tezozomoc descended the stairs toward them, as they followed him—numbed, shocked—down to the ground again, as he led them silently back to their rooms, Aaron kept seeing death, kept smelling it and hearing it and tasting it.

It would, he suspected, stay with him forever.

18

A Love Lost

As soon as the morning sun flooded the windows of the cold room they'd slept in, SStragh insisted to Jhenini that she must go see the Mutata dwelling they'd glimpsed not far from here. Jhenini had protested—like the rest of the humans, the sights of the night before had shaken and disturbed her.

Not so SStragh.

Mutata and Gairk both practiced ritual warfare. Both Mutata and Gairk also believed that at times the All-Ancestor would request an end to someone's physical existence so that the spirit might return to the spiritual world. SStragh understood what had happened last night. She'd seen that the victim had been willing and submissive. The human had known that his death would exalt him in the eyes of his gods and he'd given his life willingly. SStragh understood that. Gods were gods, no matter how strange they might be—she had been willing to do the same, had the OColi asked it of her.

She wondered why Jhenini couldn't understand all that, as well.

The male Aaron had not wanted anyone in their odd little group to go off on their own, but the All-Ancestor had decreed otherwise. Tezozomoc had come in at dawn and commanded that Aaron and Mhundo follow him. Peter and Eckels had gone out not long after for some reason of their own; Travis had not wanted to leave—he said that he felt someone should stay and watch the glowing stones they'd taken, but SStragh could smell the sickness and exhaustion of the man. She was certain that Travis simply wanted to rest and was too stupidly proud to admit it.

Such self-pride was another thing about humans SStragh could not fathom.

Jhenini had examined SStragh's burnt hands, clucking over them in that strange language of hers before wrapping them again. When SStragh had asked her again to go with her to the Mutata building, she had reluctantly agreed.

Two of the servants, making no pretense, followed them at a discreet distance: as they left the palatial grounds, as they walked out into the throngs on the plaza and the marketplace at its southern end.

This city of the humans was huge to SStragh. She had thought the villages they had passed through were extraordinarily large and far too crowded, but this . . .

The Mutata language had no numbers for counting so high. A Mutata *jhaka* with more than twenty hands of people was considered prosperous, though she had heard stories about *jhaka* in the far south with triple that number. Still, until SStragh had seen the human city, she had thought such crowded *jhaka* only a traveler's tale. Now she wasn't quite so sure.

Everywhere she looked, there were more of these humans, as endless as the leaves of the forest, as noisy as all the tree-swingers in her valley, and their mingled scents were as chaotic, strange and strong as those of the sea dunes where the Mutata nested. SStragh admitted that the city had its beauty, with its wide, white avenues and the sparkling water of the canals, the intricately carved and painted facades around them, the lake and the mountains as a backdrop. But . . . the buildings: so harsh and unyielding in their lines, not soft and natural like those of the Mutata. It was as if these humans wanted to flaunt themselves to the world, to say "You see, I too can create mountains. I am greater than you, and I defy you to crush us!"

In SStragh's experience, those who defied the gods usually lost.

So unlike the Mutata, who only wish to blend with the world. That is what we say with our buildings: "We are part of you, and we are satisfied with our part-ness."

As if echoing her thoughts, Jhenini spoke. "It's very different from your world, isn't it?"

"Yes, Jhenini, it is." SStragh paused, reflexively adding a musky sadness to her scent and lowering her stance to reflect her sadness at the loss of her home. "It must be good for you to be back in a human world."

To SStragh's surprise, Jhenini snorted like an eggling just learning to talk. "Hardly," Jhenini said. Her chin lifted as if in submission, but SStragh decided that meant nothing. Jhenini's scent, as always, did not change. "Frankly, this place is almost stranger than your world."

"How can that be?" SStragh asked, genuinely puzzled. "They are human. Like you."

"They might be human, but their customs, their religion, their beliefs . . ." Jhenini shook her head. "SStragh, don't different tribes of Mutata have different ways?"

The question was so patently insane that SStragh almost couldn't answer it. She recovered her composure and gave Jhenini a scent of rebuke. "No," SStragh answered. "How can that be? We are all the same. We all follow the OColihi. Even Gairk are not different from other Gairk."

"Well, humans *are* that different. I'm sure I'd feel differently if I'd grown up here, but I don't feel safe and I don't want to stay here a minute longer than we need to."

Jhenini glanced up to the summit of the flat-sided mountain on which the ritual had been performed the night before, shading her too-sensitive human eyes against the sun's glare. SStragh knew she looked there, for somewhere up there was the path away from this world: the Floating Stone.

SStragh hooted gently in sympathy.

The boundary between the city and the small section of SStragh's home world was sharp. It was as if a cosmic knife had sliced a perfect circle from Tenochtitlán, pulled out by the roots what sat inside it, and replaced it with an identical piece from SStragh's time. The stone flags of the roadway ended smoothly at the interface, giving way to a large circle of dirt. Several of the cycads and other tropical shrubs from SStragh's world had also been transported, but they had died. Shriveled leaves whispered dryly on their bare skeletons. This place was too cold, the air too thin and dry, the sun too weak.

The Mutata building sat off-center in the alien circle, a pale lump the height of three Mutata, as tall as the stern, square buildings surrounding it but looking somehow smaller. The humans who lived here were as crowded in this area as any other, but they gave the area a wide berth; several watched as SStragh and Jhenini approached.

SStragh took a tentative step into the circle, feeling the familiar comfort of the earth between her clawed toes. She reached down to stroke one of the cycads, but the brown frond fell apart at her touch, the pieces of leaf fluttering away in the breeze. SStragh gave a soft warble through her nasal horn—a whispering hello. She expected no answer, but she felt her frill rising as the sound echoed.

"There's no one here, SStragh," Jhenini said. "You know that."

"I know, Jhenini," SStragh answered. "Yet . . ."

SStragh went to the arched entrance to the building, ducking her head as was proper. She stopped, her frill suddenly engorged and the scent of sorrow spilling from her glands. She loosed a trumpeting bellow. "SStragh!" Jhenini shouted behind her. "What's wrong?"

SStragh moved aside so that Jhenini could see into the building.

There, on the wide shelf which should have been used for speaking with guests, someone had placed the skeletal head of a Mutata. The huge eye sockets were empty, the eye ridges gleaming whitely through strips of mummified, dry flesh. The cause of the Mutata's death was readily apparent: a long fracture split the skull, and flecks of old blood still stained the edges of the wound. The mouth was open, the lower jaw hanging loose and askew. A few bones had been placed alongside the skull, leaning neatly against the grainy surface of the wall, but nearly all of the rest of the skeleton was missing.

Lying in front of the gory array, like an accusation, was a broken weapon: an Aztec spear.

"Oh, SStragh," Jhenini said behind her. The human's warm hand touched her flank, her odd sweet scent filled her nostrils. "I'm so sorry . . ."

A shadow fell between the two of them, cold and dark.

"*Xiuhcoatl!*" said a voice. SStragh looked over her shoulder. At the edge of the boundary between earth and city, an Aztec warrior stood. SStragh could not see his features with the sun glaring between the buildings behind him, but the scent was all too familiar—it was the one who had challenged them at the bridge, the one she had sent into the lake: Acayacatl. The man spoke the strange word again—"*Xiuhcoatl!*"—pointed to the skull on the ledge with his spear, and then clapped himself on the chest, his face twisted in an odd grimace. The gesture spoke better than any words: *I killed him*, it said proudly and defiantly, a mute challenge. *I did it.*

And because SStragh was Mutata, because the OCol-ihi held her in its chains of instinct in spite of her long denial, there was only one answer she could give to such a challenge.

With her left hand, SStragh snatched the broken spear from in front of the skull. She turned to Acayacatl and lowered her stance, releasing the spice odor of accept-ance. The warrior smiled, an expression of satisfaction.

He hefted his spear in his right hand—the wrong hand and an additional insult, but SStragh was beginning to expect such crudity from humans—and stepped into the circle of Mutata land. He seemed ready to charge. SStragh could smell his intentions, could see the muscles gathering in his legs, and she prepared to strike.

When Jhenini stepped between them.

"What's going on?" Aaron asked Mundo as Tezozomoc led them through the courtyard of the palace. The golden light of early morning angled sharply through the open windows of the building. They walked alternately in shadow and light, the sun blazing on Tezozomoc's white robe and making a halo of Mundo's fur. The ape sniffed as he padded along behind the priest.

"He didn't say."

"He's not much for telling anyone *anything*, is he?"

"He talks to *me*," Mundo answered, with an innocent grin that sent Aaron's temperature rising.

"Yeah, I'll just bet he does," Aaron replied.

There didn't seem to be anything Aaron could do but follow. He hadn't liked leaving Jennifer and the others behind, but Tezozomoc had been insistent. After the bloody ritual of the night before, and considering that his best guess was that they were outnumbered by something like fifty thousand to one, arguing seemed pointless. "Hey, man," Peter had said. "If the dude wanted us dead . . ."

"I know, he could have done it before. I hear you."

They were heading for the Great Temple, which did little to help Aaron's unease. The pyramid was a massive presence in the dawn, throwing a cold shadow that seemed to spread out over half the city. The edifice was even more impressive in the day. The twin main staircases angling sharply toward the sky seemed clifflike; he was glad they'd been unable to see them clearly in the torchlight the night before. A diligent crew was cleaning and whitewashing the pyramid; another group swept the plaza with straw brooms; while yet a third—scattered up and down the slope of the pyramid—scrubbed the steps. Looking at the scene now, Aaron might have been inclined to believe that everything last night had been some horrible nightmare, a hallucination. The city was clean, beautiful, alive; yet he knew that these same smiling people had watched the death of one of their fellows last night and cheered his death.

The contrast between the two images made Aaron's head spin.

Everyone they passed bowed respectfully to Tezozomoc, who hardly bothered to acknowledge their presence. "Hey, Mundo," Aaron called. "Just how important *is* Tezozomoc?"

"Oh, he was once *very* important," Mundo said. "That's why he was allowed to help with the ritual last night, even though Techtopec and the emperor don't really like him. But it doesn't matter. Tezozomoc was important once and everyone says that he will be again, very soon. And he's my *friend*."

"It doesn't bother you that your friend helped kill someone in cold blood last night?"

Mundo shrugged. "In *my* world," he said. "I was everything: hunter and hunted, predator and prey, killer and victim. I was born, died, and was reborn again endlessly. It's all part of the cycle."

"You're not *in* your world. If you die here, it's over. Done. I seem to notice that you've developed a keen sense of self-interest since we dragged you out of your time. You still say it doesn't bother you?"

"As long as it's not me being killed."

"Mundo, I really, *really* don't understand you."

"Then we're even," Mundo said, his nose wrinkling and his long fingers smoothing the fur on his chest. "Because I really, really don't understand you, either."

Tezozomoc looked back at them. He scowled and said something. Mundo bowed and lifted a finger to his lips. "He says we should be reverent in the presence of the gods," Mundo said.

Tezozomoc, turning his attention away again, began to ascend the long stairs. Sighing, Aaron looked up at the distant summit of the pyramid. Shaking his head, he followed.

In the excitement of the night before, he hadn't remembered how difficult it had been to ascend this man-made mountain. By the time they reached the top, his thighs ached, he was sweating, and his lungs ached with the effort of drawing oxygen from this unsatisfying thin air. Aaron bent over at the waist, hands on knees. When he looked up, the breath nearly went out of him again.

The tableau spread before him was gorgeous. He looked down on the white city, the bustling and colorful crowds of its streets, and the vista of blue lake and mountains beyond. Aaron could see why the Spaniards had been so impressed with the Aztec culture, with their wealth and the depth of their culture.

One heck of a picture postcard, Aaron thought. "*Had a wonderful time at the sacrifice last night. Wish you were here.*" The only blot on the landscape was the circle of transplanted Mutata world, just off to one side of the temple plaza. Jennifer had said that she and Struth would be visiting there this morning, but at the moment it was deserted.

A hand touched his shoulder and Aaron jumped, whirling around with his face red and his hands doubled involuntarily into fists. Tezozomoc took a step back from Aaron, looking at him silently and—Aaron thought—a little sadly. The priest inclined his head toward the most northern of the two temples. Mundo was already waiting there.

Aaron turned from the panorama of Tenochtitlán; as he did so, the eagle vessel caught his eye. There was a dark, ugly stain in the bowl of the sculpture. As he passed, Aaron made certain that he didn't look at it too closely.

The altar he saw to one side of the temple didn't ease his mind. The facing wall was studded with rows of skulls set in the mortar, at least two hundred of them. Aaron shivered, not entirely because he walked out of sun into the shadow of temple's interior.

It took a moment for his eyes to adjust to the gloom. Here, torches guttered in wall sconces around the large outer room. In niches around the room, glittering jewels, masks, figurines, necklaces, shells, and a thousand other baubles were displayed.

But placed in the center of the room between two fiery braziers, drawing the eye immediately to it, hovered a broken rectangle of stained white plastic: the Floating Stone. Not caring that Tezozomoc watched him with appraising eyes, Aaron went immediately to the piece of roadway, stroking it with one hand.

"Ask him how it got here," Aaron said to Mundo. "Ask him where it *goes*."

"It was found after the first vision-storm," Tezozomoc told him through Mundo. The priest's eyes glittered darkly in the torchlight, his skin the color of beaten, fiery copper. "Found here in this very place. The vision-storm destroyed the temple, leaving behind a sandy waste and four dark men who attacked the priests—the ones the vision-storm hadn't already stolen. We took the dark men captive and built a new temple to Tlaloc, mixing the blood of the prisoners with the mortar to sanctify the new building."

With the words, the chill ran through Aaron again. Tezozomoc paused, watching him. "I lived here in Tenochtitlán then," Tezozomoc continued. "I was a High Priest of Tlaloc, second only to Techtopec, the high priest you saw last night. Techtopec and I were rivals, but

I was proud because the Emperor Cuauhtemoc had begun to listen to me, and I knew that one day I would take the robe that Techtopec wore. I was deeply in love, also. Her name was Chantico—and she was wonderful, surprising me always with her kindness and the way she returned my love. Her hair was corn silk and black as the night sky, her voice as soothing as a flute, and her skin was smooth and warm . . ."

Tezozomoc stopped. He looked away from Aaron and Mundo, gazing for a second into the guttering flame of the braziers before looking back to Aaron. "You understand, perhaps?" he asked. "You and the girl, the one with the hair of gold—is it that way with you?"

"Yes."

Tezozomoc nodded. "That day, the day of the time storm, Chantico and I were together. We both ran here when we saw the lightning of the vision-storm strike Tlaloc's temple. We both fought and helped capture the dark men, and we were both here when Techtopec ordered that the Floating Stone be moved. Techtopec was certain that the gods were speaking to us, that Tlaloc had given us the gift of the magic Floating Stone. When you touched it, you could feel its power, tingling your fingers."

"That was the temporal machinery . . . uhh, the magical 'greenstone' underneath it," Aaron said. "That's what made it tingle."

"So we found out," Tezozomoc agreed. "That day, as we tried to move the stone away from what was left of Tlaloc's temple, Chantico jumped up onto the stone to quickly get to the other side. But . . ." Tezozomoc stopped again. His gaze had gone to the stone, and there was only hatred in his eyes. "She cried out once, as if in surprise, and then . . . It was as if Chantico had gone through an invisible doorway. She . . . my love . . . disappeared."

"Did you go after her?" Aaron asked eagerly. "Where did this stone go?"

The muscles of Tezozomoc's face tightened. "I don't know. When Chantico tried to leap over the stone, the stone shook. When she vanished, the greenstone fell out from underneath at the same time. I had jumped onto the stone as soon as I heard Chantico cry out— I felt dizzy and cold for a moment, and I saw a strange landscape as if in a dream, but it was gone as quickly as it had come, and I was only standing on top of the stone. Techtopec had picked up the greenstone, holding it in awe. I knew, I *knew* that the magic was in the greenstone, and I asked—no, I *ordered*—him to put it back where it had been, so that I could go to Chantico, but he would not."

Tezozomoc suddenly slammed his fist onto the Floating Stone. Aaron jumped with the noise; the stone bobbed in response. "Techtopec said that the greenstone was Tlaloc's gift to him, as was the stone. Chantico had only been the sacrifice necessary to cause it to happen."

"What did you do?"

"I shouted, I argued. I told him that I had glimpsed another place beyond the stone, that Chantico had only gone there and that if he replaced the glowing stone, I might be able to find her. Techtopec didn't listen. I went raging to Cuauhtemoc Acamapichtli, fearing every second that was wasted, and when Cuauhtemoc in his wisdom said that this must be a decision for priests and he could not interfere, I knew I had lost her. Techtopec had already given the bright greenstone to the artisans to be made into a necklace. When I argued with him, telling him that if the stone was Tlaloc's then the god obviously meant for us to use it, he would not listen.

"Without Chantico, I had no desire to stay in Tenochtitlán; I had no ambition to take Techtopec's place. I gave blood that night, and I prayed to Tlaloc for understanding. I saw other vision-storms coming, and saw myself among the mountains. '*Go there*.' the dream seemed to tell me. "*Go there and I will give you further signs*." So I obeyed. I left Tenochtitlán." He looked at Mundo, at Aaron.

"And Tlaloc sent you," he said.

"No," Aaron said. "That's where you're wrong. Look, I'm really sorry about Chantico and all, but you've got to get this business about Tlaloc out of your head. We don't have anything to do with you or Techtopec or any of the rest. All we want—" Aaron stopped. *All we want is to use one of our pieces of temporal material on your Floating Stone. But I don't want to tell you that because I don't know that I can trust you, and I don't know what you'd do if I did.*

"Mundo told me what you want," Tezozomoc said as Aaron hesitated.

Aaron looked at Mundo, who gave one of his wide grins as if he'd just read Aaron's mind—which, Aaron realized, he probably had. "And just what did you tell him that we wanted, Mundo?" Aaron asked.

Mundo shrugged and scratched at his fur, but he never got his answer out. From outside, Aaron heard the distinctive trumpeting of a Mutata, a loud blast of distress that carried over the general clamor of the city. "Struth!" Aaron said, and bolted from the temple.

As he approached the stairs, he could look down to where the Mutata dwelling stood. Despite the distance, he could plainly see Struth and Jennifer standing at the entrance to the Mutata building. An Aztec warrior was also there, and as Aaron watched in mute despair, the man drew back his arm and launched his spear.

19

A Captive Taken

Jennifer decided that she'd probably made a mistake. Not long after she'd broken up with Peter and started seeing Aaron, she'd once stepped between the two young men when it seemed that they were about to fight. That time, her intervention had ended the confrontation. She wasn't quite sure what had impelled her to step between Struth and Acayacatl—but she was fairly sure that the impulse could have been labeled "stupidity," because it didn't seem to make any difference to the Aztec that she was between him and his target.

Acayacatl brought his arm back. From the look on his face, Jennifer had no doubt that he was about to cast his weapon.

And at the same moment that Jennifer decided to throw herself on the ground, he did.

She felt the breeze of the weapon as it passed within a few inches of her head, then she hit the ground hard, wishing Aaron had taught her how to do that aikido tuck and roll. She grunted as her shoulder jammed into its socket, but she let herself tumble, trying to look back at

Struth and afraid that she was about to see her friend killed.

But Struth was more prepared than Jennifer had been. Acayacatl had evidently forgotten just how agile Struth was. As the spear flew toward the Mutata, she stepped to the right and—in the same motion—swept her own spear left in a blocking move. Struth's spear contacted Acayacatl's weapon with a sound like a baseball bat slamming into an oak tree, and Acayacatl's spear went careening away.

Struth loosed a brassy note of triumph. "Stupid, stupid human," she crowed in Mutata. "Never throw your weapon unless you know you're going to hit your target."

Acayacatl backed away a step, glancing from Struth to where his spear, temptingly, lay on the dirt near the Mutata building. He made a feint toward it, and Struth jabbed at him with her spear. The Mutata's speed startled Acayacatl and he nearly went down as he evaded the thrust. Jennifer had managed to get to her feet by then.

"Struth," she called. "Just get his spear and forget this."

"The human asked for this *ciosie*," Struth answered firmly. "Not me. Let *him* say that it's over." Struth's bandaged hand gripped the broken spear firmly, even though Jennifer knew that the pressure must hurt the just-healed skin. Jennifer could see that she wasn't going to convince Struth; she turned to Acayacatl.

"Acayacatl." The man's ebony eyes flicked once toward her; otherwise, his gaze stayed on Struth. "End fight," she said in the pidgin Nahuatl she'd picked up on the way to Tenochtitlán. She waved her hand to indicate that he should retreat.

He didn't. She could see a crowd gathering around the circle of Mutata land, people attracted by Struth's honking and whistling. Most of them looked to be those shopping in the marketplace, but some among them were well dressed, evidently of the nobility. No one seemed inclined to stop the fight, no matter what their rank. They watched, silent.

"Acayacatl," Jennifer said again. "End fight." Acayacatl sniffed without looking at Jennifer; she didn't know if he understood her or not. He crouched.

And made a leap for the spear.

Mutata reflexes were faster. Struth stepped forward and jabbed. A short shriek of pain was torn from Acayacatl as the spear point dug deep into his thigh, and he fell to the ground. Struth stood over him, her shadow falling across the warrior as he stretched a desperate hand out toward his spear, his other hand clamped around the shaft of the spear in his leg as blood flowed thick around his fingers. Struth leaned down casually and plucked Acayacatl's spear from the ground before his quivering fingers could close around it. Struth looked at it critically.

"A youngling's toy," she said contemptuously, and snapped the shaft in two. "First blood is mine," she declared, looking at the gathered spectators. "This *ciosie* is over."

Jennifer ran to Struth and hugged the Mutata, then dropped to one knee beside the stricken Acayacatl. "I help," she told the man in her broken Nahuatl. She pointed to herself, then his wound. "I must see."

Gently, she pried his hand away from the spear. Fresh blood gushed out and Jennifer grimaced. "Struth," she called, "I'm going to need help with this. We need bandages, clean water, some needle and thread . . ."

Acayacatl pushed her away with a grimace. He said something, and Jennifer pointed at her ear. "Don't understand," she told him.

"He said that the *xiuhcoatl*—the fire serpent—must say the words first." The voice was Mundo's. Jennifer looked up with relief to see the ape wriggling through the front ranks of the onlookers. "What words, Mundo?" Jennifer asked.

"Evidently it's something that has to be recited when you take a captive in battle."

"Struth didn't take him captive."

"Doesn't matter," Mundo said. "I don't think he's going to let you help him until Struth says it."

Jennifer grimaced and told Struth what Mundo had just said. "This human *ciosie* is very strange," Struth sighed, a soft hooting. "What must I say to him?"

Mundo spoke to Acayacatl. "Say 'He is as my beloved *son*,'" he told Struth, using the Nahuatl word for "son," since there was no such word in the Mutata vocabulary. "I told him that you were going to speak it in your own language. He says that's fine."

Looking down at Acayacatl's pained face, Struth spoke the words, half whistling the unfamiliar "son." Acayacatl nodded, then grunted out another phrase in reply. "He said that you are as his beloved 'father,'" Mundo told Struth. "I don't think he has a good grasp of Mutata biology."

"What is 'son'? What is 'father'?" Struth asked.

Mundo looked at Jennifer with a look of confusion on his face. From what Aaron had told Jennifer, he probably didn't quite understand the concept himself. "A father is someone whose eggs have hatched," Jennifer told Mundo and Struth. "A son is a male youngling from those eggs."

"But why should I love my son, Jhenini?" Struth asked.

The question, asked so earnestly and with such inno-cent puzzlement on Struth's face, startled Jennifer. Cer-tainly she knew that the Mutata didn't care for their

young the way humans do, but she suddenly realized that
for the most part she considered Struth to be simply a
big, oddly shaped person—as human as herself. Struth's
question brought her face-to-face with Struth's undeniable *otherness*. Jennifer took a breath, stammered, then
glanced at Mundo, who shrugged at her.

"Don't look at me," he said. "*I* haven't any idea, either.
Sounds really stupid to get so attached to someone else."

Acayacatl groaned then, ending any comment Jennifer
might have made. She knelt beside him.

"By the way," Struth asked as Jennifer tended to the
man's wound. "Just what does one do with a captive?"

Mundo put the question to Acayacatl. "You offer them
to the gods," Mundo told them. "You kill them."

"Jennifer!" Aaron cried from the top of the pyramid,
knowing that it was useless. There was no way he could
scramble down from the summit of the pyramid in time,
no way he could stop what was about to happen. He could
only watch, helpless, as Jennifer threw herself to the
ground, as the weapon nearly sliced into her, as Struth—
impossibly—managed to knock the spear out of the air.
Aaron scrambled down the steep staircase of the pyramid,
losing sight of Jennifer and Struth as he did so. Mundo
scooted past him, the ape moving on all fours at a breakneck pace. Aaron heard Tezozomoc's heavier footsteps
behind him.

When he hit the plaza, he broke into frenetic, broken-
field running between the people gathered at the marketplace on the edge of the plaza, ignoring the shouts as he
pushed past and between them. By the time he reached
the crowd gathered around the patch of Struth's worlds,
it was already over—so much for heroics. Jennifer was

taking care of the wounded Acayacatl (though she had an unsettled expression on her face that Aaron couldn't quite decipher). Mundo had his arm around Struth's thick neck and was talking to the Mutata quietly.

As Aaron started toward Jennifer, he noticed the head priest, Techtopec, standing near the edge of the crowd. The look on the man's face as he stared at Jennifer, Struth, and Mundo was anything but friendly, and when Tezozomoc came up alongside Aaron, Techtopec's glance at them was daggered. Techtopec sniffed as if in disgust and turned to leave, the crowd respectfully parting to allow him to go. As he passed Tezozomoc, the two exchanged quick words, then Techtopec moved away into the bustling lanes of the market.

Aaron raised an eyebrow toward Tezozomoc. Whatever Techtopec had said had given the priest the face of someone with terminal indigestion.

"I don't know that I can trust you any better," he said to Tezozomoc, knowing the man wouldn't understand the words. "But Techtopec doesn't impress me much either."

20

Trapped

It didn't escape anyone's notice that the "attendants" around their rooms just happened to double in number in the wake of Struth's fight with Acayacatl, or that their "servants" were suddenly muscular and fit young men who—when they glanced at the "captive" Acayacatl—seemed to grimace disapprovingly.

"It looks like Struth impressed the heck out of them," Jennifer commented.

"Yeah," Peter said. "It doesn't look like the greatest tactical move on our part, either. I think we have about half the city on our staff here now. I wonder if Struth's friend here knows what's going on?"

Acayacatl, unfortunately, wasn't talking. To Mundo's repeated questions, he simply glared back wordlessly. "We can *make* him talk," Eckels growled.

"Man, you sound like something out of a bad B war movie," Aaron said. He was gazing from the open window out across the plaza.

The setting sun poured light like molten gold over the Great Temple pyramid. The sellers were packing away their wares in the marketplace as the last few buyers of the day haggled for last-minute bargains. Birds pecked hopefully at the cracks between the plaza stones; colorful lizards played hide-and-seek across the walls of the court-yard below Aaron. "We're not doing *anything* to Acaya-catl. Do you understand that? I don't care what he might know—he's not to be hurt."

"Hey, I wasn't talking about hurting him. I was just suggesting we *scare* him a little," Eckels persisted. "I don't know about you, but there are too many *eyes* watching us. I don't like it."

"Whassa matter, Eckels?" Travis said. The safari guide was lying on his pallet, a blanket over him despite the warmth of the room; Aaron had heard him tell Jennifer that he was "cold," something he knew had worried Jen-nifer. "Got a guilty conscience?"

Eckels looked like he was about to kick the reclining Travis. Peter, who was standing nearest the man, didn't seem inclined to stop him. Aaron pushed away from the window angrily. "Stop it!" he shouted. A coffee brown face peered in curiously from the blanket covering the doorway, and Aaron waved him away. "We're stuck in the middle of someone's else's fight—"

"Again," Peter interrupted blandly. Aaron glared at him; Peter just shrugged.

"And we're not going to solve anything by bickering among ourselves. If everyone's happy staying here, then fine—why don't you just tell Tezozomoc or Techtopec and be done with it. If you want to get *home*, then let's figure out how we're going to do that."

Aaron explained to them what he and Mundo had seen and heard at the temple of Tlaloc: the Floating Stone, and Tezozomoc's story of his lost lover Chantico.

"He isn't saying so, but I think what he's really after is a chance to go through the Floating Stone himself and try to find Chantico," Aaron said. "Is that what you're getting from him, Mundo?"

The ape nodded. "He told me that the reason he has stayed away from Tenochtitlán for so long is that Techtopec has the ear the of the emperor, and the piece of temporal machinery has become the sign of Tlaloc's high priest's office. He has been waiting for some kind of sign that the time was right to take the 'sacred greenstone' from Techtopec."

"And you were willing to help him—as long as you got a chance to go along, without us, preferably," Peter said. "You're a real friend, Mundo."

"You're mistaken, Peter," Mundo replied coldly, his black eyes glittering in his dark face. "Even if you *were* right, remember that I can read your surface thoughts— and I know you would abandon *your* friends if it meant you could get back to your home."

"That's not *true*," Peter protested loudly, but the redhead's face had colored and he kept his gaze away from Aaron and Jennifer.

"Drop it," Aaron told Mundo. "At least *we* don't need Techtopec's piece of temporal machinery. We already know that where the Floating Stones go is determined by the piece stuck in it, and we have the ones we need. We just have to get to the Floating Stone with them."

"Which is in on top of a pyramid in the middle of Aztec Central, and inside a temple to boot," Peter said. "Not to mention the goons Techtopec has placed all around this place. It's an awfully comfortable jail, but it's still a jail."

"Struth and I walked around the city today with no problem," Jennifer reminded Peter.

"That was today," Peter answered. "And Acayacatl was following you, or did you think it was just coincidence that he happened to show up? I know that when Eckels and I were walking around today, there were always a couple of familiar faces a few yards behind us. Now that we're here, I can guarantee that we're not free to leave anytime we please. In fact . . ." Peter rose to his feet and stretched. "I'll just prove it."

With that, he walked out of the room, sweeping aside the curtains of the entrance archway to reveal the startled faces of the guards outside. "Peter—" Jennifer called, starting to go after him, but Aaron stopped her.

"No, Jennifer," he said. "If Peter's right, we need to know it. Let him go."

• • •

Peter wasn't entirely sure why he'd stalked out like that, except that he was tired of Emperor Aaron and the way Jennifer looked at him. He was tired of not understanding anything people were saying around him, weary of being in places where nothing was in any way familiar. His shoulder ached all the time where he'd been shot, his stomach didn't like the strange food, and he was, yes, just a little scared.

It felt good to *do* something.

Even if it felt like a mistake.

"I'm going for a little stroll," he told the guards, for the benefit of Aaron, Jenny, and the others. The guards spoke quickly to each other in their own language, their faces suspicious. Peter took a deep breath and turned right down the corridor to where the courtyard beckoned in the last dregs of sunlight. He heard one of the guards running quickly away down another hall. *Okay, you've stirred them up now*, he told himself. *Let's just hope you don't get stung.*

Peter whistled as he walked slowly toward the opening to the courtyard. The arch came closer, and for a moment Peter thought that he'd been wrong and that no one was going to bother him at all.

A shadow fell across the archway. An Aztec warrior in full battle dress, stood there like an apparition, with the tall, feathered backplate towering well over his head. Peter stopped, licked his lips.

"I'm gonna go watch the sun set," he told the man. "Y'know, go out and commune with nature, that kind of thing. Of course, you can't understand a word of this, can you?" The man's stolid, stern expression hadn't changed. Peter smiled at him with false nonchalance. "Maybe if you get lucky, they'll choose you for the next sacrifice," he told the man. "Wouldn't that be nice? 'Course, I'll bet you'd be honored, wouldn't you, you great ugly brute?"

As Peter continued to babble, he kept walking forward as if he expected the man to step aside at the last moment like a polite doorman. When Peter was two paces away from him, the warrior suddenly snapped down the short stabbing spear he carried, the threatening tip toward Peter. He spoke a few abrupt words in Nahuatl.

"I suppose that means 'no,'" Peter said. *Well, that's what you expected*, he thought, but that didn't stop the surge of anger that came from deep within him. He knew it wasn't just this—the rage came from all the frustrations of the last few months. He suddenly didn't care that this was exactly what he'd anticipated, that he was unarmed, or that he was alone. He wanted to be *out*, and the warrior was a symbol of the whole situation. "Wave the spear all you want. I have the right to take a walk."

Peter reached out and pushed the spear head aside, striding forward. The warrior grunted something. A hand came up, grasping for Peter. The unfocused anger filled Peter now, and he did a sweeping block of the man's arm, then—as the warrior shouted at him and tried to push the youth back—Peter turned slightly and lashed out with a side kick that would have taken out a knee if it had connected.

It hadn't, unfortunately. His kick was high, striking the man's muscular thigh. The warrior staggered and grunted in pain, but Peter realized that all he'd managed to do was make the man furious. His own initial adrenaline rush had passed. The warrior flicked his spear toward Peter. The spear tip evaded Peter's frantic block; the glassy edge of the obsidian slid gratingly along the side of his forehead just above his left eye. Peter staggered backward, warm blood running into his eye and half blinding him. He didn't feel any pain. He told himself it was only a scratch and held his hand to his head.

His fingers came away coated with sticky red. The warrior was still advancing, and Peter's stomach was doing ugly flip-flops. "Okay, okay," he told the warrior, holding up his hands and still backing. "I get the idea."

The Aztec didn't seem impressed. He stalked Peter, the spear held up as if ready for another strike, the elaborate battle dress making it seem as if the warrior filled the hallway. "Come on, dude, chill. You made your point."

The back of Peter's heel caught the edge of an uneven flag. He fell heavily backward, and his head hit the stones hard.

The last thing he saw clearly was the warrior rushing forward.

Peter was escorted back to the room by a sternlooking warrior who seemed to be limping badly. Peter grinned at the group from under a long, bloody scrape on his temple. The warrior gave them all a long stare, lingering an especially long time on Struth. He sneered at Acayacatl's prone form before turning his back and leaving them, favoring his right leg.

"Let me take a look at that," Jennifer said. "Eckels, hand me some of the cloth over there, please; Mundo, bring me some of the water."

"What happened?" Aaron asked as Peter grimaced under Jennifer's ministrations.

"My friendly companion there wasn't going to let me leave," Peter said. "We had a little discussion about it, and he won. No more walks for us. They want us to stay right here." He pushed away Jennifer's hand as she cleaned the cut on his forehead. "Which means that we're stuck in more ways than one. We're captives," he said. He let go a deep breath, looking at Acayacatl. "And we already know what they like to do with them."

"I don't think it's that bad yet," Aaron said. "We're caught in the middle of Tezozomoc's feud with Techtopec, and Techtopec hasn't figured out where we fit in yet."

"Where *do* we fit in?" Eckels asked.

Peter grinned, nodding at Aaron. "*We* haven't figured that out yet. Have we, Aaron?"

"I know I don't trust either one of them. If you ask me, I think we need to get out of here before one or the other of them decides that we'd make a great offering. I just don't know how."

"But I do," Travis said grimly. "I do."

21

Into the Night

Tezozomoc arrived before they could put Travis's plan into action.

The priest, his face drawn and pale, and moving as if he were on the edge of exhaustion, entered their room as they were pretending to settle down to sleep. Tezozomoc said nothing for a time, just standing at the entrance in the dim light of the banked central fireplace. He seemed to stare into the room, but it was difficult to tell exactly at whom or what he was looking. Finally, Tezozomoc stirred, asking that Aaron and Mundo come with him. Shrugging at the others, Aaron followed the man to a small room down the hall, Mundo padding after. Guards moved with them, but Tezozomoc ignored them.

"This afternoon I gave blood to Tlaloc," Tezozomoc said to Aaron via Mundo. "I asked him to send me a clearer sign, so that I would know what I must do. It took much of my *chalchiuh-atl* to make him speak, but he did so."

"You hallucinated, Tezozomoc," Aaron told him. "Loss of blood will do that." Mundo looked at Aaron with a scowl on his muzzle, but at Aaron's nod, the ape sighed, turned to Tezozomoc, and translated.

Aaron expected Tezozomoc to become angry, but the priest nodded indulgently. "You understand only what fits into your view of the world, Aaron," Tezozomoc said. "I do not blame you for that. That is the flaw the gods have given you. That is the defect that you must correct."

Aaron sighed. "All right, Tezozomoc. Fine. This is getting us nowhere. You came to tell me about a vision? I don't believe in visions, but you know that and I have the feeling you're going to tell me anyway."

"Yes." Tezozomoc glanced at the doorway, where a guard was conspicuously stationed. He moved toward the window, glanced out at the courtyard below, and gestured to Aaron to move closer. The priest half whispered his words, cautioning Mundo to be quiet as he translated.

"In my vision, all of you were in the temple, crowded around the Floating Stone. I saw you, Aaron, with the ceremonial knife in your hands, about to take Acayacatl's life, but I could see into your own beating heart as if your body were made of crystal, and I saw a darkness there, a mark on your soul that told me that what you were doing was false. You looked at the Floating Stone, and your heart brightened as if set on fire, and that told me what you actually coveted."

Tezozomoc stopped, his head tilted. "You look distressed, Aaron," he said. "My vision disturbs you?"

"It's indigestion," Mundo told Tezozomoc, rubbing his furry stomach for emphasis. "Aaron always gets that way when he has to eat his own words."

"Mundo . . ." Aaron said warningly. He rubbed at his forehead surreptitiously. He found himself sweating despite the chill—Tezozomoc had just come dangerously close to speaking what Travis had outlined for them only a few minutes before. *Serendipity*. Aaron told himself.

Coincidence. Maybe he was listening, or maybe Mundo can project thoughts too and we just don't know it. "I'm fine, Tezozomoc. Go on. I'm listening."

"The vision was less clear after that. I saw the *xiuhcoatl* in her own world, the one you call Struth, and there were many of her kind around her. A storm swirled in the sky above, and shining greenstones were scattered at her feet. Someone took the fiery stones—I could not see the person's face, but the hands were light-skinned—and put them all together. When they did so, suddenly the storm was gone and a wall like an emerald sheet was placed around the *xiuhcoatl's* land."

Tezozomoc took a long breath as he stared out toward the pyramid. Fires had been lit on the summit at the four corners of the platform, making the pyramid look like a volcano smoldering in the night. When Tezozomoc looked back, his face was somber.

"Then the vision changed and flowed," he said. "I saw you again, Aaron, and myself. We were in the temple of Tlaloc. Now it was the Floating Stone that was formed of transparent crystal, and embedded in its jeweled depths I saw my love Chantico. Techtopec was there also, blood running down his face as if he had been struck, and he spoke to us. 'Only blood can release her,' he said. 'A sacrifice is demanded.' Techtopec placed a knife in my hand, and in the other he put his greenstone amulet. 'Choose,' he told me. 'One of you must die.'"

Tezozomoc stopped. Torchlight cast moving shadows in the valleys of his face.

"So you killed me?" Aaron asked at last. "In your vision?"

"The dream ended then," Tezozomoc answered flatly. "I came here."

"What are you planning to do?"

Tezozomoc didn't answer. He stood near the window, one hand on the wall, and his body swayed slightly. "Tezozomoc?"

The priest started as if from a reverie. "You will try to leave soon. I feel this; I know it. I want to go with you. I want to find Chantico, and I will help you in any way I can to accomplish that."

What do you say now? The question rolled around Aaron's mind, thundering, and he had no ready answer. Instead, he danced around Tezozomoc's request. "Let me ask you one thing first," Aaron said. "We're being held here for some reason. Why is that? If we stay here, what is going to happen to us?"

"You are—as are we all—in the hands of the emperor, and the emperor listens to the high priest Techtopec in matters of the vision-storms," Tezozomoc told him. "Since you have come from the vision-storm, your fate will be decreed by Techtopec, not me."

"I thought so," Aaron said. "And I already have a good idea what Techtopec has in mind."

Aaron rubbed his chin—a nervous habit he'd picked up the last few weeks since he hadn't been able to shave. His chin itched with the scratchy fuzz. *You can't trust him. You can't tell him that you're not going to wherever his Chantico is gone, and you don't want him to know what the "green-stones" we carry can do. What choice does that leave you?*

"And if we don't let you go with us, you'll just let Techtopec do whatever he pleases, right?"

"If you don't allow me to help you," Tezozomoc answered calmly, "you will not be allowed near the Floating Stone again until the time has come for your heart to be cut from your chest and offered to Tlaloc."

He's right about one thing—with Tezozomoc, we do have a better chance of getting to the path. We could use him. All you have to do is tell a little white lie. . . . "All right," Aaron said. "It's a deal. We'll open the gateway for you. If you want to go with us, you can."

Mundo looked at Aaron. A smirk touched the edges of his mouth. *So you lie too,* the ape seemed to say. *You do the same thing you've accused me of doing.* "Funny," Mundo said. "I could have *sworn* we were just talking about going somewhere other than wherever this Chantico went."

"I didn't say *where* we were going." Aaron retorted. "I just said we'd open the gateway—and we will."

"To your Green Town. Not to wherever Chantico's gone."

"Just translate," Aaron said curtly. Mundo shrugged and spoke to Tezozomoc. Aaron listened carefully, trying to understand some of what Mundo was saying to the priest in case the ape decided to switch sides again—as he'd demonstrated he could do far too easily. Mundo spoke too rapidly for Aaron's poor grasp of Nahuatl. He caught a few words. The two conversed back and forth a few minutes, with Aaron growing more irritated and worried by the second.

"Mundo," he broke in at last. "What are you telling him?"

"I was just cleaning up your little omission for you," the ape answered. "He wanted to know just how the greenstones worked with the Floating Stone. I told him it was magic and only a great sorcerer like yourself could manage the spell; he bought that."

"I wish I knew if you were telling me the truth."

"I *always* tell the truth," Mundo said in aggrieved tones. "Just like you."

The ape gave Aaron a grin yellow with pointed teeth. "Now doesn't that make you feel good?" Mundo added.

"Our visitors wish to sacrifice the captive Acayacatl to the god Tlaloc, as is their privilege. They would like to do it now."

The guards' eyes narrowed suspiciously, looking from Tezozomoc to the dour, silent Acayacatl in the midst of the strangers. The duo in the hallway didn't look especially happy at the prospect of arguing with five foreigners, an ape, a dinosaur, and Tezozomoc. At best, they were outnumbered; at worst, the *xiuhcoatl* might breathe fire on them, and it was rumored that at least one of the paleskins was a magician. A Mexica would have understood that he was a captive and remained in the room—these people insisted on being troublesome. If Tezozomoc hadn't been with them, there wouldn't have been any question about what to do: the guards would have accepted their fate and refused to allow this, fighting and dying if that was what had to be. But the fire priest complicated things.

"Has Techtopec been told of this?" one of the guards asked.

"*I* know of it and approve the sacrifice," Tezozomoc told him sternly. "That is enough. You are in my way. Step aside."

One of the guards took an uncertain step backward, then stopped. The other twitched his spear nervously. "Would you prefer that I go to Techtopec myself?" Tezozomoc asked. "Should I tell him how two of his servants prevented us from giving Acayacatl's blood at the most propitious moment? Should I say to him that two fools ruined the sacred rites of our visitors?"

The guards shuffled uncomfortably, uncertain. Tezozomoc let them squirm for a few moments, then sighed.

"You will come with us," he said. "You can guard these visitors from the vision-storms there as easily as here."

The guards jumped for the proffered compromise with obvious relief. One in front, one in the rear, they escorted the group out from the building and into the cold night air. They passed easily through the other guard stations.

If anyone noticed the fact that each of the foreigners carried a luminescent greenstone, no one remarked on it.

Struth snorted as soon as they were in the open. They'd fashioned a crude if colorful cape for the Mutata from several blankets, but the chill bit into the dinosaur, who was already half-lethargic with the night. The guards looked at Struth in alarm, then decided that the creature looked placid enough at the moment.

They moved out into the plaza itself.

Aaron had to admit that Tezozomoc's presence fit beautifully into Travis's strategy. Even though the city was quiet by night, the plaza was never entirely deserted. There was no way that their group could make it across the open expanse undetected; even less that no one would question them when it became obvious that they intended to scale the pyramid to the twin temples at its summit. But with Tezozomoc, no one bothered to do more than stare. The two guards were something they hadn't counted on, but Tezozomoc had actually handled that as deftly as possible; they'd have to find a way to deal with them, but that could wait until they saw the situation in the temple.

Aaron also realized that they'd picked up another escort: the men who had accompanied them to Tenochtitlán from Tezozomoc's village. The village warriors fell into step alongside the group; the two guards from the palace exchanged glances, but said nothing.

Aaron hoped they were on their side.

You can't worry about it now. For the moment, Aaron concerned himself only with getting their band to the pyramid—Struth kept lagging behind, and Travis wasn't moving well either.

"Jen," Aaron called, nodding to Travis. "Stay with him, okay? I'll help Struth."

Jennifer looked up at the pyramid. The double row of the staircase seemed impossibly steep and high. "I hope we're making the right decision," she said.

"Right or wrong, we've made it. And the quicker we get to the top, the better."

Aaron felt exposed as they began the climb. The wind was cutting and cold, and the torches set along the stairs illuminated them all too well for anyone with a bow. Aaron's spine tingled, and with each step he expected to hear a shout or feel an arrow plunge into his back. Tezozomoc gave no indication that he was worried; the priest strode confidently forward at the head of their procession, his stride firm and slow. Peter and Eckels followed, with the stoic Acayacatl between them, his face composed and calm. Even knowing he was going to his death, Acayacatl revealed no emotion beyond a serene pride. Despite the fact that Aaron knew the warrior had tried to kill Struth, he admired the man's composure in the face of his situation; Aaron knew that he couldn't have done the same.

Ascending the pyramid was the work of several long minutes, but at last, his breath a cloud before him, Aaron stepped up onto the platform. This time he resisted the temptation to gaze out over slumbering Tenochtitlán. Torchlight lent a sense of animation to the wall of skulls; he heard Jennifer's quick intake of breath as she noticed the display. The carved facade of the temple of

Huitzilopochtlio was a massive presence to their right; Tezozomoc, without a glance, had turned left toward Tlaloc's temple. Aaron could see no one else around.

He allowed himself a brief sense of hope. Maybe this would work after all.

Which was when Techtopec stepped out from the entrance to the temple.

22

The Sands of Time

Tezozomoc moved forward to intercept Techtopec, the amulet of temporal machinery glowing green on the head priest's chest. Aaron could see several acolytes watching from within the temple, and the odds were suddenly not quite so good. The two priests were quickly involved in a rapid conversation of which Aaron could understand nothing. Mundo was listening, however; Aaron called him back as the two priests continued to speak.

"What's up?"

"Tezozomoc's telling Techtopec why we've come; Techtopec's arguing that this sacrifice of Acayacatl is fine and all, but we should wait until the emperor gets here to watch. In fact, he's dispatched a runner to fetch our esteemed ruler—and, I'll bet—a small army of warriors."

"Aaron, we're dead meat unless we go *now*," Peter said as the others crowded around. "We may not get this close again."

"I know, I know." Aaron bit his lower lip, beat his fists on his thighs. *Should I tell Techtopec how two of his servants prevented us from giving Acayacatl's blood at the most propitious moment?* Tezozomoc's words came back to Aaron, and with them, an idea. "Jenny can you get Struth to play along here? Tell her to act upset—honk, bleat, stomp her feet, anything she can think of. Will she do that?"

"I guess so," Jennifer said. She turned to the Mutata and spoke to her. Struth snorted, paused, and then let out a shattering bass bellow that echoed from the buildings around the plaza. The dinosaur swung her arms wide, her body pirouetting wildly so that everyone had to scatter to avoid the flailing tail. Tezozomoc and Techtopec had turned to stare at the display. Mundo translated as Techtopec shouted over Struth's din.

"What is the matter with the *xiuhcoatl*?" the priest asked. "Is it ill?"

"It is the madness of the gods," Aaron told the priest through Mundo. "Acayacatl is Struth's captive, and Struth's gods demand that captives be sacrificed on the night of their capture, before . . ." Aaron looked westward, to where Venus glittered on the horizon. He pointed to the planet. "Before the brightest star leaves the sky." Aaron gestured at Struth, still capering around the platform. Jenny was shouting at her in Mutata—instructions to keep up the act, Aaron hoped. "Struth had believed that Acaycatl's sacrifice would placate the . . . uhh . . . the 'God of Vision-Storms' so that the storms would end for the Mexica, at least for a time."

Aaron glanced at Techtopec. The high priest was still listening; Aaron decided that was a good sign. Mundo waited for Aaron's next words, a strange appraising look on the ape's face. "If the sacrifice is not performed immediately, Techtopec," Aaron continued, "the god will be furious. None of us can predict what would happen then. That's why Struth is so upset."

Tezozomoc turned to Techtopec. "This is true," the priest said. "It was what I have told you all along—these people have been sent to end the storms. They have come to save us. You must listen to them, Techtopec. They cannot wait."

Techtopec stared at Aaron, at the dervish that was Struth. The Mutata thrashed her heavy tail, kicked with her great clawed feet, and seemed to snap at invisible creatures with her hands. Her trumpeting shrills threatened to deafen them.

"As you wish," Techtopec said.

He motioned shortly to his acolytes, who disappeared into the temple to emerge a few seconds later pushing the Floating Stone before them. Aaron felt his heart slam against his rib cage at the sight, and from the awed silence around him, he knew the others felt the same. The piece of temporal mechanism he carried seemed suddenly heavy, a reminder. Struth stopped her mad hornpiper dance to look.

The Floating Stone. Their one hope of escape.

Travis's plan had been simply to get to the Floating Stone, shove a Green Town-linked piece underneath it, and go through, with the last one "pulling the plug" again so that the Aztecs couldn't follow them. That plan, they all knew, had been scrapped—Techtopec, the acolytes, the guards, and Tezozomoc's own men: each of those was a complication they hadn't counted on. Aaron took a breath.

"Okay," he said, stroking the familiar texture of the Floating Stone's surface. "Someone bind Acayacatl's hands so he's not a problem. Peter, Eckels, why don't you two bring Acayacatl over here and lay him down on the Floating Stone. When I tell you, we'll roll him off the stone. Travis, you have one of the Green Town pieces, right? Keep it ready. Jenny, tell Struth to get ready to go for the acolytes; try to make sure that they don't go for weapons. Mundo, you and Peter each take one of Tech-topec's warriors; I'll try to take Techtopec out."

"What about Tezozaomoc and his friends?" Jennifer asked.

Aaron resisted the temptation to look at them. He tried to pretend that he was concentrating on the rite he was about to perform. He closed his eyes and raised his hands to the night sky, his head lifted. "We'll have to cross our fingers with them, I think," he said softly. "Okay. It's showtime, people."

Aaron clapped his hands together and brought them down again in a gesture of meditation, as if praying. Acay-acatl, his face betraying no emotion at all, was laid faceup on the Floating Stone. His eyes focused on the stars above, resigned. Aaron looked out across the plaza. There was movement at the far end: torches, and men adorned with the feathery headdresses of the warriors.

"Don't look now, but company's coming," he said in a quiet monotone, as if reciting a chant. Tezozomoc came up alongside Aaron. Without a word, he took something from his belt and laid it on the Floating Stone in front of Aaron: a large flint knife, adorned with two jeweled eyes that seemed to stare at him. Tezozomoc moved away again; Techtopec leaned in toward the group around the Floating Stone, his gaze almost eager. Aaron could feel the priest's stare as he picked up the knife, bringing it up as he'd seen Techtopec himself do, holding it poised over the silent Acayacatl.

This is Tezozomoc's vision. This is what he saw.

The blade glittered with starlight. Keen, hungry.

The emperor stepped out onto the plaza, saw the gath-ering at the summit of the pyramid, and gestured his men forward. They spilled forward, running.

Two-handed, Aaron brought the knife down with all his strength.

Acayacatl jumped under Eckels and Peter's hands, but the blade shivered point-first in the plastic alongside him.

"*Now!*" Aaron cried.

Aaron pushed the stunned Acaycatl from the stone and leapt over it toward Techtopec. He hit the priest high, sending the man stumbling backward. Techtopec tried to regain his balance, but he was too close to the platform. His foot came down on air; he fell backward down the steps with a cry. He landed in a heap on the landing from which they'd watched the sacrifice the night before.

Aaron whirled, hearing the sounds of struggle behind him. He was in time to see Peter execute a whirling back kick to the head of one of the guards. The warrior went down heavily, unconscious before he hit the ground. Peter snatched up the man's spear, driving the butt end into the stomach of one of the acolytes—who promptly sat down, all the breath gone out of him. Jennifer and Struth were keeping the other acolytes at bay, most of whom showed the marks of having been struck by the Mutata's powerful tail. Mundo was swarming over his guard like a possessed thing, shrieking and clawing. The man flung his spear aside and fled.

Suddenly, the only Aztecs left standing were Tezozomoc and his men. The priest stood with his arms crossed over his chest, watching Aaron. Their eyes met, and Aaron dropped his gaze guiltily.

"Aaron!" Peter shouted, glancing down at the foot of the pyramid. "We gotta move it! We have people heading up the stairs."

"All right," Aaron said, turning away from Tezozomoc. "Travis, let's have the Green Town piece." He tried not to look at Tezozomoc. "And guys, let's keep an eye on our allies here. I don't know if Tezozomoc is entirely with us or not."

Travis handed Aaron the glowing, broken mechanism. As Aaron hefted it in his hand, Tezozomoc spoke. "He's asking why you use one of your own greenstones," Mundo said. "He wants to know if this will open the gateway to where Chantico went."

"Tell him—" Aaron stopped. Everyone was looking at him: Tezozomoc, Jennifer, Travis, Mundo . . .

"*Aaron!*" Peter called again. "They're getting *closer* . . . !"

"Tell him—" Aaron stopped again. "I'm sorry, guys. I'll be right back."

Aaron darted to the edge of the platform. The first warriors were already a quarter of the way up. *There isn't time. Go on back*, the rational part of him screamed, but he took a deep breath and half slid, half ran down the stairs to where Techtopec lay unconscious. A flung spear clattered on the stairs below him as he scampered onto the landing and crouched down alongside the man.

Techtopec was breathing, at least, though a fan of blood was smeared across his cheek from a cut above his eye. The greenstone amulet was snagged in the priest's robes. Aaron tugged: the chain held as another spear chipped stone a few feet from his head. Cursing, he pulled harder. The chain snapped. "Sorry, Techtopec," he whispered. "Hope you don't have too bad a headache tomorrow."

With that, Aaron headed back up, crouching low and zigzagging across the steps as the warriors shouted and a few more spears struck sparks at his feet. Out of breath, he tossed the amulet to Tezozomoc.

"I lied to you," Aaron told the priest, nodding to Mundo to translate. "We never intended to go where you want to go. I'm sorry. We just wanted to go home. Put that greenstone back in the roadway after we've gone through. It'll take you to Chantico." Turning away from the priest without waiting for an answer, Aaron pointed. "Travis! Where's our piece?"

"Here." Travis tossed the glowing chunk of metal to Aaron, who rolled underneath the Floating Stone. "I'll pull it back out when everyone's gone through and close off the path as I go through," he told them as he wriggled under the hovering roadway. "Everyone ready?"

There was no light underneath the Floating Stone except for what the temporal machinery itself provided. Aaron felt the undersurface with his hands, searching for a place in which to wedge the metal. "Damn!"

"What's the matter?" Jennifer asked. He could see Jennifer's and Peter's concerned faces as they crouched down alongside the Floating Stone, peering underneath at him.

"This path's a lot smoother than the other pieces," Aaron told them. "This part must have been on the edge of the explosion. I can't attach this piece anywhere. There's a few cracks and crevices, but they're all small."

"Try holding the mechanism tight against it," Peter suggested. As Aaron did so, Peter climbed onto the roadway. Aaron heard his friend curse, then felt the path sway as Peter jumped down. "Not even a tingle," he said.

"There probably needs to be a lot of surface contact," Travis said. "Try just laying it on top of the path."

Aaron rolled out from underneath. He placed the glowing metal on the roadway and touched the surface with the palm of his hand, shaking his head. "Nothing. Let's try another fragment."

"We don't have time for that," Mundo called from near the staircase. A spear went whizzing past the ape's head in mute confirmation, and the ape scrambled backward in a flurry of snowy fur. "They're almost at the top."

Aaron looked at Tezozomoc, still holding Techtopec's amulet in his fist, the golden chain curling over his wrist. Tezozomoc nodded, and barked a command to his men.

With a yell, they bolted to the staircase as one. The sounds of battle drifted up as Tezozomoc walked slowly toward Aaron, as if there were no fight raging only a few feet down from them, as if they had the rest of the night in which to act. When Tezozomoc stood before Aaron, he took Aaron's hand in his own, palm up. Unclenching his other fist, he dropped the amulet into Aaron's open hand and spoke. Aaron looked at Mundo.

"The gods brought you here for this."

A roll of thunder accompanied Mundo's translation, and to the east, they could see a quickly moving storm approaching, walking the valley on its bright, crooked legs.

Aaron stared at the amulet. "It came from this path," Jennifer said. "At least we know it works."

Aaron looked at the others. The wind was rising; shrieking, it carried away the sounds of the struggle on the steps. "Peter? Travis?"

"I don't like the odds here, man," Peter said. "I say we split." The others nodded in agreement, all but Struth who had turned from holding the acolytes at bay to sniff the wind and glare openmouthed at the time storm. The outriders of the storm were already overhead, and the air smelled of ozone. Stroboscopic lightning illuminated the pyramid in blue light. Somewhere below, someone screamed. "What about Struth?" Aaron asked Jennifer.

"She'll come with us," Jennifer said.

"All right," Aaron said, then with more enthusiasm: "All *right*! Let's go—to wherever and whenever this takes us."

Aaron ducked under the roadway again. The Floating Stone was shuddering in the wind, and Aaron had to hold it steady with one hand. The amulet slid easily into the largest of the crevices under the path; Aaron could feel the energy surging through the Floating Stone as the greenstone fell into place. Thunder grumbled its basso complaint.

"Go!" he called to the others. "Now!" He could feel the path bounce as, one by one, the group jumped on. Each time, a flare of verdant fury that matched the lightning sparked through the underside of the roadway. Aaron counted the flashes: Peter, Jennifer, Eckels, Travis, Mundo, and (an eruption of glittering electricity) Struth.

"Tezozomoc!" Aaron shouted into the gale wind. "Go!"

He could see the priest's legs, but the man had moved away from the stone. Aaron rolled out. "Tezozomoc!"

The priest was staring out over the city as the time storm broke around the pyramid and shifting fragments of a hundred realities flickered into existence among the buildings. The man, Aaron realized, was crying. A single tear tracked Tezozomoc's furrowed cheek as he gazed out at his home.

"We have to go!" Aaron said, grabbing the man by the arm. "Come on! I have to seal off the path before they follow us!"

Someone stepped onto the platform only a few feet from them: a towering backpiece, pleated cotton armor, a jabbing spear already running blood, and an expression of strange eagerness on his face. He saw Tezozomoc and Aaron and shouted. Another plumed head appeared behind him, and another. Aaron knew that there was no way he or Tezozomoc could reach the path before one of those spears found their backs.

"Only blood can release her . . . A sacrifice is demanded." The rest of Tezozomoc's vision came back to Aaron. *"One of you must die."*

Tezozomoc stared at Aaron, and he knew that Tezozomoc remembered the vision, too. "Chantico," Tezozomoc said. His eyes were dark as the stormclouds and full of pain, and Aaron saw that the man had picked up his ceremonial knife again. The stormwind whipped Tezozomoc's hair.

"One of you must die."

"Chantico," Tezozomoc said, more firmly this time, and pushed Aaron with his free hand at the same time. Surprised, Aaron staggered backward toward the Floating Stone.

Tezozomoc, without another look backward, raised his knife and ran toward the approaching warriors. "Tezozomoc!" Aaron shouted. "No!"

Aaron saw the spear tip rip through Tezozomoc's abdomen, hearing the priest grunt with pain and fury even as Tezozomoc slashed his knife across the man's throat. The priest glanced back to Aaron. "Chantico!"

Tezozomoc howled as another spear pierced him from the side. His eyes still on Aaron, pleading, Tezozomoc staggered. Then he turned to face his attackers, his knife high.

"I'll . . . I'll find her!" Aaron shouted to Tezozomoc. "Chantico! I'll find her for you!"

He didn't know if Tezozomoc heard or understood him.

More warriors were clambering onto the platform. The storm threw mad shadows and wailed its lament around the temple. Aaron ran desperately, flinging himself flat on the ground under the Floating Stone as spears ricocheted off the roadway. In one motion, he yanked the amulet from its crevice and scooted out from the other side. The Floating Stone shivered and threw off a firework display of sparks as the gateway began to close. The Aztec warriors were rushing the stone, heedless of the storm or the pyrotechnics or Aaron.

Aaron leapt onto the path as a half dozen spears arrowed toward him, their aim true.

But Aaron was already somewhere else.

Dinosaur Warriors Sketchbook

A Record of My Adventures
by Aaron Cofield

Page 272: The Mutata capture the time machine—with Jenny, Peter, Eckels, Struth, and Mundo inside.

Page 273: Jenny talks with Struth.

Pages 274 and 275: Wings of a fly, body of a wasp, glow of a firefly—the deadly mechanical insect is about to attack.

Pages 276 and 277: Our first view of the saorod world.

Pages 278 and 279: Our second view of the saorod worlds—this time after the saorods dumped us at the foot of the cave where we met Salisos.

Page 280: Struth has a nasty fall down a cliff.

Page 281: A Gairk ore-smelting furnace. Part of our tour of the Gairk *jhaka* on the way to our meeting with the Gairk OColi.

Pages 282 and 283: Our arrival at the Aztec *alteptl*.

Pages 284 and 285: We watch in horror as Techtopec prepares to perform a human sacrifice.

Page 286: Peter's excellent idea of hang-gliding with saorod corpses in action.

One Million Years B.C.

Glossary of Mutata Terms

The Sounds of the Mutata

The sounds made by the Mutata (a race of sentient dinosaurs most similar to the duckbills of our pre-history) are produced through their long nasal horns. In the novels, they are omitted for the most part. However, the most common sounds are a nasal bleat, a snort, a full roar, and a trill.

Pronunciation Key

The Mutata language has been transcribed into an approximation of phonetic English. Most consonants are pronounced as they would be pronounced in that language. In most cases, "a" is pronounced as the "a" in cat; "e" as the "e" in meet; "i" as the "i" in dim (though an ending "i" is pronounced as the "ee" in meet); "o" as the "o" in solo; "u" as the "oo" in moot; "ai" as the "i" in ride; "ei" as the "ea" in heaven; "ah" as the "a" in tall. Some of the Mutata sounds cannot be adequately reproduced by the human larynx. In those cases, the closest English sound has been used, as in "jh," which for the Mutata is a glottal stop much like a very rapid "jeh-eh," the last syllable being a quick aspirant. In some cases, a literal translation of the Mutata word has been substituted, as in "Speaker" or "Giving." There are also subtle posture and scent aspects to the Mutata language which, unfortunately, must be lost in the written form and which humans can never imitate. Any human must always be partially mute and deaf to the Mutata language as spoken by the dinosaurs.

aii   An imperative: to be performed immediately.

Amath   The Mutata god of death, who comes to bear the soul of a dying Mutata back to the All-Ancestor.

Baosiot   Unintelligent predatory dinosaurs—the allosaurus, possibly.

bhieye   "Thank you."

broaii   The Gairk war club, a massive wooden mallet tipped with several protruding blades of obsidian. The Gairk will usually carry two, one for the right hand, one for the left. Like the Mutata, the left hand is used when striking another sentient creature; the right is for "non-intelligent" lifeforms.

chodoe   "Follow me." An imperative, used only by a superior Mutata to his or her social inferiors.

ciosie   A demand for satisfaction. Ciosie means literally "The decision of the All-Ancestor"—in other words, letting the right or wrong of an issue be decided by combat, with the All-Ancestor's influence supposedly determining the outcome.

daii soo   Literally, "Pause (or wait) several breaths."

ehei   To go outside a dwelling. Also, to wander.

Eikels   Eckels

Floraria   Unintelligent predatory dinosaurs, possibly the Tyrannosaurus family.

gaedo   An affirmative given by a younger to an elder. "Yes."

Gairk   The racial name for a species of sentient, small allosaurs.

geedo   "Yes." As spoken by peers.

geiree   "Come here," or "Approach me." An imperative form.

gheodo   Literally, "I cannot do that," with the added emphasis that the refusal is based on a superior's orders.

Giving   Translation of the Mutata phrase meaning "The time when the spirit

	is given to the All-Ancestor." The funeral rite for Mutata.
iado	"Animal"—more specifically, an unsentient creature, without language or anything more than animal intelligence. The type of being killed with the right hand rather than the left.
jhaka	The village in which Mutata live, each under the rule of its own OColi.
Jhenini	Jenny.
jhiehai	Scavenger proto-birds—these are deliberately enticed to feed on the bodies of dead Mutata.
khiisoo	A demand for obedience: "You must obey!"
LongDay	Or OGhielas. The summer solstice. As with almost all human cultures, the Mutata and Gairk also mark the solstices for religious celebration and ceremony.
Mutata	The racial name for SStragh's species of sentient dinosaurs.
niijeks	Mouselike rodents which feed on the stored grains within the Mutata encampments.
OColi	Literally, the Eldest. The ruler of a particular Mutata tribe is nearly always the oldest among them. Gan be either male or female, though the males generally live the longest.

OColihi   The Ancient Path. The code of
ethics and behavior which governs
the Mutata. This code is handed
down via a verbal tradition
through the OTsio. The begin-
nings of the ritualized OColihi are
lost in the long centuries of the
Mutata past.

oei   A modifier. When used in
conjunction with other words, it
indicates "many" or "a large
amount."

OTsio   Teacher. Each youngling Mutata,
when the tribe has returned from
the first Nesting Walk after their
hatching, is assigned an OTsio to
guide its development. The OTsio
becomes a parent-analogue,
though a Mutata of that age is considered independent.

otsioiue   The OTsio's student.

Raajek   SStragh's OTsio, and a propo-
nent of the OChiihi, or New
Path—a mindset at variance with
the old ways of Mutata behavior.

saitie   A flying insect. Each dawn, they
chirp noisily as they rise from their
nightly sleep in the leaves of the
fern-trees.

saorod   A species of pterosaur in Dinosaur
World, with about a 3-inch
wingspan.

skyfire   Or "Holata." The sun.

Speaker   Translation of the Mutata title-phrase meaning "One who speaks the words of the Eldest."

SStragh   The Mutata who finds and captures Jennifer, Peter, and Eckels, and who befriends Jennifer.

Tiafer   The original name of the OColi who preceded Raajek.

werada   A death caused by a Mutata—specifically, the left-handed type of killing, not the right-handed killing that would be done to an animal.

werata   Pain.

whiaso   A "right-handed" killing, or the killing of a simple, unintelligent creature.

yeie   A modifier, indicating a negative: "I will not" or "This is not so." Also used as a quick denial: "No!"

zhiotae   The Gairk "Reader of Omens" or shaman. Functions as an adviser to the Gairk OColi in spiritual matters. The Mutata have no analogue occupation.

We want to hear from readers!

Your opinion of the Dinosaur World series is important to us. We welcome all feedback about the series.

Write or email to the editors at the following address:

J. T. Colby & Company, Inc.
Purveyors of Time Travel Instruments and
Accessories™

Manhanset House
Dering Harbor, New York 11965-0342
bricktower@aol.com
bricktowerpress.com

RAY BRADBURY, one of the greatest writers of fantasy and horror fiction in the world today, has published some 500 short stories, novels, plays, and poems since his first story appeared in *Weird Tales* when he was twenty years old. Among his many famous works are *Fahrenheit 451*, *The Illustrated Man*, and *The Martian Chronicles*. He has also written the screenplays for *It Came from Outer Space*, *Something Wicked This Way Comes*, and *Moby Dick*. Mr. Bradbury was Idea Consultant for the United States Pavilion at the 1964 World's Fair, has written the basic scenario for the interior of Spaceship Earth at EPCOT, Disney World, and is doing consultant work on city engineering and rapid transit. When one of the Apollo Astronaut teams landed on the moon, they named Dandelion Crater there to honor Mr. Bradbury's novel, *Dandelion Wine*. Recently Mr. Bradbury flew in an airplane for the first time.

STEPHEN LEIGH is the author of several science fiction novels, including *Crystal Memory*, *The Bones of God*, and the best-selling *Alien Tongue*. He is also a contributing author to the Hugo-nominated *Wild Cards* shared-world series. Currently Mr. Leigh lives in Ohio.